LUCKY BREAK

CHARLOTTE CROSBY
LUCKY BREAK

**When you only get one shot…
you've got to dive right in**

Harper North

ALSO BY CHARLOTTE CROSBY

Me, Me, Me
Brand New Me
Me, Myself and Mini-Me
Live Fast, Lose Weight
30 Day Blitz

HarperNorth
Windmill Green
24 Mount Street
Manchester M2 3NX

A division of
HarperCollins*Publishers*
1 London Bridge Street
London SE1 9GF

www.harpercollins.co.uk

HarperCollins*Publishers*
Macken House,
39/40 Mayor Street Upper,
Dublin 1, D01 C9W8, Ireland

First published by HarperCollins*Publishers* Ltd 2025
1

Copyright © Charlotte Crosby 2025

Charlotte Crosby asserts the moral right to
be identified as the author of this work.

A catalogue record for this book is available from the British Library.

HB ISBN: 978-0-00-877649-7

This novel is entirely a work of fiction. The names, characters and incidents portrayed in it are the work of the author's imagination. Any resemblance to actual persons, living or dead, events or localities is entirely coincidental.

Set in 10.5/15.5 pt. Sabon by Amnet

Printed and bound in the UK using 100% Renewable Electricity by CPI Group (UK) Ltd

All rights reserved. No part of this publication may be reproduced, stored in a retrieval system, or transmitted, in any form or by any means, electronic, mechanical, photocopying, recording or otherwise, without the prior permission of the publishers.

Without limiting the author's and publisher's exclusive rights, any unauthorised use of this publication to train generative artificial intelligence (AI) technologies is expressly prohibited. HarperCollins also exercise their rights under Article 4(3) of the Digital Single Market Directive 2019/790 and expressly reserve this publication from the text and data mining exception.

This book contains FSC™ certified paper and other controlled sources to ensure responsible forest management.

For more information visit: www.harpercollins.co.uk/green

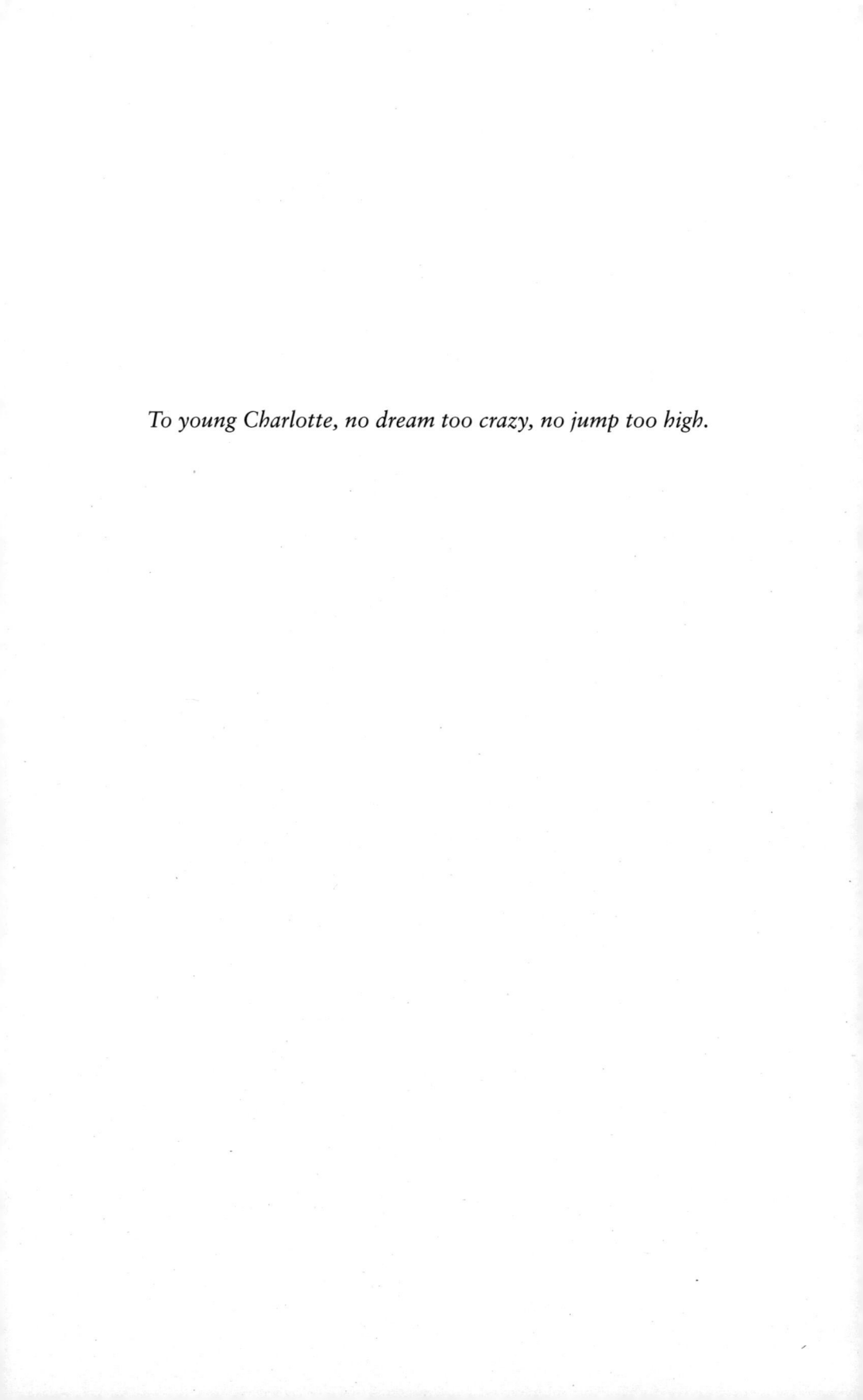

To young Charlotte, no dream too crazy, no jump too high.

Prologue

"Number sixty-eight, come forward, please. Stand on the white cross, look down the camera and tell the world why you want to be a star."

Angelica Clarke took a deep breath, blinked beneath the glaring spotlight that was zeroed in on the stage, and stepped forward.

"Hi *North Stars*," she began, urging her jangling nerves to settle, "I'm twenty-two years old, I work in an old people's home…whenever I sing to them or just have a chat, they're always telling me I belong on the telly. I saw the ad in the paper and it said you were looking for people with star quality. If you want someone who knows how to party, how to have a laugh and who's young, free and single and ready to take on the world, I'm your girl."

Angelica grinned, relieved she'd nailed the lines she'd practised. It sounded a lot more convincing than "I've moved back in with my mam and dad, I'm heartbroken and determined to prove to my stupid ex that he was wrong when he said I'd never make anything of myself." Before the fresh tan she'd applied last night, and the new set of lashes she'd put on to stop herself crying over that waste of space, she'd just been dumped Angie from Oakdene. Now, the auditions were here, she was ready to show everyone who she really was. World, meet Angelica…

PART ONE
2011

Chapter One

My heart won't stop beating. I know I want my heart to beat, it can't not beat. I'd be dead then – here lies Angelica, she had a rabbit called Jeffrey, could drink a shot out of her cleavage and knew the lyrics to every Spice Girl song, ever. Not much to leave behind, is it? No, what I mean is, it's beating really, really fast. Like, too fast. Boom, boom, boom it goes, jack-hammering away in my chest...and I regret everything.

How did I get here, wobbling on my patent platform shoes, in some club that's all done up like the jungle? One minute, I was just sipping my cocktail, trying to be sensible Angelica, and the next I feel like I'm flying. It's slowly dawning on me what I've done...and what I've put at risk.

I should have known Samantha was up to something. She's been nagging me for weeks about being a goody two shoes, for never touching the pills she keeps stashed on her. When we met during the first day filming *North Stars*, over two months ago, I thought she was so sophisticated. Samantha Savoy, already a local radio presenter, had been hired as the voice of the show – she was meant to be the professional out of all of us. But that very first night at the club before we'd even started filming, she pulled a white baggie out of her bra. I wasn't naive, I'd seen it from the sidelines, but it was never my scene, and I'd thought no one would be that blatant.

Of course, tomorrow, when the whole country watches the premiere of our new reality show, no one will see that. I learnt pretty quickly that what's edited out is almost as important as what's filmed. I'm not one to judge how people get their kicks but I steered clear of the hard stuff – that first night, and all through the series. I'm trouble enough when I have a drink without adding any more mayhem in. So tonight, the night before *North Stars* hits TV screens, I was fine with just sticking to the vodka tonics and a promise to be in bed at a (vaguely) decent hour. After all those weeks of being told 'not to be boring' or 'go on, one won't hurt', I could stand firm and refuse for one more night. It wasn't like I wasn't curious though, tempted even, sometimes. I imagined what Damon would say if he saw me finally give in and try it. Alright, I know, so sue me. Angelica sometimes thinks about doing stuff to impress lads, who doesn't?

So when Sam had pulled all us girls together for a selfie then recoiled, saying I had death breath and rattled a tin of mints at me, I'd not thought twice about necking one, washing it down with a bit more vodka and shouting NORTH STARS CREW at the lens.

Then, not long after, the nausea and the racing heart thing happened. Look, I'm no stranger to getting trashed but I knew right then it wasn't the booze. Sam had slipped me something, I was sure of it. I tried to pull myself together, after all, Sam had been necking all sorts for the entire series, and she still managed to keep going. It was her typical checklist for a big night: nails on, tan glowing, tits out, pills popped.

Anyway, now I'm standing here looking out at the dancefloor thinking this is meant to be the last night out before our lives change forever, before the world knows our names, our faces, our secrets. I feel like I'm underwater. My best mate Madison's dancing on a table, she keeps yelling over "Angelica, get up here." But I can't explain what I'm experiencing, I'm in this bubble, and it's just me, my heart beating and the voice in my head screaming that I've made a big mistake. It doesn't help that everyone in this place is so busy posing and then there's me. I only seem to fit in with Madison, sparkler in hand, newly-whitened teeth almost glowing in the UV light, so tanned she's practically mahogany. But that's Mads for you, she knows real is sometimes overrated and she rocks her look: fake lashes, fake tan, fake hair. But I don't think either of us want fake men.

None of the lads have bothered to show up. They *promised* us they'd be here. That's why we've got this massive booth, a treasure chest full of booze sitting on the table, which was brought over by all these people waving sparklers, dressed up in Tarzan costumes. The whole club is draped in plastic ivy that keeps hitting me in the face every time I move anywhere. There's some kind of Aztec temple disguising the doors to the loos and I think Madison is now twerking with an inflatable toucan.

What time is it? I've no clue. I don't want to ask Mads, she always says I'm putting a downer on the night whenever I want to check and, mostly, I agree. I met her on Day One – she's a runner on the show, which she explained meant she handled whatever the crew needed to keep filming running smoothly. I should have known we'd end up best mates – she's been the one keeping me sane throughout, and even though she works so bloody hard, she has the energy of ten men. She's always the first to pull, the last to go home, and the first one with the stories the morning after.

But now, I really need to know what time it is, as it's the launch tomorrow and they're playing the show first thing in the morning, before it airs on national telly, to a bunch of really important journalists and reviewers. Then they're going to interview us, in a line-up. One by one, being grilled with questions like…well, I don't know.

Madison always says I'm too honest, but I figure life's too short to not be straight. What would I ask if I was them? What's your favourite cocktail? How low can you go in a slut drop? But whatever they ask us, I'm now going to have to answer while I'm on a comedown from a dodgy pill that Samantha probably bought off some guy with a moustache. I'm sweating now. My tan is definitely going to be all streaky come morning. *If* I even make it to morning. The pill, the booze, the music – it's all too much – everything down here is louder, stronger, wronger than what I'm used to back home. I need to have some water, cool down a bit. Better to look like streaky bacon than dead I suppose.

"Angelica! Angelica," Madison has jumped down from the booth and she's thrusting a phone in my face. "The lads, look, they're in Jewel, Reed's just posted a pic. The slimy bastards aren't even coming."

My stomach lurches. I feel sick and stupid. What did I expect? Really? That Damon was going to show up here, see me in this dress that I bought in the Jane Norman sale with my last twenty quid, and decide that yes actually, he does want me. Why would he do that? When there's been so many girls, ever since we started filming the show, with supermodel legs, glamour-model tits and perfect bubble butts just waiting to seduce him? It'll be even worse when we're on the telly. Even the ugliest of famous men marry stunners. And Damon isn't ugly. Far from it.

"Are you OK?" Madison is asking me, as if she herself wasn't hanging out here, whooping and dancing on tables, waiting for Marc to walk in and see her, looking fit and having the best time ever. The lads can be thoughtless sometimes, but we have to put on a front, even with each other, by pretending we don't care. "Nah, I don't give a shit about Damon," I say. I may be young, but I know enough about heartbreak already to know when it's too raw to even speak about.

"It's alright if you need a little cry, you know," Madison squeezes my arm. She's one of the good ones, I know that for sure, even if we did only meet a couple of months ago. Funny how a few weeks can change your life.

Chapter Two

"Madison Mount, I'll be your lifesaver on the show. As long as I'm doing my job right."

She stuck out her hand for me to shake. With her long, swishy, lilac hair, pastel nails and matchy-matchy outfit, she was like a My Little Pony, all rainbows and perfume and lashes that went on for miles. I was already missing my normal mates, and as she introduced herself in her broad Scouse accent and talked me through all the cameras and mics and what everyone was called in the crew, I knew I could trust her. But I'll admit I didn't know I'd found my ride-or-die best mate until I told her I was so nervous I thought I was going to throw up and she shrieked with laughter and told me some of the others already had.

She made it OK to be scared about filming. I was terrified that first day when I laid eyes on the cameras. We were thrown into a house with eight strangers and our *every move* would be filmed. It wasn't that I was all sweet and innocent. Ask my mates, I've a reputation for being an idiot sometimes. I can't tell you the amount of times they've found me spewing up in some nightclub toilet. It's not only when I've had a drink either, I once climbed up onto my parent's roof in protest when my dad finished the leftover roast I'd bagsied (if you've ever tasted my mam's roast you would have done the same). But doesn't everyone do crazy shit when you're a teenager, figuring out who you are – and the first time you get an allowance and the chance to spend it? The difference was, none of that was caught on camera.

I'd known about the idea behind *North Stars* before I auditioned – I read a flier, signed some forms, got my head round the concept: eight people, chosen from eight cities across the north, all up for one hot summer of partying, flirting, and having a laugh while the cameras rolled and the temperature in the house rose. We were all picked because – so the producers told us – they wanted real people, people who'd be themselves on-screen. I'd got nothing to lose, a summer of fun was just what I needed and I'd signed up without worrying about what would come next. The house was in Manchester's Northern Quarter but they told us we'd be filming in cities all over the place, having nights out in all our home cities. So far, so straightforward. But when I learnt only four would make it to the end of the series, and those four would get a chance at being returning cast for a second series, I realised this might be more than just a few weeks of free drinks and VIP entry to bars. Before I'd even got to the start of filming, the stakes had been raised.

That day, I wasn't only facing meeting my new housemates, I'd have to work out who my competition was. I'd met loads of people on the audition day, queuing down the block to secure my shot. The bosses had already told us that every week the 'siren of shame' would blare out inside the house and Sam, the voiceover girl, would get her moment of fame, her voice echoing through the house to reveal the housemate deemed too boring to stay. I dreaded those days. I knew how to have fun – but it's different when you know the cameras are on you. It's tough to be fully yourself, or at least, it was at first.

We were so aware of the crew on day one, particularly as some of the cameramen were seriously fit – the strong, silent types. Their arms were so muscly from lugging that equipment about. But soon enough they blended into the background (just as well, as we were strictly not allowed to chat up the camera crew, we had to pretend this group of gorgeous men weren't even there, how unfair is that?) and, as we got used to them, we could lower our guards that little bit more. It was an eye-opener to me that it was often the crew who were wilder than us housemates, but it meant we soon stopped being self-conscious around them.

Madison gave me a rundown of who I'd need to know. She gestured to Samantha, our queen bee and voice of the show, sitting on the other side of the green room getting her face done. At that point, everyone else was just a name, sex and age. Layla, a massage therapist from Newcastle who said she was great at relieving stress; Bobbie from Hull, the baby of the house (who ended up being evicted first, which was for the best as she said she missed her mam); Ella, a receptionist from Blackpool who looked like a model, and the lads: Reed, Shane, Marc and Damon. She told me the men entering the house were hot, but I hadn't even blinked when she read out Damon's name. If I'd known then that boy would turn my heart inside out, I wonder if I'd have been knocking on the front door to get in the house even faster – or turned and run away. Every day I wish I could 'be more Madison' when it comes to men. She's gorgeous, and yes, she told me from that first morning that she'd already decided the hottest guy in the house was Marc from Sheffield – she flashed his application form with a Polaroid attached – half-Yorkshireman, half-Italian, 100% horny, flash bastard. But even then, she gave me some advice. "It's OK to fancy them, Angelica, fuck them if you want, but don't, whatever you do, fall in love. These guys are here for a good time, not a long time."

I've spent so much time these last few weeks wishing I could be more like her – 'thank you, next' is her mantra. But though I pretend it's not true, there's only been one guy in the house for me. Damon Greene.

"Damon Greene is twenty-five and from Otley. Blonde, 6'2" and once had a trial for Leeds United." Madison had read aloud. "Claims he's had more birds than hot dinners. I'd stay away from that one, babe. You don't know where he's been. Or what he's caught."

If I'd have listened, maybe everything would have been different. Or maybe I'd have ended up with a crush on sweet Reed from Carlisle, or harmless if gormless Shane instead of Damon, the emotional equivalent of dynamite. But instead, I'd remembered what Anika, my best mate from school had said when she'd phoned from the cruise ship where she was working as a personal trainer. "Be loud, be proud, be you, Angel-face. No bullshit, no bitching, no regrets."

It was that last part I was struggling with now.

Chapter Three

What am I doing thinking about men, and especially Damon, when this night is meant to celebrate friendship and freedom? I should know by now just the mention of these guys brings me down. I reflect on all the silly things I've done to get their attention – including letting Sam spike me because I was too preoccupied to check what I was swallowing. Aren't these stupid pills meant to make you happy anyway? When's the ecstasy part of this pill going to kick in? So far, all I've felt is like I'm going to puke. I've got to fix this. This can't be how this night goes. So, the lads aren't coming. So what? There's got to be something I can do to turn this night around. After all, we've got a literal treasure chest full of booze, our own roped off area that everyone's dying to be invited to and tomorrow, our show is going to hit the screens and we're going to be overnight celebrities. That's what the producers tell us, anyway. They say they show is rocket fuel – and that we'll be proper famous, like can't go to the shop for a pint of milk famous. We need to celebrate this moment.

I shout to Madison, tell her we have to go find Layla, the other girl who made it to the finals with me. After all the so-called 'Dump Days', there were just four of us left in the last month – me, Layla, Damon and Marc. And our host Samantha of course. Can't forget her – she loved the power of being the one who saw all the footage, who got to announce the name of the dumped housemate, and make her trademark jokes about all the wild stuff we got up to, although I swear sometimes she was just a teensy bit jealous of the fact we were the ones with all the air time.

I scan the crowd for Layla, who's like the mam of the group. She gets trollied like the rest of us, but is always on hand to hold our hair back when we think we're going to be sick, cook us a fry-up when we get home and offer bits of advice, like "never trust a man with small hands."

Layla's at the bar, chatting up some lads that are twice her size. At five-foot-nothing she's a pint-glass of a girl, with these big blue eyes that are impossible to stay mad at for long. Not that anyone ever really gets mad at Layla, from the moment she stepped into the house we all adored her. "I can't find Samantha anywhere," Layla's saying now. "She promised one of these lads some action and I don't think I can handle both," she winks at them, before carrying on. "Where the fuck have you been?"

"Exactly where you left us, you're not that short to have missed us," Madison says, but when I look over, towards our booth, all I can see is fake vines, a rubber python and a sea of heads that blur before my eyes. "Samantha's gone home, though."

"What?" I say. "But she gave me this big speech about not being boring and making this a wild night?" Not to mention the other thing she gave me. Although I realise now I've been a fool.

Layla and Madison both just shrug. We stopped long ago trying to guess Samantha's next move at any given time. When we arrived for our first cast and crew briefing, I was in just a tiny pair of frayed denim hotpants and a faded t-shirt, holding a case with god-knows-what flung in, and she had, I kid you not, four huge *matching* designer cases full of bandeau dresses, heels, shimmery tops and belt-like miniskirts. But sometimes classiness is just a topcoat – as filming went on she would regularly blow her lid, at any small thing. One of the guys who left early had a soft spot for her, but Samantha was the queen of Play-It-Cool, like a stereotypical lad. Sam was all 'don't catch feelings' while this lad, Reed, followed her around like a puppy dog. Until he got the boot in the final dumping. How's it all going to look to the audience, I wonder? I've lived it – but I've no idea how it will all look onscreen.

I work out what the strange feeling in my stomach is – it's not the cocktails, and I don't think it's Sam's stupid pill. It's anxiety. Tomorrow morning the critics will watch our show – decide how many stars they'll assign us in their reviews – and tomorrow night, well, the world watches us. Or maybe they won't? Right now, I can't work out which is worse – everyone I know watching me get wasted and snog Damon on national telly…or everyone ignoring us? My mam tells me not to get my knickers in a twist – she says I should know what's expected to air, as I was the one they were filming. But that's the magic of TV – you really do forget about the cameras after a while, and then there's the editing…

It's been eight weeks of non-stop partying and to be honest, it's all a bit blurry, considering we were getting mortal pretty much every night. But I loved it. We could get into any club we fancied, the drinks were free, everyone wanted to be our friend as, even though the show hasn't aired yet, if you rock up with a camera crew people know that you're a *somebody* and (what pleased my mam the most) the producers arranged our cabs home. Though, back home was when the *real* trouble began, when we'd all pile into the hot tub or, if we'd got lucky, would head up to the penthouse. We called it private time, but nothing was ever really private in the house.

I look at the girls and suddenly just stop worrying. After all, I'm in a club with my two best mates, legends the pair of them, and they look so pretty, there's this soft gleaming light falling on our faces and, is it just me, or does this fake ivy just really bring out the colour in everyone's eyes? There's something so beautiful about it all, it properly does feel like I'm in the jungle. And the floor! It's all shimmering and glowing, just like my future could be. If the last eight weeks were just a taste of how great the next few months will be, I'm determined. "We've made it," I say to Layla and Madison, gripping their arms. "Seriously, girls, I love you so much! This isn't just the end of the season. This is the beginning of an incredible journey!"

We squeal and they pull me into the most blissful hug. I just feel so happy, like nothing in the world could ever possibly go wrong. Is this what confidence feels like? Or maybe this is what ecstasy feels like...

* * *

Chapter Four

Where am I? I don't recognise the wallpaper. It's not the patterned paper of the *North Stars* house, the lilies climbing up the walls. I would joke to Damon that the closed ones were like little vaginas, tiny vaginas on a vine. Damon! Is he…? Am I…? Did we…?

There's someone beside me, I can hear their breathing, the hot little puffs of booze-scented air they're expelling. Very gently, so as not to wake whoever-the-fuck-it-is beside me, I turn in their direction. The lump their figure forms is hench, Damon-like, but as he rolls over I see a flash of alabaster-white skin. Damon would never leave the house without a tan.

My stomach drops, there's a dark feeling squirming inside of me, whispering and trying to tell me that I'm no good. Damn Samantha and that damn pill, leaving me like this, questioning everything. What goes up, must come down and all that. Oh, that's given me a flashback! This guy beside me, his willy went up, but just for a second, and then it went down, down, down. Too many tequilas, he'd shrugged and rolled over, and that meant we didn't have sex. Phew. I've got enough to worry about today than having to walk like John Wayne. It all clicks at last. Of course, it's the big launch day, with all the press. I'm in London, that's my hotel room's wallpaper and, wait, is that Layla, curled up and snoring in my bathtub? My brain is not functioning yet. What happened last night?

I pat my face, one rogue falsie has tumbled down my cheek, settling itself just above my lip, like my own dodgy moustache. "You don't belong there," I say to it, peeling it off and dropping it to the floor. But my words unsettle the gentleman (wishful thinking) beside me and he begins to mutter something. "Ssshhhh," I say, tapping his head like my mam used to do. "Go back to sleep." I have absolutely no intention to ever see him again, particularly as I haven't the foggiest who he actually is, but still, I don't want him to wake up and see me missing one eyelash with my (once backcombed to perfection) hair now, by the feel of it, a big ball of tumbleweed on my head. I gently tiptoe into the bathroom, and begin to prod Layla. She's so little she fits in the tub perfectly, reminding me of one of my old Polly Pockets, perfectly tucked up in her case. "Layla," I whisper, but she doesn't stir. "LAYLA," I bellow. "Don't make me fart in your face!" Confession: I did do that a couple of times in the house.

She creaks one eye open. "Where am I?"

"You're in my hotel room, don't ask me how we got here."

"Cause it's a tragic story, or because you don't know?"

"Because I don't know."

"Well, why have you even woken me up, if you're not going to tell me a funny story? Wait, did you bring a guy back? I woke up in the night and could hear you at it."

"Yeah nearly, but if you must know, we didn't shag. Anyway, that can wait – we have to be at this press junket thing, remember?"

Realisation flashes across Layla's face. "Oh shit, what time?"

"I...can't remember. One o'clock maybe?"

It's at that moment that the hotel room phone rings. And the guy, the mystery one, is answering it. Layla and I exchange a look. She also has an eyelash stuck to her cheek, which I pluck off her.

"Alright, chill out man," the mystery man is saying. "I'll just get her, errrrrmmm," There's a pause. "Ange? Angela?"

There's going to be a time where I'm so famous no man ever forgets my name. Now there's a life goal. I dash through, deciding I have to not care how this man sees me, plus my ass looks great in this pair of hot pink knickers. "They sound mad," he whispers to me, handing over the phone. At least now I can see his face, not bad, but wait a minute, is that a...whisper of a moustache?

"Angelica Clarke." It's one of the producers. Gerald. The strict one. The one you get when you've done something really bad. I only spoke to him once in the house, but I'll never forget telling off I got. "It's half past eleven. The driver for your car has been waiting in the lobby for you for half an hour. Your phone is dead. I presume you've kidnapped Layla as she is also nowhere to be found."

There's something about Layla's size, and those big blue angelic eyes of hers. No matter what she does, she gets away with it. I swear, Layla could go to Gerald and say there's a dead man in the hot tub, I killed him by stuffing my knickers in his mouth, and Gerald would say 'did Angelica put you up to that?'

"I'm so sorry, time...um..." My slow head is scrambling for a decent excuse but all I can come up with is that my watch broke. I don't own a watch. And it's not 1995, it's 2011, we have phones now.

"I couldn't give a shit, just get your ass down here, and bring Layla. Now."

With that, he hangs up. Rude. There was no need to bring my ass into it.

"Layla! We have to be downstairs. The car's waiting for us."

"When do we need to be downstairs by?"

"Half an hour ago."

Cue a mad dash from the pair of us, as we attempt to make ourselves look respectable, while last night's pube-moustache guy just sits on the edge of the bed, watching, baffled. Layla's scrambling through my suitcase, trying to find a dress of mine that doesn't come down to her knees and I'm slapping on so much highlighter, to try to look fresh, dewy and like I've had eight hours sleep, that I end up going too far the other way. "I look like an embalmed corpse," I say sadly to my reflection.

"A tanned, fit corpse," Layla yells back at me. This is why you need your girls. They always offer the much-needed confidence boost, at just the right time, but don't let you get big-headed.

It takes us ten minutes (OK, fifteen) but we manage to make ourselves look semi-decent, hustle this strange man out the door, with a (fake) number of mine inserted in his phone before we're down in the lobby, where our sweet driver tells us that we're "very beautiful ladies."

When we get to the hotel where the press view is, Gerald is waiting in the lobby. He takes one look at me and says "Jesus Christ" while kissing Layla on both cheeks. Fuming. As he ushers us along the corridor he fills us in on how everything is "actually absolutely fine because Samantha swooped in and saved the day, by chatting with each journalist one by one and totally, totally charming them."

Sure enough, when we get into the press room Samantha's there, her hair done perfectly, beaming at everyone and generally looking like butter wouldn't melt. How does she look so glowing? She was out last night with the rest of us.

"Round of applause for them," she says, at the sight of us. "Though I think we could smell you before we could see ya. *Eau de Jägerbomb* is it?" But I can't even be mad at her, that'll have to wait, because there he is. Damon. Laughing with Marc, his gleaming white teeth shining like a light bulb across the room. When's he had time to have his gnashers done? It's worked though. My stomach flips and I curse it, and my damn heart which begins to pitter patter once more. Bloody attention-seeking heart. I can't help it. I just crave being near him. He spots me, and waves. God, I'm so weak for that man I could suck him off in a club bathroom and kid myself it counts as romantic. In fact, come to think of it, I have.

Now that the gang's assembled, we begin to walk to the cinema where they're screening the first episode, plus a montage of the rest of the season. I catch up with Samantha. She isn't exuding alcohol from her pores like me and the girls. No, she smells fantastic, like candy floss mixed with coconut.

"Where did you go last night?" I ask. "How come you're not hanging like the rest of us?"

She turns and smiles that perfected fake smile of hers and says, "What do you mean? I opted for a sensible early night, unlike some people."

As if it wasn't her conning me into getting off my tits! "But you gave me...a pill?" I drop my voice to a whisper, but still determined to let her know that I know what she did. Sam thrives on knowing more than everyone else. I began to notice this during filming, she'd spend days watching the rushes and filming voiceovers, then come out on the town with us at night, pleased as punch that she'd already seen all the footage, practically hopping with knowing what everyone had said. Not that she always used her knowledge for good. Sometimes Samantha would massage the truth, hoping that the amount of shooters we'd downed would blur our memory of how things happened. She'd drop little hints about things caught on camera that had been edited out, or she'd exaggerate the embarrassing things I'd done to make me feel bad. But tough luck on her, I embarrass myself so much it takes an awful lot to make me feel that way! This time though, it's just confusing. She's always been proud of being able to get hold of uppers and downers and even uses it against us sometimes, claiming she's the one that always gets the party started.

"Pills? I didn't have any pills last night," she looks at me quizzically, the picture of innocence. "Why would I give out drugs the night before the big launch? That's just loser behaviour."

"But you did! You gave me one..."

"Oh I know that happened...You saw me with my Smints, you had one, too and then just because you got wasted on voddie, you jumped to conclusions." She reaches into her bag and pulls out the same pink diamante encrusted tin she had last night, which rattles with tiny white triangles. She takes one out, pops it into her mouth and then hands one to me. I sniff it, suspiciously.

"Do you really think I would try to drug you? God, they're mints, Angelica." She breathes her spearmint-scented hot breath on me. I decide to chance it with another 'pill', take one and lick it. It is, indeed, a mint. But last night it was definitely different, I remember it. It was a little round tablet she gave me then, and even at the time I thought it wasn't minty enough! She obviously wanted to look the best today, so decided to give me drugs while she remained sober. Surely that's illegal somehow? Tricking someone into taking a pill? But it's not like I can go up to Gerald and tell him what happened, we all know who would get the blame, and who would deny it. I'm so angry but I have to remain calm, as we're ushered to our seats. I'm very aware that it's an all-eyes-on-us scenario so I have to appear smiling and happy to everyone.

The *North Stars* title music rolls and as I try to imagine what little Angelica would think of me now. Or Angie, as I called myself back then. My mam always said I was away with the fairies – playing games, fancy dress, the whole singing-into-my-hairbrush shebang. I used to say I was going to be a pop star – I always nabbed the lead in school plays, one time I even went busking in Piccadilly Gardens. But all that changed when I met Robbie Thompson. He was my first love – proper teenage puppy love. I'd have done anything for him – I even lost my virginity to him in the back of a Fiat 500. And that takes flexibility, I'm telling you. Then, the night before my 21st birthday he told me he was leaving – not just me, but the whole country. He was going to Australia to audition for a TV show called *Beach Life*. At first I thought he was inviting me – but then he told me I was holding him back, that I would never be a singer, or anything much, for that matter, that I was mediocre and a dead weight. I cried so much that night – and I've never sung a note in public since. Unless you count me leading the old dears at the care home in a few choruses of 'We'll Meet Again'. I wonder whether Robbie knows about *North Stars*. He'd never have believed I'd have had the courage to even audition, let alone get the gig. But I suppose there's some kind of justice in knowing it was partly him ditching me that gave me the idea in the first place.

Even though my heart is in my mouth waiting for the credits to end, I think – no, I know, little Angelica would be proud of me. Maybe not the times where I've spewed in a club toilet, and she'd have definitely pulled a face at the constant snogging, but she'd approve of the dresses and the make-up, the friends and most of all the fun. I sit back in my chair. Who cares what this audience thinks – this isn't for them, it's for her.

They play our first episode and it's bizarre to revisit my first impressions of the house and who I predicted I'd get it on with. I thought Reed was absolutely gorgeous and I'm there telling the green screen I think he's the one I'll fall in love with! I mean I do love him a lot, he was proper class on the show and I hope we stay in touch, but just as friends. No matter how good someone looks, you always need a spark, and the spark was definitely always there with Damon. I sometimes wish it wasn't, as Reed treats girls so much nicer, but maybe that's why there's no chemistry. I even said it in my audition, "I've got with loads of men, and the bigger the arsehole they are, the more likely I am to fancy them."

I don't think anything prepares you for seeing yourself on a massive screen. I'm trying so hard to keep watching, to be grateful for being here, and the opportunities this show is going to give me, but I can't help cross examining myself. I'm scrutinising my nose from the side now and, God, has that bump always been so noticeable? And do my hair extensions really look stringy in certain lighting? These were from an expensive salon up town, not the ones you glue in yourself following a YouTube tutorial. I'm looking at Layla and Samantha and I just think they look absolutely gorgeous onscreen. Even on the nights out where I was *sure* I looked nice, and spent ages getting ready, I'm now wondering 'why did I choose that dress?' and 'how come my lips are so thin?' It's this agonising running commentary in my head, like one of those football pundits, only it's an Angelica pundit and she's being a right nasty piece of work. I'd do anything to switch myself off right now, and I sink lower into my seat, my head pounding, wishing it would swallow me.

Then there's the scenes where Damon is talking to the camera, in the green-screen room. It was opposite the main house and producers would come and collect us, ask all sorts of questions, for hours on end. It didn't matter what you were doing, or wearing, if they came to usher you to green screen you had to go, immediately. That's why there's some shots of us in towels, or our pyjamas. We'd always come back and wind each other up, claiming we'd said loads of nasty things about the others. Except it wasn't true. At least, it definitely wasn't true when I was saying it, I was just teasing. But Damon, it turns out, wasn't. I have to fight the urge to turn round and glare at him as I listen to some of the stuff he comes out with. When he calls me easy, tears well up in my eyes. It's not that I'm ashamed to say I like sex. And it's not like Damon was complaining at the time. It's the way he phrases it and his smug tone – like he's entitled. He even says that he sees me as his safety net, claiming he can rely on me, at any time. So if he doesn't get his first choice of bird, he'll just shag me. *I'm worth so much more*, I want to yell…it's just, he doesn't seem to see it, does he?

But I'm not the only one screwed over by the lads in the show. They do something clever, squishing all of the episodes into a forty-five-minute highlight reel, so the press will have a flavour of what the series has to offer. Bearing in mind we were in the house for eight whole weeks, which has already been condensed into just one series, so watching it squished even more makes for some wild viewing. I discover the things Damon was saying to me on the green screen, but at least I already went through a lot of my heartbreak in the house. Damon was not very good at hiding his shags, and it's not fun to see them all over again, so I'm watching through my fingers. But it's no surprise.

Whereas Layla is getting with loads of lads in the first three episodes, having the time of her life when Shane set his eyes on her. He decided then that he wanted her all for himself. He was gorgeous – a proper Greek god, so, of course, when he started moving in on Layla she was like putty in his hands. It's so obvious while watching the show how much he played with her. Played with all of us, as I had no idea that he'd hide girls behind the hot tub, then as soon as Layla was asleep, or one of us was holding her hair back in the toilet (something that was often my job) and sneak them into his room. But Layla didn't know, neither did we. Only the cameras did. We all watch on as Shane enjoys a threesome in the hot tub, with the camera cutting first to Layla in the green-screen room gushing about how she has 'tamed the beast' to then her snoring in bed, before switching back to the girls thrashing about in the hot tub, necking on in neon string bikinis while Shane looks on smugly. I try to crane my head around to see Madison, realising now she must have known – no wonder she told Layla she was well rid of him when he got dumped from the house. But instead I see Layla. I don't manage to catch her eye, she's just staring straight ahead, her lip slightly quivering.

Mads is transfixed, too. She'd be the first to admit she's under Marc's spell. He's a dead ringer for Chad Schmidt (yes, that Chad Schmidt, the Hollywood movie star who's featured in the World's Sexiest lists for years now). Marc is a little rougher round the edges, I'll admit – even if Madison would slap me for saying so – he's more like a Chad Schmidt dupe, a Poundland Chad Schmidt.

When the screening finishes, we receive a polite round of applause from the journalists, while everyone from the cast and crew is up on their feet, screaming and applauding. The head of the network, this serious-looking old guy called Edmund, gives a little speech about how this is reality TV like it's never been seen before. "Real people, real lives, and getting absolutely mortal," he says, in his super posh accent and I can't help but laugh as the word 'mortal' should not be said in an accent that's clearly more used to saying words like 'caviar'. But he is right. I've never watched anything like this before. There's obviously *Animal Farm*, that show where they shove all those people in a farmhouse and lock the doors, but we've got our freedom in this. I think that's why I applied. It wasn't an experiment – it was our lives, but bigger and bolder and more banging than ever before. We go out, get absolutely off our faces and bring people back to the house for raging parties. Plus, we're northern and I swear that means we're just less uptight. I certainly don't care that people are going to see me at my drunkest, wildest, rawest. I'm grinning now, because I can already tell the show's going to be massive. Which makes my tummy feel funnier than Damon ever managed…until I wonder how many people are going to notice the bump on my nose?

As soon as the screening is over, during the five-minute break they give us, I search for Leo. I have to make sure that neither Edmund nor the producers, particularly Gerald, see me as we're not meant to 'fraternise' with the crew. That's what they told us on the first day, and even though it's not like any of us are rule-followers their tone was so strict we all took it on board. So we're friendly with the cameramen and producers, but they're never allowed to hang out or party with us once the cameras stop rolling. They don't seem to mind us spending time with Madison – after all, she was their go-between and the whole show would have been lost without her running errands and generally keeping the show on the road. But Leo's different. He's one of the quietest cameramen, and I couldn't help but find myself drawn to him. There's something different about him. I mean he looks different than the other lads for a start. In the middle of all the oiled and buffed guys, he's sort of rumpled and unbothered. He's a few years older and he's just, well, comfortable in his own skin. His tan lines come from filming outside, not a spray booth, and the curls of hair that peek out of his plaid shirt are unusual in a sea of waxed pecs and t-shirts cut to show off gym-toned biceps. It's not like I've broken any rules, though. He's come to be a friend, a proper one. He was just… there for me, in the house, and out on the town. This one time, I was so trashed, I kept passing out in the club toilets. Pretty standard practice for me, but Leo, once he learned some girls were trying to humiliate me by taking pictures, urged Madison to check on me before apparently shooing everyone away and carrying me out in a fireman's lift, like a proper white knight, to the car.

But after watching episode one, I'm frustrated he captured so many side shots of me. I find him leaning against the back wall of the screening room. "You could have chosen more flattering angles," I mutter at him, eyes darting to make sure no one spots us chatting, relieved it's dark up here. He does smell nice, he's got a spicy, woody aroma that always smells like soap and leather and, for a very brief second, I feel a little spark fly between us. This fleeting moment of connection makes me yearn for him to scoop me up in those arms again and carry me out (while I'm conscious, so I can savour it this time). But then he starts saying all these *nice* things. Which means I can't possibly believe he's sincere.

"Your nose is perfect, Angelica, stop stressing about that," he proceeds to tell me that if I'd just paid more attention to the audience reception rather than analysing every out-of-place hair or side angle, I'd have noticed all the journalists in the room loved me. "They laughed at everything you said, and they clearly thought you were the sweetest one," he says. "There's just this directness to you, you know, it's very endearing, an innocence somehow."

Now I know he's taking the piss. Innocence? Me? Most of the time on camera I'm going on about who's shagging who, or what I want to do with Damon's willy. Something I think is going to come back and haunt me – my words I mean, not Damon's tackle. But only because it's clearly boosted his ego, as when we enter the next room for the line-up of interviews, he's there already seated, in his white tank-top, chest clearly freshly waxed, looking like he's the King of England, his legs spread so far apart he almost needs two chairs. I want to say, "hey, there are more interesting things about Damon than what's in his pants," except that's not strictly true. It sometimes used to feel like there were three of us in our relationship, if that's what you could call it: me, Damon, and his dick. He used to say it had a mind of its own but I think that was just another on of his excuses for getting it on with other women.

The interviews are exhausting. The journalists don't ask me questions about what I want to do next, or even the stages of my coveted tanning regime. Nope, instead they're all focused on one thing. The fact they all, just half an hour ago, watched me have sex on camera. Except technically they didn't, they just caught a glimpse of some vague out-of-focus movements under the sheets. It's hardly the sequel to Paris Hilton's sex tape is it? But still, it's all they can ask about. "How do you think your parents will react to you shagging on TV? Do you think they'll be proud?" is a common one. My answer? They just switch over at those moments and besides, it's all under the covers. I'm a grown adult. I doubt my dad will even watch – all he ever tunes in for are science and programmes. When I told him I was auditioning for *North Stars* he thought it was an astronomy show. Oh, and the press are also obsessed with how drunk we get on the show. As if most of them don't reach the same levels of wasted every Saturday night, we're just doing what everyone does but, if anything, we're doing it better given it's the VIP areas of the north's best night-clubs. These aren't pound-a-pint nights, they're classy places. No, it's just the same questions over and over again and while I'm happy to be here, I really am, I just wish they'd ask me something else.

Particularly as, when I get up to find the loos, I eavesdrop on some of Damon and Marc's interviews. And they're not being asked about all their shagging! Even though they copped off way more in the house than all the girls did. One time, Marc shagged an actual old woman round the back of a supermarket. Or there was the time Damon had the audacity to be banging some girl while I lay there in the same room, asleep. Or, at least pretending to be. I was fake snoring so loudly, hoping it would turn the girl off and she'd climb off his dick and go home. But sadly, my snores seemed to motivate her even more, as she moaned louder with every thrust. Not that it lasted long.

I'm fuming about the boys' questions, but I do overhear something very juicy. "So," the journalist asks Damon. "You and Angelica were clearly the big romance of the house, with that cliffhanger ending leaving the door open for season two. Is there going to be a second series? And is all your talk of her being a backstop just bravado, when you've clearly developed feelings for her?" Yes! Thank you, journalist! I like her. She's asking all the probing questions I've been dying to ask Damon myself, if I wasn't trying so very hard to pretend I'm not bothered about him in the slightest. I didn't think this would be a benefit of fame, journalists being nosy and forcing guys to confront the truth on my behalf. Maybe

I can plant some in his room, lying in wait under the bed and behind the wardrobe with notepads to hand, ready to quiz him with bombshells like "Damon, would you ever consider marrying Angelica?" Damon looks down, and up again, meeting her in the eye. "Well, there's obviously a lot of very beautiful women in this world, yourself included." Sleazebag! "But, Angelica cracks me up. I love the bones of that girl, I really do. So, I guess…watch this space."

I scamper back to my seat, the biggest smile across my face. I can barely hide it. Maybe my fifteen minutes of fame is going to be fun after all.

* * *

Chapter Five

I should've asked for a bed in the driver's carriage of the train down south, considering the amount of times I've travelling to London since the show started airing. It's only been two weeks, and this is the third trip already. It's been fun, and I'm not complaining, but I don't think anyone ever warned me how much work this whole 'celebrity' thing would be. And, I don't mean to sound arrogant, but I am. A celeb, that is. Viewers absolutely love the show, I keep getting stopped in the street by random people, for the first few times I would reach to the back of my skirt, to make sure it wasn't tucked into my knickers, or look down to my shoes for stray toilet paper. I couldn't believe that anyone was stopping me in the street for anything other than to point out something embarrassing. It's a brilliant feeling – and I love the fact that real people are buzzing about the show.

When people stop me to ask stuff, I soon realise the questions fall into three main groups: how to get into TV (I've got no magic answers here, I just tell people to be themselves); what the secret is to dancing in insanely high heels (I don't know why anyone would ask me this if they've seen how often I fall over) and the thing they really want to know...are Damon and I an item? That last one? That's the killer question.

I'm not proud of the fact that the night after the press interviews, when the cast were staying in the same hotel and once we all went to bed, after drinking loads of course, there was a knock on my door. It

Lucky Break

was Damo and, well, every TV viewer in the country now knows how weak I am when it comes to that man...

Ever since then he's been messaging loads, non-stop even. But have we managed to *physically* see each other again? No. He keeps saying he's busy and normally I know that sounds like a fob off, but I've seen the lad's schedule – it really is jam-packed. They keep getting booked for these things called PAs, as in personal appearances. A more accurate term for them would be Pussy Ambush considering it's just hordes of girls queuing up for a piece of Marc and Damon. Even the lads who got dumped from the show in the early weeks, Shane and Reed, are doing them. I've seen all the pictures and videos online, shots of all the girls, lining up at these dodgy nightclubs where the carpets are sticky with WKD, Smirnoff Ice and worse for all I know, desperate to meet the boys. Damon is being pretty insistent in his messages that he doesn't want any of the girls hounding them, just says they're fans and he's only being friendly. He says as soon as his schedule allows, he'll take me out on a proper date, something much fancier than the pair of us eating beef Monster Munch in bed (which was our morning tradition in the house, Monster Munch and a little cuddle, while venting about the others.)

Us girls don't get booked for that many PAs, the promoters claim that lads don't really show up in the same way. Not because we're not fit, of course. But just cause, I think, lads aren't really into the whole *fangirling* thing, are they? They either just want to see us in their magazines at home or go out to pull real birds, rather than spending an hour in a line for a peck on the cheek from me. It's a shame though, as the PAs pay really well and, despite being stopped in the street and being on one of the biggest contemporary shows on telly, I am officially skint. Yesterday in Boots, my card got rejected, but the girl behind me recognised me and offered to pay! It was so embarrassing, particularly as my order was thrush cream and a pack of chewing gum. I pretended to the girl that there was a problem with the banking systems and took her number so

I could pay her back. But I don't know when I'll be able to, as my balance has dwindled down to £4.45 which I need for a hangover sandwich and fizzy drink for the train home.

Thankfully, things are looking up. I'm in London for a photo-shoot, with the biggest celeb mag in town, *Flair*. I'm so obsessed with this magazine that right now I wouldn't even mind if I ended up in their Ring Of Regret, the famous page where they draw circles round stains on celebrities' clothes, or slag them off for having dodgy tan lines and chipped manicures. I'd take it as a sign I'd made it! Well, I would have before today, when I actually *have* made it, as they've invited me down to take my photo and then quiz me on all things *North Stars*. When I get to the studio, I'm just so excited by it all. The place where I get my picture taken is all white, with a big sloping wall, and it's so pristine, like being on an untouched snowy mountainside. I run straight to it and start pretending to ski, before the photographer comes over and tells me off for marking the floor with my trainers. Oops. I'm ushered upstairs where Hollywood style mirrors line the corridor walls, the ones with the lightbulbs studded around them, and a lovely make-up artist called Verity, who's going to be doing my glam for the day! But first, the clothes...

There's a whole rail of them for me to try and a stylist who'll choose different things for me to wear. I'm praying I can keep some of them afterwards. I'm given a handful to try first, as they want to see what I'm wearing before deciding on my style of make-up. Which is how I find myself with only a thin curtain between me and the make-up artist and stylist, in a dress that doesn't zip up, and a bare make-up free face. This isn't how I pictured the day going. I'm trying so hard not to stare at my reflection but when it's on three sides of you, that's really hard. It's like I'm trapped in a haunted house of mirrors, except instead of scary clowns or skull faces it's me, looking an absolute fright. I decide that there must be something wrong with the dress, perhaps it was labelled with the wrong size, so I unhook the next one from its hanger. But it doesn't even go over my head, getting stuck around my tits. So I try shimmying it up my knees, but it won't budge past my hips. Great.

"Everything alright in there?" It's the stylist! But I'm too ashamed to confess, not yet, I'll try the other two dresses first and if they fit, I'll pretend I liked them best. So I just mutter a "fine, thanks" and try to step out of the dress now trapped around my knees. All I can think about is that episode of *Friends* where Ross can't get his leather trousers up and covers his legs in slippy lotion. I scan the makeshift changing room (again, avoiding the actual sight of me) for some lotion. How is it that I'm *seriously* considering that?

I know this is a struggle everyone's endured. I've certainly been here before, lying on the ground in changing rooms, trying to force up the zip on a pair of jeans. It's not a nice feeling but it's not earth shattering. Yet here, in this studio, miserable on a day I was so excited for, that's exactly how it feels: earth shattering. Because a voice hisses in my head that I'm fat and ugly. Not just look, but *am*. Like Angie and everything I used to be, and stand for, is gone. It doesn't matter that I have friends and family who love me, that I'm nice to people and that I always offer a quid to the homeless. That's cancelled out by this grim reality: I'm just a fat, ugly blob of a being, who's worth absolutely nothing. Before, even when Robbie broke my heart and buggered off to Oz, I used to be able to quiet the hissing voice, assure myself I was being silly, of course I was hot, that it was silly insecurities maybe brought on by my period or something. But I can't do that, not now I've read everything people have been saying about me. I know I shouldn't, that it's the equivalent of taking a pair of scissors and stabbing them in my thigh. But what I've been doing, every night the show airs, is searching my name on Twitter and on this new Instagram app, following the hashtag #NorthStars. Leo's right: there are plenty of people who love me.

I only watch this for Angelica.
Angelica's way too good for that himbo Damon.

> She might party hard but you can't deny she's a genuinely sweet soul.
> She'd be top quality on a night out. Love her.

Even so, there are people who really, really don't like me. Or, more specifically, really don't like the way I look. They're contradictory too, one minute they're calling me a beanpole, the next insisting I'm piling on the pounds. I know I shouldn't read the comments, as it's a lose-lose situation. But it's hard to stop myself, considering every single bad thing I've ever thought about myself is being reflected back to me by hundreds of people.

> Her body count is probably higher than her IQ.
> She's like a bus, everyone climbs onboard her and she's getting wider than one now.
> Angelica needs to close her legs and the fridge while she's at it.

And now, my one chance to show the world (and Damon) I'm hot stuff has finally arrived and yet none of the clothes fit. I'm yanking at the fabric of these lovely clothes and sweating profusely. I try the final dress and nope, the zip just won't budge past a certain point, no matter how much I hold my breath. I have to admit defeat.

"Excuse me," I say, but it comes out a whimper and I have to repeat myself. "Excuse me, Tash, can you come here a minute?"

The stylist pulls back the curtain and I retreat into the corner, as I've taken my underwear off in the hope that it might shed a few inches off of me, allowing the dress to fit. Unfortunately, this does not work as my bare ass is just reflected back, out into the studio, for the young camera assistant to see and quickly divert his eyes (out of politeness, I like to think, rather than disgust).

"The clothes, ermm, they just don't fit."

"Oh that's odd, you sent your sizes, right?" She pulls out her phone and finds the email, reading my message aloud. They *are* all my sizes but, I realise with a slow dawning dread, my sizes from before I entered the house. And I've probably eaten enough kebabs doused in garlic sauce to feed an elephant, and drank enough to fill the river Thames. I can feel the redness travel up my body, itching at my neck and spreading to my cheeks. I've probably turned the shade of beetroot as I say, "I must have put on a little weight."

"Not to worry. We can order the next size up," Tash says, breezily.

"Are you sure?"

"Absolutely hun, it's no bother. Silly of me, really, I normally order a range to be on the safe side. We can have them biked over in no time."

She's making me feel better, but also worse, as I don't want her blaming herself for what was definitely my mistake. "It'll be about an hour though, so we can sit you in the chair with Verity, then we've lost no time at all."

Verity waves me over, ushering me onto this tall chair, my legs dangling off it like a child. She talks me through all the products she's going to apply, and begins by rubbing this incredible soothing cream across my still-blazing cheeks.

"So, tell me about your show," she says. She's older than me and isn't wearing a speck of make-up herself. I like that. She's so stunning she doesn't need it, with these big wide eyes and a heart-pucker of a mouth, but she must also be pretty bloody confident in who she is, knowing full well that she could do her make-up if she wanted to, but that she doesn't *have* to.

"Erm, it's called *North Stars* and it's reality TV, really," I say.

"Oh so who do you play?" she asks, and I realise she must not really know what this newfangled reality TV is.

"Well, I guess, myself. They film us doing all sorts of things, like having romances and going to parties."

"That sounds fun!" she says. "And I've seen you today, you're a sweet girl, I bet people absolutely love you."

We chat a little more and she tells me she's been doing make-up for the past twenty years, how she at first used to specialise in prepping catwalk models, then spent a few years travelling around the world with pop stars (most of whom I haven't heard of, but it's exciting to know Verity is a proper MUA to the stars) and now mostly she does magazine stuff as it's flexible so suits her family life, with two little girls waiting at home for her. "I've seen what fame does to people," she tells me, while dusting powder on my cheeks as I try not to sneeze. "So, I hope you don't think I'm being too pushy here, but because of what I've seen and the people I've met, I worry about people in this business, particularly people like you, who are new to it all."

I tell her I don't mind and that I'll take any advice I can get, so she carries on.

"There are a lot of cruel people in this world. It's not necessarily their fault, they're damaged or hurt, or have been bullied and, instead of using that as motivation not be bullies themselves, they decide they'll take all that anger out on others. They don't like to see others living full, happy lives and, so, they'll do all they can to tear them down."

I begin to think of all the nasty things I've read about myself lately, and how often they came from accounts that were either faceless, or, even worse, from women who had things like 'be kind' or Bible verses or motivational quotes in their bios. Women who I looked at, smiling back at me from a tiny circle of pixels and thought "why do you hate me?"

"And the thing is," Verity's saying. "You're just human and there's going to be times in your life when you don't feel confident in yourself, or your body is going to change, as that's what bodies do. They go up in size, and they go down in size and, that's OK, it's natural but, unfortunately, people tend to get angry at celebrities when they don't match up to the impossibly perfect standards pushed upon them."

"How do the people you've worked with cope with that?" I may not be wise, but I'm wise enough to know that the answer isn't always found at the bottom of a shot glass.

She shrugs. "The ones that cope well are the ones who develop a really thick skin, who only care what the people around them think, not random strangers. Have you got family, friends you trust?"

"My mam's a legend," I say. It's true. She kept me going when I was mess after Robbie left, and I stopped singing in the pubs and clubs and then got the job at the care home while I tried to work out what on earth to do. She told me she didn't care what I pursued as long as it made me happy and didn't hurt anyone…but she doesn't stand for any nonsense. Get working, get busy, get happy, she told me.

"And there's Anika," I tell Verity. It's shit having a best mate working on a cruise ship. She texts me pictures of when they get into dock at all these glamorous resorts. But I don't know when I'll next actually see her – or even what time zone she's in. She says she's running fitness classes for the passengers. Aqua-aerobics in a pool with a swim-up bar doesn't sound that bad, but I miss her. "I've got new friends, too," I add. "Layla, Madison – they're other girls from the show, so they get what this mad thing we're doing is all about. They're my squad."

"Well, keep them close," smiles Verity. "They're your real diamonds, true friends. Those kind of mates don't try to twist themselves in knots trying to be what others want them to be. They listen to the voice in their heart, not the voices on the internet…"

"The voices on the internet are pretty loud right now, they're quite hard to ignore." I say to her and she looks me dead in the eye, and says: "I know, it'll get easier, I promise."

But it's hard to believe her, as surely the more I chase my goals and the more famous I get, the more people will have their eyes on me and have something to say. As it's not even falling asleep in a club loo, or the sex on telly, I don't really mind people ribbing me for those things, as I'm having so much fun. It's the comments on my appearance that are really settling in right now, digging at me. It's almost like the words themselves are pinching at my belly fat, jiggling my thighs. It's like the words have jumped out of the computer screen and crawl all over me, mocking me. I need to learn to swat them like pesky insects. Quickly. The stylist hauls in three more bags of clothes and gestures for me to come and try them on again, so it's time to venture back into the mirror room.

The clothes fit! No more sausage-skin vibes. Verity's also done my make-up so nicely, I'm all glowing and tanned and the way she's done my lip liner makes my lips look way more pouty than normal. I feel myself standing taller. It's fun being in front of the camera, moving from pose to pose and laughing with the photographer who tells me I'm a 'natural'. With each camera flash, I begin to feel better about myself, every now and then the mean words slip in but I try to just bat them away. Tits, teeth and tan, baby! I've got all three and I'm feeling myself, strutting around the studio in these huge heels. It's then, out the corner of my eye, that I spot them. Madison and Layla, all dolled up to the nines, their hair back-combed and high, sooty, spider-leg lashes framing their eyes and frosted pink lips. Better still, they're holding up a bottle of white wine each and whooping at me.

"What are you two doing here?" I holler, too excited by their surprise appearance at the shoot to consider the unflattering shots the photographer could be capturing of me.

"We wanted to celebrate your first big shoot and the girls from *Flair* said we'd be welcome to tag along!" Layla yells back and the photographer beckons them over. We end up doing an impromptu shoot with all three of us, plus the bottle, pouring wine into each others' mouths and showing the photographer, stylist, and, of course, Verity, how to do all our famous moves. There's the slut drop of course, which the photographer finds he absolutely cannot do in his mega-tight Indie-boy jeans, he only makes it about a quarter way down. We're all laughing so hard and no one from *Flair* seems to mind at all. In fact, they're delighted: three *North Stars* girls for the price of one. Having the girls with me on this big day really reminds me of why I want to keep doing all of this: because it's such a laugh. With my girls beside me, I really do feel unstoppable and as if we're here for a reason. I never used to see people like me on the telly, young girls who do stupid stuff like get tipsy and obsess over lads while still holding their heads high. It's not rocket science, sure, but it feels good. Like something's shifting.

I drape my arms around my friends and we lean towards the camera on my phone. "Say *'moist'*, ladies," I shout. I read somewhere that's what Victoria Beckham always says in photos to get a perfect pout. I quickly upload it with one line: HERE COME THE GIRLS.

* * *

Chapter Six

Once the shoot is over, we decamp to a nearby pub, and nab the best spot right by the window. Verity spritzed a special setting spray across my face and practically choked me with hairspray, so my 'look' will stay put for the night. We tried to beg her to come on a night out with us, I'd been telling Madison and Layla all about her wisdom, but she said all she wanted was a bath and huge glass of wine. Which is a pity as I really could do with her fairy godmother ways, when, one bottle down, Madison has a suggestion. She tries to say it all casual, like it hadn't been in her mind all along, and she was just waiting for the wine to loosen up me and Layla enough that we'd agree to it. We exchange a look as she says it, Layla with one eyebrow raised at me.

"So, I was on socials earlier, and guess who has a PA tonight?"

"If you're going to say Marc, you have to do a shot," Layla says, as back when we were in the studio we made an agreement: no talking about the lads. And anyone who so much as mentioned them had to do a shot. Which, considering we all love getting a drink in, isn't that big a punishment.

"You're the one who said his name!" Madison says, but even she knows her defence is weak.

"Alright, so it isn't Marc, then?" Layla retorts. "By some miracle you've forgotten all about him and instead it's the *Born In Buckinghamshire* boys who are doing a PA nearby?"

It just so happens that, at the same time our show launched, two similar reality TV shows hit screens (I say similar, as ours is clearly the best one). There's *Born In Buckinghamshire*, which features all these posh types who are all related in some way or another, either by actual blood, or because they're shagging…or in some cases, both (not, you know brother and sister stuff as that would be minging but like aristocratic-third-cousin type things). It always feels like the mega rich don't have family trees, they have a shrubbery of shame.

"UGH, no, as if," Madison squeals. "He's so pasty he probably uses factor fifty in a tanning salon."

"Yeah they're so pasty, they look like the inside of a Gregg's sausage roll."

They're right. The *Born In Buckinghamshire* lads are so not our type. You'd think with all that money they could afford to get a tan, or at least some decent clothes. They're all dressed in white, skinny jeans, shirts in weird colours that are better suited to an Easter egg than clothing. And the shoes! These slippy, poo-brown things that are called 'boat shoes' but I've never seen anyone on that show go near an actual boat. They're mostly just in fancy bars and having lunch and getting hammered, only they don't call it that, they call it getting 'sloshed' or, as one girl put it, 'absolutely waaaaahhssssted' really elongating the word, for absolutely no reason at all. That's the thing about *Born In Buckinghamshire*, they act like their show is better than ours, but theirs is exactly the same, it's just fighting, shagging and getting drunk, only they get drunk on champagne and we get drunk on Smirnoff Ice.

"OK, so not them lot," Layla says, playing along. "Though I wouldn't mind tearing the polo shirt off of that Sebastian lad. He looks ripped under those sweater vests."

The other show is *Carry On Chelmsford*, which is a little like *Born In Buckinghamshire* as it follows an actual group of friends around, but, like us, they're a lot less posh. They also love to get proper glammed up for nights out, but a few of them have managed to get some amazing deals lately. One of the girls got her own clothing line. I'd love to do something like that, as I know this whole 'new kids on the TV scene' thing can't last forever. I mean the PAs might pay the boys some wedge right now but it's not like when the lads are in their forties women will be queuing up to ogle them in nightclubs. Or maybe they will. I once queued up for four hours to meet Harold from *Neighbours,* but not because I fancied him (I'd have to have serious daddy issues for that, and I don't! My dad's been my hero and around all of my life). I just queued because it was funny, and I got this brilliant picture of me licking his head, something I am sure there was a reason for at the time though I can't, for the life of me, remember what it was.

We gossip for a little while about the other shows and who we've heard is shagging who, until Layla points out we've gone off topic and directs her attention back to Madison.

"Fine it's fucking Marc, OK? But it's not just him who'll be there. Reed will, and…Damon." She gives me a pointed look. I try to rearrange my features in a way that doesn't expose my excitement but also doesn't show that Damon, in all of the back-and-forth messaging we've been doing, didn't mention he was doing a PA in London. We could have met up last night. Or this morning and had a shag in a fancy hotel room. My room has this massive shower, one of those ones that makes you feel like you're standing under rain. Not freezing Mancunian rain that frizzes up your hair and makes you feel minging, but luxury, tropical rainfall. The type of rain you see in the movies, during the very last scene, when the main hero of a character (so, me) is chased in the rain by the love of her life who's messed up (so, Damon) and she looks exquisite in it and he tells her how she's the only one for him, and then they kiss and…

She then appeals to Layla's weakness. "Come on, it's all of the lads, we can get together, be a family again."

That's always what Layla loved most about the house, bringing all of us together as a group, lads *and* lasses for huge nights out. They were always the most fun, well, until they descended into snogging, gossip, chaos and, usually, at least one of us puking or worse. I'm feeling classy today though, in my shoot make-up, so I'm not going to reflect on that for long…

"Except it won't be all the family, will it? Samantha won't be there."

I try not to roll my eyes at Layla, who seems to be the only person not annoyed by how quickly Samantha has tried to distance herself from us since the show aired. *Voice and host of North Stars*, her new Instagram bio reads, and her following has climbed massively. She's barely replied to any messages from us. I don't consider her one of my 'family' because that word means something to me: loyalty and loving someone unconditionally. Samantha's not shown me either, and she's definitely not shown Madison that. Some pictures appeared in the papers of her proper snogging Marc, even though she knew how much he meant to Madison. And she was also there for the fall-out after the screening, after Madison saw, on screen, the games Marc had been playing with her.

I try to deflect from the fact that I do, actually, really want to go to the PA, as I don't want the girls to figure out that I shagged Damon again. I mean, knowing them, they've probably sussed it out already, there's something psychic about the pair of them when it comes to shagging. They can just tell. "Why do you want to see Marc anyway, Madison? Like, seriously, he was fucking awful to you."

"Why did you shag Damon again?" Madison replies, in an eerily accurate impression of me.

"Yep, of course we know," chimes Layla. Watch out Mystic Meg, the Psychic Shaggers are about.

"I'm not..." I try to say but they both just look at me and I sigh. "How did you know?"

"One, your hair the next day"

"Two, that smug look on your face, like the cat that got the—"

"Come on," I interrupt and shove them as they keep fake humping and laughing. They both break down in giggles and I can't help but join in.

"Fine, let's all do a shot for Madison talking about Marc."

"Then another round for Angelica talking about Damon," Madison chimes in.

"Then we'll go to the PA. Family reunion!" sings out Layla.

As soon as we arrive at the PA, I get this dread in my tummy that tells me it was a big mistake coming here. I can't walk quite as straight as I would like to, and as we approach the nightclub, this petite blonde in frayed dark denim shorts approaches me with a flyer. She's very pretty. She has a little button nose, big Bambi eyes and, worse still, is actually incredibly friendly and funny and sweet. My problem since getting to know Damon in the house as both his friend, and part-time… whatever we are, is that I also got to know who is type is. I know he likes frayed shorts, as I was wearing them when we first laid eyes on each other, and unfortunately, I know he likes petite blondes who can get away with wearing hardly any make-up, as he told me multiple times, saying that I wear too much (but then OTT gasping when he does see me without it). I'm also trying to block out the times I watched him pull girls exactly like this chatty wee thing in front of me, pretending I'm the cool girl, that I'm chill about who he pulls, totally unphased, even when I'm clenching my jaw so hard I'm seeing stars. I look at this doe-eyed girl again. I hope they haven't met. Except, that's what she's telling me has just happened.

"Oh my god, and they're like so fit and so nice," she's saying, while I'm suddenly clocking just how long the queue of women snaking out the door is. The lads were not exaggerating.

It's also about halfway through zoning her out that I realise that Madison and Layla have completely disappeared and that this girl has absolutely no clue who I am. "Did you watch the show?" she's saying. "Sure, the lads came across as dickheads sometimes, but they're actually so sweet. Don't tell anyone, as he told me not to, but I think I might be in there with one of them…"

Don't say Damon. Don't say Damon. Don't say Damon.

"Damon! Can you believe it?"

She's waiting for me to say something, and I'm wondering what the hell I should do. Tell her who I am? That would be so humiliating. Not just because I'm clutching the flyer she gave me that has my own show typed across it, but also because anyone's who watched the show has seen me snot-cry about Damon multiple times, before totally and utterly denying that he means anything to me. On the other hand, I do need someone who works here to know who I am as there's no way I'm joining an hour-long queue to meet people I've shared a toilet with, especially as I don't know if I have enough money in my bank account to pay the entry fee.

Thankfully, Madison begins yelling my name, saving me (kind of) from humiliation. "Oh my god," the girl says, even shriller this time. "Angelica's here, no way, where?" Before it slowly dawns on her, just as Layla's grabbed me by the arm, that I am, indeed, Angelica.

"Oh fuck," I can hear her shout after me. "It's just you look…so much nicer than you did in the house?"

Madison and Layla have spoken to the club promoter, explaining we thought it would be fun to have a family reunion with the lads. We're all ushered through the queue, some of whom exclaim in anger at our skipping, others who begin to scream when they realise who we are. Once inside, we dash up the spiral staircase and onto a balcony overlooking the whole club, where an ice-bucket of drinks is waiting for us in our VIP section. The club was obviously once a grand ballroom, or perhaps a theatre, in its glory days, when ladies would get dressed up for gentlemen to take them dancing. Which, I guess, nowadays it kind-of still is, all the girls I can see are definitely dressed up, and they're dancing but not in a way I can imagine would gain much approval from any fancy Lords or Ladies. We can see the stage, and below us, there's hordes of girls in bandage-dresses and skin-tight tiny tops, their hair teased high, waiting for the lads, *our* lads, to come out. When they do it's complete mayhem, the crowd rushing to get closer to the front as they begin pulling girls up onto the stage, twirling them around, picking them up, so the girls are wrapping their legs around their waist, and Damon has even taken his top off and is just in the midst of squirting whipped cream on his chest for some girl to lick off when…

"Actually, you're in for a treat tonight, as, there's some surprise guests in the house," the speakers blast out. "The most famous – wait, did I say famous? Of course, I meant *infamous* girls from the whole of the North... The *North Stars* girls are in the house!"

It's at that moment that a huge spotlight swings round and bathes us girls in bright light, and the lads look up from the stage – Damon with his whipped cream can in hand, fangirl already on her knees – in shock. It's not the look I'd have wanted from him, but very quickly he regains his composure and a grin spreads across his face. He grabs the mic out of the host's hands and says, "Belting! If it isn't our favourite girls, cough, sorry Samantha..." and the audience all begin to laugh and cheer, waving up at us.

They continue their act, including the girl licking the cream off. But I don't mind as what else was he meant to do, see me and ask for a towel? Damon is the kind of lad who gets his pecs out without any encouragement, let alone when he's got a girl ready to treat him like dessert. But also, there was that smile on his face when he saw me. It really did seem so genuine. Something I'm slurring at Reed, after all the lads head on up to our VIP area. Marc's nowhere to be found, despite Madison checking every single toilet cubicle for him. I had followed her around, trying to stop her, or so at least I could be there when she eventually discovered what she inevitably would. We witnessed two lads furiously jerking each other off, one girl passed out on the toilet with what looked like Apple Sourz sprayed all up the walls, and at one point we even thought we'd found Marc shagging someone else. But after a raging Madison pried the pair apart, it just turned out to be another Chad Schmidt lookalike. Turns out you only really need a man-bun to be the dead ringer for a Hollywood hearthrob these days. Damon is chatting to, but I swear not chatting *up*, the barmaid (she's definitely not his type...I think, despite her having a pulse, a tiny skirt and a massive rack – all Damon's usual requirements) while Layla and Madison are twirling each other round.

"Yeah, it was genuine," Reed's saying back. "But just be careful will you, I don't think he's exactly ready to settle down yet."

Reed's a good friend as he's genuinely mates with Damon, but he will also call him out when he's behaving like a knob-head, as well as, gently (and probably far too many times) telling me when I'm taking it a little too far. "Anyway, Angelica, come out with me to the cash machine, I've got to, well, you know…"

I don't actually know. With Reed you're never quite sure what he's scheming, he could be getting cash out for magnums of champagne, or he could show up, after meeting a man in a local garage, with two homing pigeons he's decided he'll raise.

"Yeah sure," I wave at the girls to tell them where we're off to, and we head out into the night. It's one of those inky blue nights, where the stars are almost twinkling at you and encouraging you to misbehave. It could be Damon's grin, or it could be the shoot today, but I suddenly feel content, as I link Reed's arm as we stumble down the street together, having one of our typical silly Reed and Angelica conversations all about what aliens might think of us if they were to land here tonight. It's as we're debating whether aliens would love or hate kebabs that we pull up by the cash machine and I notice it: five missed calls from my mam. I ring her back straight away, it's late but I know she'll be up.

"Mam, is everything OK? Are you OK? Is Dad OK?"

"Oh, we're fine," she says, but her voice is shaky. It's obvious things aren't fine.

"Then why did you call?"

Reed looks over with concern, but I gesture at him to carry on withdrawing his cash.

"Oh it's just, I wanted to know if you were going to be home for Sunday dinner this week?"

I can hear the wobble in her voice, and yes, my mam's roasties are the best. But she wouldn't normally be calling at nearly midnight to check if I wanted extra Yorkshires. "What is it, Mam?"

"I don't want to worry you but it's…well…you know how Mr Marner is always threatening us with how he could get so much for the house if he sold it?"

"Yes…" The man that we rent our family home from, have done for years, fancies himself as the Alan Sugar of the north. He seems to owns half of Manchester – even the *North Stars* house is leased from him, so of course he thinks he's Mr Bigshot. But he's actually called Callum Marner, and he's got a ton of businesses as well as being a dodgy landlord, including a chain of basement tanning shops that, I swear, must use actual vegetable oil or something in their fake tan mix as I always come out absolutely stinking of chippie (and am incredibly attractive to seagulls) whenever I leave one. Come to think of it, I don't know why I keep going back. He doesn't need our rent, or the money he'd get from selling the house, but that doesn't stop him from calling round every now and then to remind us just how 'lucky' we are that he's letting us rent what he calls a 'premium executive home'. When really he's the lucky one, my mam's kept the garden in perfect condition and even put in the most amazing rose bushes, while my dad's the one fixing any problems that come up.

"He's done it," Mam's saying. "He says if we can't increase the rent to the silly money he's asking, then he wants us out in a month. And I don't know what to do, I just don't think we can afford the deposit on a new place on top of all the cost of moving, and what about my roses…"

All the while she's talking I'm craning over Reed's shoulder for a look at his bank balance. At first I find it comforting, thinking that, like me, he's got about tenner in his account. Then, I realise that the extra 0s are not a result of my drunken eyesight. He's actually got £10,000 in his account! Ten-thousand-effing-actual-pounds? How is it that Reed's got so rich? He's a scaffolder from Barrow, not a banker. Surely that can't all be PA money?

"I hate to ask, love," my mam continues. "You know we'd always pay you back but—"

"Mam, you and Dad raised me, made sure I never wanted for anything, you'd never have to pay me back a penny," I promise her, knowing exactly what she's going to ask.

"Are you sure, petal? What with your show and all those lovely shoots and things, and you know we're so proud of you for that, would you be able to lend us the money for the move?"

Without hesitation, I tell her that of course I will, that she doesn't need to worry and I'll sort it ASAP. I say all of that knowing I've got less than a tenner in my own account. But I don't care. I will sort it. They're my parents. I just need to figure out how…

* * *

Chapter Seven

One month. One measly month to pack up our family home, put our memories into boxes and erase all traces of us from the house that I took my first steps in, the house where I used to make a slide out of the stairs, bump, bump, bumping down them in my Simpsons sleeping bag. There's marks on the wall, proudly sketched in pencil, a record of my height for each of my twenty-two years. We're going to have to paint over that, I think, and even pay for the paint.

I've been trying to keep myself together and be strong for my mam, who keeps crying every two seconds, as we fill up boxes. "Oh but this is where you threw a carrot at your dad, because he was trying to get you to eat it," she'll say, pointing out a random patch of carpet, and filling me in on a memory that my childish putty brain definitely didn't absorb. But, every now and then, I have to go into the bathroom and have a small cry myself. I know it's just a house, and that the most important thing about the house is us, as a family, and no one, not even a sleazy landlord, can take that away from us. We carry the memories, the walls don't. But still, I don't want to leave this place. It feels silly, but I almost want to whisper to the wallpaper, to the doors, even to the skirting boards, 'don't forget us.' I can't imagine a new family in here, making their own memories, both good and bad. Because there have also been bad moments, these doors have been angrily slammed by me (sorry doors) and Mam and I have had screaming matches over too-short skirts and late-night sneak-outs, facing each other on these carpets, with me stomping my feet that she's being 'so unfair.' Then there's the mounting pressure that I promised them I'd pay the deposit for a new place. I'll find a way to do it, I know, it's just I'm not quite sure how yet.

But I know who will help. The day after the PA, I had a voicemail on my phone.

"Angelica, this is Felicity Johnston. But you can call me Fliss. All my clients do. Call me back – I think we could do great things together."

And that was how I met my agent, Fliss. From our first conversation I knew she and I would get along. So far the *North Stars* producers had handled all the media requests, but it was always just a list of what to do that week. What I loved about Fliss was that right away, she had a long-term plan. And she took me seriously. Perhaps more seriously than I take myself. Already, she's offered me so much wisdom and advice as to how to turn my five-minutes of fame into a long-term career, and she promises me that while the lads might be making a mint now, that won't last. There's a look in her eyes like she sees me as a human being rather than a quick buck, a person not a payout. I guess I might not have been in this game long, but as Fliss told me, if I can sniff out a phoney, I'll survive longer.

So now I've got all these long-term plans, like how eventually I'll host my own show, maybe have my own clothing line and be the face of a make-up brand, and I feel really excited about the future. The problem is that all feels really far away, and I can't let my parents down. It's just not even a possibility.

Life lately has mostly either been packing and panicking when I'm in back home, or living a glam celebrity life on trips down south while pretending everything's fine. Take tonight. I'm currently covered in dust from crawling under my childhood bed to clear it out (and getting really distracted by my old diaries, honestly Damon should read these and see he's really not that special, since the age of twelve I've had some obsession or another with a boy). But I need to hop on a train to London soon (told you it's practically my new home) as this evening we've been invited to the BTA's! They're the biggest telly awards around, and all of the *North Stars* lot have been invited, even the crew, so it'll be epic.

We're being put up in a swanky apartment overlooking the Thames and of course, getting all glammed up before walking the red carpet and watching the awards surrounded by all the other celebrities. I can't wait. Me and Mam have been chatting non-stop (in between the crying fits over all the memories we keep packing away) about what celebs I might see tonight. She's convinced that all these stars are going to meet me, and either fall instantly, deeply in love or offer me a gig on their shows. I'm not so sure.

When we arrive at the apartment that the *North Stars* production company have rented out, us girls can't stop running around screaming. Even Samantha joins us in excitement, grabbing my hand and pulling me through exclaiming "have you seen the hot tub?" and "oh my god come jump on this bed with me, it's sooooo soft." The flat is on the 14th floor of an all-glass block, and it's the penthouse suite so the lift opens directly into it. It's got floor-to-ceiling windows and a deep, wraparound balcony, so you can walk from each bedroom out onto it and use it as a walkway to the living room. And the views! The London Eye is so close to us I swear, if I was some sort of stunt woman, I could jump from the balcony and grab onto one of the pods and go for a ride. The Thames is below our feet and there's bean bags and sunloungers and heaters out there. Not that we need to turn them on. As soon as we arrived in London, we could feel it. Sunshine! It's been cold and rainy for months and while I always say I don't mind bad weather, that us northern girls are made of tough stuff and can go out in plummeting temperatures, sleet, hailstones and wind without a coat, feeling those golden rays on my face made me realise how much I'd missed it. Everyone else clearly has too, as it's just making everyone so cheerful. The whole of London has their legs and arms out, and the city swelters with sex in the air. All four of us girls were making eyes at so many men from the moment we stepped out of the station. Maybe Prince Charming really is just around the corner.

The lads are on later trains, so they won't arrive for an hour or so, and even though Samantha let slip that they *chose* to go later, as they didn't want to travel with us, I've decided not to believe her. Damon says he can't wait to get here and I'm excited to show him a different side to me. The dress I've chosen for tonight is nothing like the clothes I wore in the house, where admittedly I was too busy having a good time to spend eons getting ready. But tonight's different, I'm different, this dress is different. It's cherry red, and it swoops to the floor. It's even got a high neck so most of my skin is covered, but the way it clings to my body, you can tell what's underneath is banging. Or at least, *will* be banging once I've wrestled myself into the Spanx my mam has leant me. Then, at some point, I'll have to figure out how to wrestle myself out of the Spanx and into the tiny thong I'm going to carry in my handbag, without Damon noticing, if I'm going to avoid a Bridget Jones big knicker disaster. It's a pity as I wouldn't mind wandering hands under the table during the awards, but getting through these Spanx is as hard as escaping a high-security prison. This evening, my fairy is under lock and key. Which both Mam and Fliss would be happy with, considering they both keep telling me Damon is no good for me. I guess it's hard for them after watching me cry so much over him in the house, but they've not seen this new side of Damon. He saves that just for me.

I've also got Verity coming over to do my make-up. The production company said they were arranging hair and make-up, so I suggested her. She was so nice to me on that shoot and gave me such great advice, I'd love it if when I'm proper, proper famous she does my make-up all the time. Particularly as she's got a rare mix of common sense and juicy gossip. As soon as she arrives in the house and starts setting up a station in the apartment's vast main bathroom, which is basically all marble that I just know I'm going to slip on later, she begins to tell me Hattie from *BiB*'s 'spiritual retreats' mostly involve white power and shagging each other. "And then Tarquin's laid-back personality is secretly hiding a gambling addiction."

I've never thought about it before but make-up artists hear *everything*. They know who's secretly gay, who's shagging who and who's a total bitch. Verity's even told me sometimes people fake relationships. Maybe I'm totally gullible, but before I entered into this industry I just assumed that everything I read about in the papers was basically real. "No, sweetie," Verity's saying while dabbing powder on my cheeks, baking it in. "What happens is, say someone has a show to promote, or they need publicity for whatever reason, then their agent will find someone else famous for them to start a relationship with."

"Like matchmaking?"

"Not exactly. Take that singer, Kady James. Her last relationship, her and Cosimo Drake? That was all fake."

"What?" screeches Madison from the corner. "I loved those two, I was devastated when they broke up."

"He's gay," says Verity. "His actual boyfriend is a really good friend of mine. He works in finance, totally non-showbiz job. Huge dick."

"Dollar and dick," sighs Layla. "Isn't that what we all want?"

"If you girls keep going the way you're going, you'll be drowning in both," Verity says. "Just keep your eyes on the prize, develop a really strong bullshit detector and only take advice from people you really love, *not*," she taps her brush on my nose, "total strangers."

When our hair and make-up is done it's time for us to get into our dresses, which we'd carefully coordinated so that when our photos are taken on the red carpet we match but still look unique, showing off our personalities. Layla suggested we go with jewel-colour dresses, "because we're the northern jewels" and I'd bagsied red straight away. I wanted to be the ruby, all shimmering and tempting. Layla's gone for sapphire blue and I'm determined to forge ahead with my masterplan of turning Mads into as much of a star as us lot that were on camera, so she's dressing in style too. Madison went with emerald green because it matches her eyes, and she's in a gown that sweeps all the way to the floor, but of course because it's Madison, is frighteningly low cut. We're all on tit-watch tonight, if one falls out we're under strict instructions to quickly jump in front of her, while one of the other jewels helps her wrestle it back in. Earlier, we'd even had to rush to the local corner shop as it became very clear that the tit tape that Madison packed was not going to cut it with her double Fs. It was far too flimsy. So the secret is – and totally invisible to anyone else – that Madison's boobs are being held up and together by some very heavy duty masking tape.

Samantha's decided to be an elusive pearl. Her dress is off-white and is almost magical when it catches the light, revealing that it's made of miniature sequins all over. Except…she's just sashayed into the room and she's not in the white dress we *all* agreed on. Nope. Instead she's in red, the exact same red as mine, only hers is much sluttier. It's covered in slits, like Edward Scissorhands has had a go at it, but Edward Scissorhands if he worked for Versace, as all the slits are in the sexiest of places, one thigh high, one across her hip, another under her left boob. To stop it being too revealing there are gold safety pins fastened to each slit, it's a red homage to that dress that Elizabeth Hurley wore, the one that *made* her career. Samantha looks jaw-dropping in it, we're all absolutely agog when she comes waltzing in and not just because she's messed up the plan and is wearing *my* colour.

"I thought you were wearing white," Layla's saying to her and Samantha just shrugs, like it's no big deal.

"Yeah but I felt like a fucking bride in that dress, I decided to swap last-minute. This one is much better, don't you think?" She does a little twirl. There is, of course, a slash just across the top of her bum, revealing a shot of, *damn*, perfect bum cheek.

"But I was supposed to be the ruby," I say, but it comes out a whisper. I feel like a silly child, I know it's just a dress but already I can see us walking in front of all the photographers together, and I know who's going to grab their attention. Why did I decide I should be classy? Everyone knows it's the slutty dresses that make the papers the next day.

"What's that?" Samantha says, her tone switching from sweetly excited about her dress to aggressive in an instant. "You got a problem, Angelica? You can't own a colour, you know."

"Cut the crap, Samantha, we all agreed Angelica would be the one in red, you're just trying to upstage her, like you always fucking do." I'm grateful that Madison has my back, particularly as we all know you have to be bold to go against Samantha. Whenever things didn't go her way in the house, she'd not hesitate to get right up in people's faces, yelling so close that whoever was on the receiving end would get a whiff of her tequila-and-fags breath.

"Alright boulder tits," retorts Samantha. "As if you're one to talk when it comes to attention seeking, I'm not the one who's trying to distract the press from the fact you're just a runner by letting my tits enter a room before I do and who will whip off her top as soon as any lad, even a minging one, is nearby."

With that, we're all yelling, trying to get our voices heard above the din, and the warm, fuzzy, girlie friendship feeling we had earlier has dissipated. But whose fault is that? If Samantha wanted to match with us three, as she's now claiming this is typical and we always gang up on her or leave her out, then she should have stuck to the plan.

"Cat fiiiiiight!" It's Damon, he's arrived with the lads in tow and their presence is enough for all of us to stop fighting – for now at least. They're already in their tuxes and Damon looks so handsome. I've got all-over flutters just looking at him and I have to pry my gaze away before, oh, oops they're already there, my head is full of Damon-themed fantasies, in that suit, at the end of an aisle, waiting for me. We're all hugging and kissing, when I spot out of the corner of my eye that Leo is here too! He also looks handsome in his suit (though not as handsome as Damon, of course). His floppy, sandy blond hair, which is usually so messy, is perfectly tousled and the navy blue of his suit brings out the cobalt shade of his eyes. I don't think I've ever noticed just how beautiful they are before, they're like the colour of the sky, just before it turns to night. I rush over to say hello, so pleased that now we're not filming we can chat without having to hide it. Although a part of me wonders what it's like having watched and filmed everything, but having done so while sober. He probably remembers it all better than I do. I suppose that's why the crew are like the parental part of the family – they're with us all the time, but also just on the periphery.

"What are you doing here?" I ask.

"Before I answer that, I have to tell you just how beautiful you look, Angelica. Proper breathtakingly stunning."

"I guess I scrub up well," I reply, smiling and suddenly conscious of a feeling that grabs at my stomach, but it's gone before I can identify exactly what it was. Probably just a need to fart.

"We're up for one of the techy awards – the ones they don't televise! 'Best post-production.' But you know what the production company is like. Never waste an opportunity. When they invited me and some of the rest of the crew, I realised it wasn't just a knees-up. They've sent me to do some filming as well," he gestures to his feet where his trusty camera-bag sits. It's covered in all these patches, collected from all the locations he's filmed all over the world. He told me quite early on in the series that when he comes home, it's a tradition for him to sit with his mam as she sews them on and tell her all about his travels. "They think that for season two, some of these big moments might make for good cut-off scenes."

"So there will definitely be a season two, then?" I ask, thinking of Mam and Dad, and all the money I desperately need.

"Are you mad, Angelica? You're so loved, I mean…" he stutters. "The show is so loved, of course they're going to sign off on a new one. There's just a few paperwork things that need sorting, I hear. I'm sure you'll get your contract soon."

I'm fizzing inside. When I'd quit my job at the care home to do the show, so many people had said I was crazy to jack in a steady job for some flash in the pan chance to embarrass myself on national TV. When I'd handed in my resignation, my manager had said I'd been on course to become a supervisor. But the old folk I looked after? They were my biggest cheerleaders. Mavis, who I reckon was a bit of a goer in her day, held my hand in hers and told me the only things I should ever regret were the things I'd left undone. I mean, I might have taken that too literally when I was passed out in the corner of the Tiger Bar after multiple vodkas, but I take her point, and I think she'd be proud that I've stuck with it. A second series in the pipeline shows people must be loving it.

Fliss has also said that she'll try to get me more money this time. We hardly got anything for the first season, which is mad, as she pointed out, considering we had to quit our jobs and abandon our whole lives in order to go on the show. I'd never considered it like that before, as the way I saw it, I was getting to go on this mad adventure, get all free booze and VIP entry into the best nightclubs. At the beginning, honestly, I'd have paid them just to participate.

I'm about to ask Leo another question when Damon jumps up behind me, slapping me on the butt. "Ass looking good," he whispers in my ear, before announcing to the room, "Angelica's pancake butt is more of a cupcake today," and laughing. I laugh too but I notice Leo doesn't. He's never been great with lad banter, Damon always calls him boring… he'd even say that in the house. I always told him to shush, you never know when the cameras were eavesdropping, and I'd hate Leo to hear anyone saying anything bad about him. We're fair game as we signed up for this, knowing full well we'd end up bitched about, but he's just trying to do his job.

"Right, limo time," Gerald's at the door. He tries to give us pointers on how we should behave when the cameras are focused on us, and how yes there's wine on the table, but that doesn't mean we need to drink all of it, but we're all too excited at the prospect of a limo (with a very hot driver, as it happens) to properly listen. Besides, Gerald was sometimes the one who would come into the house while we were all falling over or screaming at each other and replenish the bottles of Apple Sourz. He can hardly make us change our ways now, can he? He made us who we are, and that's why the world is falling in love with us! They can see we're just like them, people having fun, because we're young, silly and

Lucky Break

want to laugh. As we pile into the limo, which has a ceiling of lights like twinkling stars, and a huge ice bucket in the middle containing a bottle of prosecco waiting for us, I realise something. Damon didn't tell me how beautiful I look, just my ass.

* * *

Chapter Eight

"Angelica, over here, Angelica!" There's a gaggle of photographers, just to the side of the red carpet, and they're all calling my name. Seriously, it's a like a wall of them, jostling with each other, their cameras hanging around their necks, the flashes brighter than any night club strobe. "Give us a pose, Angelica, that's right darling," they're shouting, and it's almost like listening to a football chant, I can hardly hear what they're actually saying, there's that many of them talking to me at once. The people-pleaser in me wants to shout, "What? What do you actually want me to do?" as I just want them to get a good shot, have a picture in the papers tomorrow that my mam can tear out and pop on her (hopefully soon) new fridge.

But when I do lean forward, to ask what pose I should do, I'm shouting with my mouth open and then I hear one of them say, "that's right love, open your mouth like usual." I recoil back, looking around to hear if anyone else heard him, or will tell him off. But no one does. And I don't have time to let it bother me, as all of a sudden Damon is by my side. He travelled over in a different limo to ours, and his presence beside me is comforting. I want to cling onto him, and have him guide me through this throng. Being on this red carpet, the camera flashes lighting me up, it's the spotlight I've always wanted. But at the same time, it's stressful handling it on your own. Am I doing it right? I keep trying to shake off this out-of-body feeling of being an imposter. So Damon's arm, pulling me in by the waist, feels grounding. I never want him to let me go.

Lucky Break

The snapping noise from the photographers' cameras gets even louder then, the flashing even more insistent. "Angelica and Damon, reality TV's golden couple," shouts a journalist, rushing up to us, a huge microphone in hand. It's all fluffy, like a cuddly toy on a stick, and she's thrusting it in our faces. "So, do you think you can forgive him for the way he treated you?" she's saying to me, but before I can answer the photographers are yelling at her to get out of the way and they need to get their pics in first.

"Don't worry, darling," Damon says to her. "It'll be your turn later." Was that a wink I saw? I don't know. The camera flashes are making my eyes all dotty, and Damon is wearing a different aftershave from the one he wore in the house. It must be more expensive, it smells of cedar and a deep, dark vanilla. It's intoxicating. "Go on, give her a kiss," one of the photographers yells, and Damon does this big showy display, dipping me back like we're ballroom dancers, before pulling me right in, the taste of his lips just as addictive as when I first felt them on mine. Soft but unyielding. He pulls away and looks me dead in the eye, and people can call me a mug all they want, but the desire burning in his eyes, during moments like these, reveals his true feelings. I can see it, clear as day.

Then, in an instant, the cameras are suddenly pointing at someone else. We turn to see Samantha, and conveniently one of her straps has slipped down, revealing a hint of raspberry-pink nipple. "Oops, sorry about that boys," she giggles, as the photographers elbow each other out the way to get the shot.

Damon keeps holding my hand all the way along the red carpet, standing close by my side during all the press interviews. I look around for Madison and Layla, I want them to see this, how attentive he's being. But they're already inside, no doubt getting stuck into the free white wine. Still, at least there's all this actual photographic evidence of us. "We're going to be all over the front pages tomorrow," Damon says, pulling me in for a squeeze. "You're the best Angelica, honestly, I don't know what I'd do without you."

With that, he's gone. Marc's ushered him to follow him into the bathroom and I'm left with just the lingering smell of his aftershave.

The *North Stars* lot are spread across two huge round tables, and we're really near the front of the stage. I always remember Mam telling me you can tell how important you are at a wedding by how close your table is to where the couple sit. At the awards, I think the stage counts as the top table so we must be flavour of the month. I can practically smell the presenter's breath (mouthwash covering a base layer of gin). He's up there now, practising his cues and being informed where different people will stand. The whole show is airing live on TV tonight and, even though I've watched it every year so I anticipated I'd feel vaguely familiar with what's going on, I forgot we will get to see all the things that aren't shown on the TV. Like, what's going to happen in all the ad breaks? Before the awards and show begin we have a three-course meal, for all the celebs and VIPs who are here. I'm trying so hard not to crane my neck and goggle at people but it's hard. On the table next to us is Alexis Vonnette. She's absolutely tiny, but has this glow to her that I swear must be injected into her somehow, there's no way she's getting that from a bottle. It's like she's got this rich aura that just leaks into the air surrounding her. Even if you had absolutely no idea who she is, or you were an alien from another planet, you'd set one eye on her and just know she was rich and famous.

"Have you seen Kristophe Spruce?" Layla whispers, or at least she thinks she whispers, but it comes out more of a boom. "He's so fit. I'd risk a restraining order." I've been sitting with Layla to one side of me, and Madison the other. Leo's sitting on our table, but across from me, so I couldn't speak to him without yelling anyway, but even he keeps making faces at all the different celebrities around us. He texted me to tell me that when he opens his eyes wide that's his cue for an A-lister nearby, and then he sticks his tongue out in the direction they're walking. At one point he even went cross-eyed trying to show me that Harry Styles was one way, and Tom Hardy the other. I was in stitches.

Lucky Break

We have a big metal bucket at the centre of our table, full of clinking bottles of wine and fizz. We don't even have to top up our glasses ourselves, the lovely waiting staff come around and do it for us. Though I bet they're gutted to be placed on our table as they've got twice, or maybe three times, the amount of work to do compared with the other tables. We're necking our wine quickly, because we're playing a game with the other table, which has Damon, Marc and Reed on it, as well as Samantha. I don't know how she ended up on the table with the lads, but she looks fuming as none of them are paying her much attention. We have to take a sip every time someone is caught on camera not smiling, take a gulp every time someone thanks God and/or their mothers, and down our drink if someone wells up during their speech. We also have to manage all this without Gerald suspecting a thing. It's easier for us as we don't have him on our table, mind you, he's up and down so much, saying hello to all his industry friends, that he's like a pogo stick.

Layla whispers to me, "this is well boring," during the awards themselves, and admittedly, it does drag on listening to the presenters announce all the nominees for each award, and then having to clap, before the big drawn-out suspense to see who has won. But, it's all worth it to watch people actually win the awards. I just love it! I always have, when we used to watch at home when I was little, Mam, Dad and I would bet on who we think would win and then afterwards I used to do a range of performances, each pretending to be someone different. I'd get them to vote for who they thought should win and then take it a step further, clutching one of Mam's vases, while Dad announced "and the winner is…" before standing in front of the sofa and giving a heart-felt, dramatically-fake speech. I'd even then pretend to be the losers caught on camera, and either do polite clapping or storm off in a huff. So I can't believe this is for real. My head is swinging this way and that, as I like to watch the winner's reaction on the big screens that are set up behind the presenter, so I can see what Mam and Dad see at home (and also, admittedly, see if I end up in any background shots) but also I want to see the stuff that isn't shown on the telly. At one point, I managed to catch a famous actress' face when she learned she hadn't won Drama Actress Of The Year and she really did display some drama. I couldn't hear what she was saying but she was turning to her boyfriend, scowling and swearing, then he tapped her to show that the camera was on her and she was suddenly all smiles and gracious claps! I would have given her an award for that acting alone. It's also so nice to hear people's speeches and really see, with my own two eyes, how much winning means to them. I love hearing the speeches thanking their mam and dad and all their friends, and I couldn't help but enter into a daydream as to who I'd thank if I were to win an award and what it would feel like to stand up, hugging everyone at my table (Mam and Dad first, obviously, then the girls, the production team, Damon, and maybe the inventors of fake tan). I daydream so much that I end up not properly paying attention, and Madison has to poke me in the rib with her fork and loudly whisper, "look alive, they're talking about us!"

Sure enough, a trendy comedian is on stage saying how much reality TV has really taken off this year, in ways that no one could have expected, pulling in all different sorts of audiences and making national treasures out of the people on the shows. Then, on the big screen, to this audience of celebrities and all the people watching at home, they play a montage featuring our escapades, alongside memorable moments from *Born In Buckinghamshire* and *Carry on Chelmsford*. There I am, pulling a face as I apply my lashes. Everyone's laughing but kindly, like they're laughing with me. If I was Samantha, I wouldn't be happy watching this, there's so many shots of us but the montage music covers up most of Sam's funniest lines. But when I glance over at her, she's grinning ear to ear, an immaculate smile for the cameras. From the other shows, the person who comes off worse is Sebastian from *BiB* due to an infamous incident where he who wore his father's army uniform to a party, then ended up stripping for a bunch of girls and pinning his dad's medals to his boxer shorts, right where his willy was. The girls kissed and he got a hard-on while the medals clanged and jangled, all on TV, and people were so offended there were even protests outside the TV studio fronted by ex-veterans demanding he got sacked. I do not know how he managed to squirm his way out of that one, but he's sitting at a nearby table. Mind you, he is so oily it looks like he could slip off his seat. When the camera pans to him afterwards, he does make an 'I'm soooo sorry' face at the camera, but then I see, because I see *everything*, as soon as the camera leaves him he makes a wanking motion to his table mates and laughs. What an entitled sod – he probably thinks he's too rich to care about what anyone thinks.

As the montage ends, huge searchlights strobe across the crowds, stopping on Reed, then Sebastian and finally Samantha. A drumroll thunders through the speakers as they announce that next year there's going to be a new category: Reality TV Star of the Year.

"Oh my god, Angelica you could win that," whispers Madison. Leo leans over, and says, "I heard from an insider that the TV execs will be watching you, Samantha, Damon and a few from *COC* and *BIB* over the coming months, tracking how your popularity grows. It's a real money-spinner too, whoever wins this award will be showered in brand deals and there's a charity donation, too."

So, it's more than just that moment where I can thank Mam and Dad on stage, in fact, it's an opportunity not just to pay for their rent but maybe even buy them their own house so they never have to worry about rent again. I can almost see the possibility, the trophy shining bright in my future. It feels within reach. Then I glance at the other table. Samantha winks at me.

"What's that about?" I ask.

"One of my friends on the other table was saying she's already started campaigning," Leo says. "She thinks she's going to have lobby even harder since she's the voice rather than the face of the show. Why do you think she's on the other table? She switched name tags so she could be near Gerald! She wanted him to introduce her to all his industry friends."

We all look over to the table, and I'm relieved to see that Gerald is not getting charmed by Samantha, but instead he's standing up, gently stroking both the chihuahua and the bicep of a man holding a little goggly-eyed dog. She's sitting with her arms crossed, frowning and scanning the audience – presumably for anyone important enough to buttonhole.

"It's a stupid plan," laughs Layla. "Gerald would not want anybody cock-blocking him. He's determined to go home with someone tonight, he told me in the limo."

I laugh – all the supposedly scandalous things we got up to in the house? Everyone else in the industry is doing it too. Just not on film.

It's then that Samantha sidles up behind me. "Oh, hi," I say. "We missed you on our table!" It's not entirely false, Samantha can be hilarious, when she's in the right mood. In fact, I bet its why she'll be in the running for the award despite not being on camera. Her voiceovers are often genius - even if she did get all her best laughs and lines riffing off the silly stuff I got up to! But she doesn't look like she's in a joking mood now.

"Yeah right," she says, before lowering her voice, and whispering into my ear. "If you think that award's yours, think again."

* * *

Chapter Nine

I thought that things got pretty wild at the award ceremony: a soap star challenged his ex-fiancee's new fella to a fight instead of giving a thank you speech, and Alexis Vonette overshadowed Samantha's puny little nip-slip on the red carpet when, during her performance, her dress, which already had a huge slit up one side, got caught on one of her dancer's earrings while he was crawling around on the ground below her. In a desperate bid to shake him free, the whole thing ripped off. Her dancer tried to cover her dignity by jumping up onto his knees, so his head covered her downstairs…but the cameras never miss these things. Everyone had caught a glimpse. Then someone ran on stage and quickly tied the dress back up again, fashioning it into a sarongstyle mini, and all the while she kept on singing, pitch perfect. I took note: if you're a true star, the show must go on, come what may.

But after the awards, came the after-party. That was where the stars seemed to really kick back. Once again, I mistakenly thought that things had reached peak wildness. I spotted three people cheating on their partners, or at least, I guess that's what I think I saw…as Verity says nothing in showbiz is actually what it seems. Layla was busy trying to pull the mean and moody one from a new boy band, Madison was receiving posing tips from a glamour model, and I was happy just taking it all in. I'd not seen the boys for hours but finally I felt like I was fitting in. Actual famous people knew who I was. A really gangly serious actor who'd been the star of some grim police drama even asked for a selfie with me.

But you live and learn, and I've learnt that the after, *after* party is really where it's at. There's definitely something in the air tonight, as I just know it's going to get even wilder. I should have known it was going to get messy when Gerald, high on something – lust, viewing figures or gin, who knows – agreed, when Layla oh-so-sweetly asked if we could invite 'one or two' people back to our mega apartment. After all, it needs to be shown off. The *Born In Buckinghamshire* lot have been making snide remarks all night, saying things like we've never encountered food that's not deep-fried or that our onscreen antics are so extreme that it means we've only got fifteen seconds on our timer of fame, and we've been determined to show them just how wrong they are about us. They're not wrong about the things we did on camera, that's clear to see, but they've broken most of the ten commandments on screen too. Shagging someone on camera isn't any more sophisticated just because your ride has a double-barrelled surname. Anyway, have they not seen our ratings? But what's even better than us smashing them at ratings is how our apartment is so much better than theirs. They're in cabs on their way here now and I can't wait to see their faces when they walk in. It's the one thing that's united me and Samantha. After her seething comment, I pulled Madison and Layla into the bathroom for a quick girls meeting. I didn't know what to do, Madison wanted me to declare all-out war with her but Layla said to hang back and just carry on being myself. "There's something about you that's obviously got her intimidated," she said. "All your success so far, it's come without trying. Just you being you. And I think that drives her wild. Let her do the running after the award – she'll wear herself out and you can just keep being you."

So, I've just been being myself, almost acting as if she said nothing at all. It clearly got to her as now she's beside me, as part of our welcome party for the *BIB* lot. She may see me as an enemy but she sees them as one even more, and we grin at each other as the group enter. Olympia Mountbatten's face on entry was priceless. Her jaw literally dropped wide. "Welcome to our humble abode," Samantha says sweetly to her. "Oh, but we have a no-shoes policy, sorry, can you take those off?" she says, looking down at Olympia's black patent Louboutins.

"But, but..."

"Sorry, house rules," Samantha insists, knowing full well she's standing there in a pair of six-inch platform wedges. Olympia reluctantly bends over to take her shoes off, leaving her much shorter, and less commanding, than she was when she walked in the room. I give Samantha a sneaky high-five before setting off to find out where Damon has got to.

My tour of the apartment is like walking through a reality TV zoo, where each room is a different cage of feral television stars. The COC lot are already here, and they've stripped off and clambered into the hot tub. Only someone thought it would be a good idea to add some bubble bath to it, which has caused a riot of foam, spilling out all over the floor. The flat has practically become a foam party, which I know means however wild things look above the bubbles, the foam will be hiding much worse. There are two girls, one who's a famous soap star and the other a politician's daughter, rolling around, kissing on the floor, soaked in the foam. When I go into one of our bathrooms, I find Sebastian from *Born In Buckinghamshire* with some of his posh mates lining up shots. "We're going to play 'I have never,'" he shouts after me, after I turn around. "For every label you don't own, or country you've not visited, you have to down a shot." It's not my scene and I shut the door. I've never really had the opportunity to travel much so far, and I've certainly not had the cash to splash on designer labels.

In our bedroom, I'm relieved to find something more my scene, in the form of Madison and Layla, apparently changing into their second outfit of the night, but sidetracked into a slut-drop battle. Say what you like about my girls, but no one can say they've not got thighs of steel. I'd like to see fellas try doing squats in stilettos.

"Guys, you know that Adam Tanner is here, don't you?" I can't get over the fact that people I've watched (OK, and lusted after) on

TV are here in our apartment, drinking our booze, and in the case of period-drama heartthrob, Adam Tanner, making every woman he speaks to melt. I'm so used to him speaking in a cut-glass accent and either clutching a top hat awkwardly or riding a horse past a stately home that I can't quite believe he's here in a tux, bowtie now loosened to reveal a distracting glimpse of chest through his opened shirt. Plus he's actually got a rolling Irish burr rather than some aristocratic English drawl. I was so disconcerted that after I'd said hello to him at the door I'd beaten a hasty retreat in case instead of congratulating him on the award he won tonight, I blurted out what I was actually thinking – which was to ask him if he rode women as well as he rode horses.

"He's hot, sure," Madison says, "But I want to find Marc tonight and show him what he's been missing," while Layla shouts over the top of her, "Angelica, stay, we need you to judge who's going lower."

I tell them I will, in a minute, just once I've found Damon. "Have you seen him, maybe him and Marc are nicking all the good booze somewhere?"

"No, but Angelica…" Madison starts but I'm already out the door before I can hear what she was about to say.

I'm about to enter the next room, where I can hear some very strange noises coming from behind the door (it really does sound like I'm about to enter a zoo; is that an elephant I can hear? Followed by a lion's roar?), when someone wraps their arms round my waist.

"Damon," I say, turning slowly around, "I've been looking for you." But I'm not faced with Damon's hazel brown eyes, or breathing in his delicious new scent. Instead, I see a pair of small, wide-set, sludge-colour eyes staring at me, not blinking, and am hit with the sharp tang of an aftershave that's pure midlife crisis.

"Ben," I say, trying to breathe through my nose and not choke. Ben Bradshaw is the hotshot agent that every reality TV star wants to be signed by. He's got Jimmy Sharpe from *COC* on his books, and the world has fallen in love with him. Jimmy's got the body of a Ken doll, and everyone assumes he has the brain of one, too until they get to know him. Mums want to look after him, all girls think they stand a chance and the gay audience all think he's secretly closeted and they're in with one, too. Everyone's saying his fame is all down to Ben's secret formula, and that without him Jimmy wouldn't have secured half the brand deals he has. But I've met Jimmy a few times on the circuit now and whatever the X factor is, he's just got it. He's a properly nice guy who treats everyone like they matter. That's what's made him a star – not Ben Bradshaw's dirty tricks. Ben got lucky, it's not the other way around.

"So, Angelica, I hear you're one of the top contenders for Reality TV Star of the Year…"

If it was anyone else, I'd tell them I actually don't care that much about the vote – sure it sounds like fun but it's really the chance to get the kind of contracts that mean I can stop my folks having to worry about the roof over their head. Well, that and the fact it comes with a hefty donation to a charity of your choice and I can think of so many places that deserve it. Ben is still droning on, but with his eyes firmly on my boobs rather than my face, so I'm not inclined to listen too carefully.

"…You know with me by your side, I can practically guarantee it…"

Wait, is he offering to be my agent? Everyone says Ben is so picky about who he works with, and will only sign on those who he really thinks will make him a lot of money. After all, he takes even more than industry standard of earnings, a fat 30% cut, I hear.

"I've already got an agent," I say, scanning behind him for Damon. I don't like how close Ben's standing or the fact one of his hands in his pocket is doing something I really don't want to picture. I wouldn't want Damon to come into the hallway and get the wrong impression. Or maybe, thinking of the way he spoke to the journalists earlier, I would…

"Fliss Johnston? She can't take you to the next level, she's old-school. She wouldn't know Instagram if it came up and slapped her on the arse."

"That's just not true," I say, shaking my head. "When you say old-school I think you just mean she cares about her clients, and she absolutely knows social media, like she's got me on Neos and everything. And you know that's invite only. It's the social network for the elite…"

"Of course," trills Ben. "I can also totally get my top-tier talent on that."

I know he's bluffing as I just made Neos up on the spot. But still, I decide to play on a little longer, maybe I can get some insider information for Fliss on what he's got planned.

"I guess I could be persuaded to come across to you though," I say, flipping my hair. Ben looks me up and down, I can't tell if he wants to eat me, sell me or worse. I try my hardest not to shudder. He begins to jabber on about the different shows that he thinks I'd be perfect for, which brands are in dire need of someone like me, and they're all very kiss and tell, sell-my-soul suggestions. Fliss' plan for me is much more original, and I am barely listening until I hear him say: "of course, we'd have to clean up your reputation."

"My reputation?"

I notice that some of the foam has started to leak into the hallway, and is beginning to spread like a frothy river over towards our feet. Layla better be on her best charming behaviour tomorrow, Gerald is going to kill us.

"Yep, I mean it's no news to you, is it Angelica," he looks me up-and-down again.

This time I do shudder, and decide I can blame the apartment being cold. "Is it me or is it chilly in here?"

"Well it's a bit nippy, I think it's safe to say," he says widening his eyes as he looks at my nipples, which I admit are making their presence felt in the tight dress. "But that all fits with the reputation you've built. Let's pull no punches. You're a bit of a slut."

What a wanker! Just because I got with a few guys in the house, and had sex with someone who I really, really liked, he thinks he can call me a slut to my face? And, even if I'd shagged more people than that, as long as no one is getting hurt, it's all consensual, and everyone's having a nice time, there's nothing wrong with that.

"And what do you propose we do about my *slutty* problem?" I ask, and he doesn't notice that my voice is dripping with sarcasm.

"Well, we'd set you up with someone pre-approved for a PR relationship, a nice cosy acceptable boyfriend type, you don't have to actually like the guy. Then, you can do a couple of interviews about how devoted you are to him, how you've left all of that *nastiness* behind and you're now a one-man woman and all that jazz, plus we'd make sure that anyone you shag on the side keeps quiet so it doesn't get out there that you're still the tramp you always were." He finishes with a wink.

When Ben first started talking I was shocked that anyone – any man, especially, thought they had a right to pass any comment on my sex life, but now, I'm simply furious. How could he even think I'd want to sign over 30% of my hard-earned cash to someone like him? But he clearly can't see the rage that's rising, how my hands are shaking with it, I'm flushing, my disgust at him clearly manifesting itself in my body, as he's still droning on.

"You will quickly learn though, that this industry is *all* about favours, Angelica. My clients know that I will do them a lot of favours, so I tend to ask we seal the deal with a little favour for good old Ben…"

He's staring at me, so intently now, but I'm too furious to reply so he carries on. "I make a nice little sideline in selling stories, and I'm sure you hear all kinds of gossip. So be a good girl and give me a little titbit I can pass to my contact, and there could be some extra cash coming your way."

"OK Ben, I'll do you a favour," I say, horrified by how casually he's inviting me to spread rumours for money. He grins. "If you do me one…" Then, in one quick, sharp movement, I knee him, right in the balls. "And get the fuck out of my apartment."

* * *

Chapter Ten

From a river-view penthouse to a half-packed house, heading home means coming back down to earth with a bump, literally. Most of our furniture is already piled up in the dining room ready to be loaded into a moving van when we can find somewhere in our budget, *if* we can find somewhere in our budget. Our 'sofa' is currently some scatter cushions propped up against a wall of boxes, and a blanket flung on top. For a brief moment it's comfortable but then one of us, Mam, Dad or me, moves and a strategically placed cushion topples and the whole set-up is compromised. I've taken to lying with my head in my mam's lap, my legs stretched out in front of me, while she gently strokes my hair, or plaits little braids in it. I need her motherly warmth, to be honest. We returned from the telly awards, hungover as anything, with all our clothes sopping from the hot tub incident as the foam, eventually, ran into the wardrobes too and got everything wet. Gerald said it served us right for doing something so stupid, despite the fact it wasn't even us who put the bubble bath in the hot tub, it was one of the COC lot. I'd put my money on Sebastian. Mam and Dad came and collected me from the station, they said I looked like a sopping, sad sheep in my fluffy wet tracksuit.

Since then, I've been helping Mam and Dad call round estate agents asking about new rentals. But that also means I've been trapped by my phone. Even when I'm meant to be looking at property, I can't stop checking gossip sites. Finally, I'll get so sick of the scrolling, I'll throw it to one corner, exclaiming to Dad to "set the timer, I'm going to manage half an hour without checking it, OK?" and then I sit, itchy, shaking my legs out, trying to concentrate on something – anything – else, a magazine, a book, but absorbing none of the words. Mam even pointed out that, one time, I was holding the book upside down. My record so far, before I give in and retrieve the phone from the corner, is ten minutes. Dad thinks I can do fifteen this time, but I'm not so sure. What if something major has happened? What if Samantha has announced she has nits? To the whole nation? Or Beyonce is touring and decided she needs a new backing singer? So, of course, with visions of tabloid headline gold in my mind, I rush over and open up all my apps, before checking the newspaper websites. Sigh! She's not announced she has nits, I guess that was wishful thinking. But nothing has changed in the past ten minutes.

This obsession started after the telly awards. First, I just wanted to see what people thought of my dress and how I looked in those red carpet photos with Damon. So as soon as we got home and settled on our 'sofa,' Mam and I quickly opened up the websites together. We'd promised Dad we'd wait for him but he'd driven to get the take-away and, oops, sorry Dad, we just simply couldn't wait. I looked, as Mam insisted I looked "drop dead gorgeous" in the pictures. I was trying really hard to see it and in some, I almost could. Especially this one with Damon, where I'm looking up at him, and he's grinning at the camera. I have this soft smile on my face and he just looks so, genuinely, happy. "You do make a very attractive pair," Mam had said, before warning that I shouldn't fixate on looks. "Cleopatra and Marc Anthony looked very fine together," my dad said, appearing suddenly in the doorway. I didn't know much about them and asked what happened. "They died," Dad said, bluntly.

What I should have done, like Verity told me to, is just listen to the words of the people I love. But I did not do that. Instead, when Mam nipped to the loo, I scrolled all the way down to the comments.

> *That much slap could plaster a wall.*
> *Someone get her a mirror... and a stylist.*
> *She looks like she's been Tangoed.*
> *Someone needs to lay off the pies, she needs to spend less time partying, more at the gym.*

I really did manage to throw my phone to the other side of the room then, and I left it there for a whole night. After seeing those comments, my brain only honed in on the nasty ones lurking there on my toxic phone, and every time I considered going near it, it seemed like approaching an electric fence coated with barbed wire. Something that was guaranteed to damage me. But after a restful night's sleep, I knew I had to face my fears. For one, I was waiting for a message from Layla to tell me what she'd been up to. She'd carted one of the waiters from the award-ceremony home with her, even making Gerald pay for his train ticket up north. Last I'd heard they'd done it eight times in one night, *in her parent's house*, and she had the worst UTI ever, so instead of getting at it again, she'd sucked him off in the local car wash. That's what I loved about Layla – she didn't give a damn about what anyone else thought, she was always living her best life regardless. And I knew she'd have me in hoots of laughter telling me what had happened next. I also, admittedly, wanted to see if Damon had messaged too. I'd eventually found him at the party, he was in the room where I'd heard all the weird animal noises, and he said he and these girls had been playing zoos. So, I joined in, I can do an amazing monkey impression, after all. And Damon knows I'm always up for a laugh.

So in the end I gave in and checked my phone.

```
OMG, send help and cranberry juice. My bladder is
on fire AND he wants to shag again tonight! He is
so freaking hot but my kitty is even hotter right
now. CHRIST ON A BIKE!
```

Then, before I'd even known I was doing it, I was back surfing the press and gossip websites. No pictures of me glowing from my phone this time. Was that good or bad? Was it better to be talked about than not – even if the press were trash-talking me? I knew I should stop scrolling but instead I saw a familiar face and clicked the link. Samantha. She was in three new stories, already, and it was only 10a.m. Samantha has friends in London so she had stayed down there after the awards, and already it was clear that was the best way to get papped. There she was necking on with a male model, in Hyde Park. I've seen him on billboards on the motorway, his pants are so tiny in those pictures I'm amazed there's not been a car crash. Then, the next story was Samantha necking it on with a supermodel this time, a girl who was the face of the perfume of the magazine sample I'd rubbed on myself that very morning. They were spotted stumbling out of that jungle nightclub and then kissing in the back of the car. The photos make it look like they thought they were being sneaky, holding up a clutch bag to shield their faces, but Samantha knows where cameras are at all times, she definitely knew what she was doing. Even when her tongue was down the model's throat I could tell she'd planned which side of the car to sit on so the paps could get her best side. I have to admit she's a genius at this stuff – she's way better at playing the game than I think I ever could be. The final story she was featured in was less scandalous, just her leaving a restaurant in London with Ben, her agent in tow, still with a smug look on his face. Though I bet Sam doesn't take any shit from him, she might be ruthless but she's also ballsy. She doesn't let men walk all over her. I sometimes wish I could be as tough as she seems. But the only comfort I can take from that is the message I received from Samantha later that day.

> Just so you don't worry about me going quiet on Insta, my new manager says he can get me on a new invite-only social media site, Neos. It's so private you can't even google it. Once I'm a member I would give you one of my invites, babe, but it's so exclusive, and I already promised the BiB lot I'd let them in on it.

Seeing Samantha all over the papers made me feel all funny inside. I tried to tell myself it wasn't jealousy as I didn't want that much attention (you should see the comments she got…half of them were worse than mine) and that I was much better off, up here, hanging out with people who loved me instead of all those fakers who party to be seen rather than to actually have fun. But, at the same time, I know what I want. Freedom. The kind of money that gives you choices and means you never have to worry again. A life of adventure but also the comfort of knowing I'll be looking after my family. And right now, the only way to get that is to secure as many tabloid pages as possible, if I want the interviews, the sponsorships and the screentests to come rolling in. It turns out that the secret to success actually isn't that much of a secret – it's hard work. Fliss keeps telling me that this buzz we're all experiencing now, unless there's a season two, won't last forever. "We have to capitalise on it while we can," she says, as if I'm a banker or something.

It's easier for Samantha though, not only with her mates in London who she can crash with, but the fact that she is natural at all this – she's like a shark, she never stops. I can only get down there when there's an event or a shoot, and the production company will pay for my travel and hotel. But I stop scrolling the Sam stories when something else hits me in the face. If I thought that Samantha getting all that attention was bad, nothing has prepared me seeing Damon's stories. TUG OF LOVE reads one headline. He's been spotted with Imelda, the same model that Samantha was papped kissing. Apparently they left a hotel together, at 6a.m. and he shouted "I'm not with her," when the paps took his photo. I can't help but zoom in on the picture. She's hanging back, her lipstick all smudged, shielding her face from the photographers but not the love bites all down her neck. I'm blinking back the tears and trying to persuade myself once again to put down my stupid phone when it vibrates in my hand.

```
Babe, you'll have seen the pics of Immy I bet. Don't
worry, she's nobody to me. Ben thought it would be
valuable to be seen with her, but she's a full blown
lesbian, which is why she was noshing Sam. You've
nothing to worry about. You're my number one girl.
```

Lucky Break

I've still not got used to the novelty of seeing my friends in the papers. It's so funny, their photos are just there, published alongside other celebrities like footballers, or film stars like Chad Schmidt casually hanging out on his yacht, and then the serious news stories. It's like I'm living out this surreal dream, where all the things and people that I thought were totally untouchable are within reach. So, in some ways when I'm comparing myself, my scrolling is a lot of fun. I'll be sitting, head in Mam's lap, like now, and laughing away at some of the comments people are saying about Damon, or Madison, or Layla. I'll scowl and say "what do you know?" if anyone says anything mean, out loud, as if the random avatar can hear me and will change their ways. It's funny as whenever anyone comments something cruel about Layla and Madison, I can see how totally ridiculous they are, and how the person must be seriously unhappy with their own lives to write something so horrible. That, or they're half-blind, and can't see how stunning Layla and Madison are. But, the thing is, I can't do that for myself. No matter how hard I try. But then, more and more stories about Damon have started appearing. At first, the girls were just in the background of the pap pics and I'd zoom in on them before managing to convince myself (buoyed by Damon's texts) that he wasn't actually *with* those girls and that they just happened to be in the back of the shot or posing for a photo or hanging out in the same crowd.

```
That's just the waitress, she's not a patch on you.
She's a wannabe, I didn't touch her
Great PR opp to be seen with that fox
She jumped on me
```

I wanted so hard to believe him. But sometimes I couldn't think what to reply – I didn't want to be jealous, sound possessive or like I didn't trust him. But the photos and stories kept coming. Sometimes, silence was all I had. But that didn't help.

```
You didn't reply to my last text, so I wanted some
company! But they're just friends, you know me,
babe, I'm a touchy-feely guy.
You've left me all alone, staying up there, you
don't want to be boring, do you?
```

But I couldn't win. When I did comment, he made out to sound like I was some kind of crazed stalker.

```
Obv, they're just fans who asked for a picture, stop
being so paranoid.
I can't help it if the ladies love me!
It was a networking event! You have to be friendly!
It's not what it looks like. Her boyfriend was just
out of shot.
```

Over the next week, the girls seemed to move out from the background and closer and closer into the frame. Until they were standing with their arms round him. Or getting him to sign their boobs, or drink a shot from their abs. These girls were really pretty, too. It's like there's a scale of hotness, and there's hot but approachable, which would be like a club promoter girl, or a barmaid, who are basically 'popular girl at school' pretty. Then there are these girls don't seem to have another job beyond working the party circuit – they must spend every hour of the day preening themselves, plus they all seem to be six foot tall and skinny enough to hide behind a lamppost. And weirder still, most of them don't even smile. It's not like I don't know how to get my glam on, but I usually know the vibe of the party scene up here. Normally the bars are full of friendly, blonde, short but curvy girls with a wardrobe full of all the best stuff from Topshop. They know how to style their hair bouncy and bombshell, and the bouncers on the doors let them skip entry. That's the sort of girl I'm used to being weighed up against in the clubs – and I can, when I've had my tan done, and popped on my best boob-tube dress, rival them as I have my secret weapon: I'm silly, funny and up for a laugh. I don't mind if I wreck my make-up, or have a piggyback ride even if my bandage dress is too short. Damon once said that "no one makes me laugh like you do, Angelica." But how can I make him laugh, remind him of all of that, when we're barely seeing each other? I've had my commitments up here and he's had his, erm, commitments down there.

My phone problem isn't helped by Madison and Layla who are also keeping an eye on the papers for me, texting any new activity as soon as it breaks, as if I'm not already immediately seeing it each time I hit refresh. They're not just looking out for Damon, but the others, too. Like me, they can't afford to be down there all the time, so we're having to think of inventive ways to make sure our names stay in the press and, until season two is announced, people don't forget about us. And Madison, who as a runner doesn't have the same contracts we do, has started to become a name in her own right. I'm so damn happy for her. She'd said if she didn't start to get papped she'd have to go take another runner job – she'd heard that a dead serious politics show was hiring. I couldn't imagine her delivering coffee and cleaning make up stains off politician's collars, so I'm so happy she's getting recognised too.

Although Madison has her not-so-secret weapon right there on her chest. She's just done a photoshoot with *Balls*, the supposed football magazine that's 80% naked girls, 20% football. As for Layla, she's a lot more chilled about the whole thing. She says that long-term she'll set up a business, maybe a chain of salons. But I still don't know what I want. I love the idea of a clothing range, maybe even a make-up deal, and I'm too scared to tell Fliss that I used to sing. *Balls* have emailed Fliss a few times, saying they'd be keen to shoot me too. But I've said no every time. It's not that I judge Madison for doing it, she looks *incredible* in the pictures and, as a bonus, she's getting to shag so many footballers.

It's just I don't feel sexy, not in that way, especially not in a bare white studio with the lenses trained on me. Don't get me wrong, I'm sexy when I'm with a guy, as long as I'm lost in the moment. I just can't perform sexiness. Arching my back, and licking my lips, shaking my bozzies in people's faces, for everyone to see. I'm meant to be all pouty and seductive and I just get the giggles. But Madison can really switch it on, as it's not a performance with her, it's just who she is, through and through. She's OTT and doesn't care if people don't like it. I've seen her pole dance round a golf umbrella, do a striptease on a packed train, and even attempt the splits on stage in a club when she wasn't wearing any pants. But it works. She always gets the guys she wants – and she won't let any of them tame her.

But somehow, I am managing to remain in the papers, without doing much of anything. They say all publicity is good publicity, but I'm not convinced that's the case here. Every time Damon is papped with a different girl, the papers print the old pictures of us in the house or at the television awards, alongside headlines like:

ROMEO DONE. The reality TV lothario had an on-off relationship with sweet but gullible Angelica during the first season of North Stars. The pair looked very loved up at The British Television Awards, but haven't been photographed together since. It was the romance that captured the nation but by the looks of our exclusive pictures Angelica may end up heartbroken once more.

Sweet but gullible! Is that how everyone sees me? What am I meant to believe in this new world? Old Angelica, I like to think, would definitely have slung Damon to the kerb if I'd seen him out on the town, with all these girls. I wouldn't believe any of his excuses. Let's face it, I've always lost my mind a little when it comes to boys, but I wasn't raised to take any nonsense. But now, I know what Ben's game is. I know what the fame game is. And it means I don't know who or what to trust – even when it's a photo in front of my eyes. I was ready to be famous for being me – but am I up for all these stunts and tricks? Anyone who watched me on *North Stars* can clearly see how obvious it is when I like someone (sweet but gullible!) I'm not sure I could fake that. As much as I may have wanted to be an actress when I was younger, I just don't have the skills for it. Seriously, you should see me when I'm lying. Oh and you should definitely hear when I try to do accents, Jamaican comes out Irish, Irish comes out Australian, I even once tried to do an impersonation of myself and it came out South African. But Damon is a good actor, I know that much. So, it would suit him to be out every night, pretending to be with a different girl, when really he goes home, tucks himself up in bed at the hotels, and dreams of me.

Mam says I'm being delusional. That this whole 'PR stunt' excuse is very convenient for someone like Damon, it's just another way to twist reality, and with it, my heart. But I'm not sure. This has all happened so fast. We thought we were prepared for being celebs, because of everything that happened during filming. When we went out, because of the cameras, the other people clubbing with us knew what was going on. It led us to believe we understood fame. I remember, before the show even aired, Layla and I were walking around her local shopping centre, convinced that everyone who looked our way did so because they knew we were famous. But now I know they probably were looking because we were tottering about in barely any clothes, laughing loudly and trying to get people to look over our way (and also, because we really are hilarious). Now that people actually recognise me, and fame, of even a small degree, has landed on my doorstep I can see I didn't know anything. I was not prepared. How could I prepare? All these headfucks are so out of this world, and far away from my life here.

Everything's changed around me, but I haven't changed. All of these mad things are happening but they're still happening to me, Angelica, the girl who thought, when she was asked to sing a solo during the school carol concert, that it would be a good idea to casually swap' Hark the Herald Angels Sing' for a bit of Britney and hope that the audience didn't notice (they did).

Mam tells me I have to trust my instincts, and tune into them. "They're the smartest friends you've got," she says. I try to tune into them all the time, but they'll be telling me one thing while another part of me tries to shut them up. One part of me really believes in proper fairytale love, really believes in Damon. The other part? Well that's the same part of me that was howling and sobbing when Robbie dumped me. The part that tells me to protect myself and not let anyone into my heart again.

But when I sit down and really think about what I feel, I suppose it's not one way or the other. I do believe that people can change, that life is confusing and we're all easily swayed, and when he makes mistakes I should give him the space to learn and change. That's what I'd want Damon, or anyone, to feel about me. After all, I'm going to mess up. I already have messed up so many times and the people that love me gave me a right telling off, but then they forgave me. I want to do that for other people, just live full of love and fun and hope. But how can I do that without other people taking me for a mug? I don't want them to see my optimism as weakness, or stupidity. Is that possible?

I'm zooming in on one of Damon's pictures, trying to figure out whether that's lipstick or just a nasty rash on his neck, when my phone rings. It's Madison, which sets off an alarm bell because she never calls. I pick up straight away.

"Angelica, babe, have you seen?"

"Yeah, I have," I say. "But it's OK—"

"How, how can it be OK?" Madison, I realise, is wailing. I'm beginning to think this isn't about what I think it is.

"It's a rash, not lipstick, so it's fine."

That manages to break Madison out of her tears and into laughter.

"Not that, you eejit! And it's definitely lipstick. It's MAC. Lady Danger."

Madison's knowledge of make-up is unrivalled. Still, she could be wrong about this one.

"Anyway," she carries on. "There's no time to be analysing Damon and his sexploits. The house has burned down!"

I don't know what she means at first. I even begin to look around the house I'm sitting in, searching for smoke. Then it slowly dawns on me.

"Our house?"

"Our house! The *North Stars* house!" she's wailing again. "It's going to be all over the news – the production company have been trying to keep the story out of the press overnight hoping it could be controlled, but it went up in flames last night about 3a.m. and once everyone saw the grey cloud, well you know what they say about no smoke without a fire…"

"Oh my god, imagine if we'd been inside," I say. "We could be toast!"

"Nah," says Madison. "We would have just got in the hot tub and the water would have protected us."

I'm not sure if that's true. But I like to think that perhaps that hot tub could have at last been responsible for saving someone…after all the trouble it caused. Thinking about the house and it all going up in smoke has brought tears to my eyes, I realise, as I try to blink them away. First I lose my childhood home, now the *North Stars* house.

"What happened?"

"They don't know yet, but it's definitely dodgy. The only line I've seen so far says the fire didn't come from a natural source."

"So someone torched it? Who would do that?"

"Who knows? Could be kids messing around, or it could be an insurance job. It's owned by the same wanker who owns your place, the dodgy one, what's his name?"

"Callum. Yuck."

"Yeah, that's the one. But the worse thing is, I had a call from the exec producer and..."

"And...?" Even when it's just us Madison is the queen of dramatic pauses, as if she's in a soap opera or announcing results on the *X Factor*.

"They've canned season two!"

* * *

Chapter Eleven

"Stop wallowing, Angelica!" Mam's at my door, a huge mug of tea in hand.

"I'm not wallowing!" I yell, my voice muffled from beneath my duvet. I have, indeed, been wallowing. After Madison called yesterday, I've decided to, like a sick Victorian woman, take to my bed. It's also the only room Mam hasn't boxed up yet so it might be my last chance. The *North Stars* house has gone up in flames and with it any possibility of season two, and me actually making any money to get us a new place. Then there's Damon, I phoned him straight after coming off the phone to Madison and he didn't answer. So I phoned him again, and again, and *again*. When he eventually answered, he sounded pissed off to hear my voice, barking "what do you want?" down the line. I would have thought I'd have been the first person he called when he heard about the house, as it was more than just the place we filmed, it was also the setting for so many memories we made together. He just didn't seem to care, and sounded so cold.

"You may need season two, Angelica, but I don't," he'd said, sounding like he wanted to hurry me off the call. "I've got so many opportunities flying my way. There's a new alcopop that wants me to be the face of the brand." He put on a weird marketing voice as he continued. "The affordable alternative to champagne that guys want to be seen with. It's called 'Stud Suds'."

I'm glad we're not on that new FaceTime thing as he'd have seen me wincing. Stud Suds? Puke. But I stopped. In the background, I could hear giggling. When I asked who was there, his barking turned to something more like yelling and I knew he must have been drinking all day. Hopefully not his gross-sounding new alcopop. "That's none of your fucking business, we're not even a couple!" and then, he hung up.

Not even a couple. The words had been like a slap to the face. I mean I knew he loves to flirt, but I'd been doing all that 'if you love something, let it go,' bollocks to give him the freedom I thought he needed to realise that I was the one who really knew him, the one who'd be there waiting for him. But was I being a prize idiot waiting for him while he was shagging his way to sponsorship deals and a regular booking at the STI clinic?

In despair (and to stop me from doing something stupid) I took the SIM card out the back of my phone and threw it into one of the open packing boxes that filled the living room.

A day later I do feel a bit silly for doing that. I miss my chats with my girls. I'd also like to see if Damon has messaged a hungover apology.

Mam comes and sits at the end of my bed, and hands me the mug. "Look love," she says, taking a loud slurp of her own tea. "I know this is a disappointment but this," she gestures to the hovel I've managed to create around me. There are empty packets of crisps that crinkle and spread crumbs whenever I move, littered around. There's a lot of other debris too, including three sachets of face mask that I shoved on, in a row, hoping that they'd fix me. I really think a face mask can fix a lot, but these are cheap and seem to have brought me out in a (Lady Danger style) rash around my chin. "This is not Clarke family behaviour."

"You said sometimes a wallow is good for us!" I protest, reciting another one of mam's lessons she distilled in us growing up. "We can take twenty-four hours to recharge."

She taps her watch. "Yes, and your twenty-four hours are up." She glances at a streak of brown smeared across the white duvet cover.

"It's chocolate! I swear!" I scramble around for the empty Maltesers box for evidence, but it's nowhere to be found.

It's then I hear a chuckle at the door and look up, in horror, to see Leo standing there. I frantically grab for the duvet to cover myself up. I'm wearing a Forever Friends t-shirt, pyjama bottoms covered in sloths drinking coffee, exclaiming SLOTHEE MORNING, which even I can admit is a shit pun and there's two holey, mismatched slipper socks on my feet. Pulling at the duvet unleashes an avalanche of even more junk – some Haribo packets, a flattened McDonald's carton, ooh some cold squashed chips that, admittedly, I'd eat if Leo wasn't standing right there and…the Maltesers box.

"See!" I point to it, as if it holds the power to return me my dignity. "Chocolate!"

"What are you doing here?" I say, and I glare at Mam. "And why didn't you tell me I had a visitor?"

"Oh, Leo popped by an hour ago, your dad's been talking to him about Mary, queen of Scots," Mam says. "I'm surprised you didn't hear them."

"Knowledgeable bloke, your dad," Leo says, smiling. "I wanted to call round and see how you're coping. After the fire?"

"Call round? You live in London, not at the end of road!" I don't know why I'm being so grumpy. After all, it is sweet of Leo to check in on me. No one else has. Well, actually, everyone has. Apart from Damon. So… Oh, I'm wallowing again.

"I couldn't get hold of you by phone, and I had some work to do up here," he says. "And by work, I mean taking you out of this hovel and cheering you up. I thought we could take a road trip - go and see Layla?"

Mam looks at me, and her eyes say it all. *Get up, get on with life, we Clarkes don't let the world grind us down.*

"OK, give me ten minutes, I'll get ready and be down."

Mam looks over at me, taking in my ratty hair and the mask rash on my chin, then back at Leo.

"Best give her half an hour, love."

I don't know where we're going. Leo told me we were stopping somewhere on the way to Layla's. But what I do know is: Leo has a very nice car. It's a zippy little two-seater thing, don't ask me to name the make, I'm not that kind of girl. But when we get off the motorway, it has a button you can press, so that the roof folds back and it's just warm enough for us to do it, even if it is a bit windy and my hair is a mess again, after finally managing to tame it this morning. I don't mind though, Leo was right, I needed to get out and have a laugh. Leo's even let me take control of the music, so we're blasting out Rihanna's 'We Found Love' and for once I'm not thinking, like I usually do, about me and Damon and how this song – and every song, come to think of it – perfectly describes our love. Instead, I'm enjoying the sunshine on my face and how Leo's answering all the silly questions I'm firing his way, like, 'would you rather be eaten by a shark or a person?' (Person, if it would help keep his friend alive) and 'if you were a dinosaur, what dinosaur would you be?' He really considered that one, before saying: "if I'm going to be honest Angelica, it would be the diplodocus. He's vegetarian, reliable and sturdy and, well…" Leo raised his neck, really pronouncing it. "I've also got quite a freakishly long neck. But…" He paused, and kept his eyes fixed firmly on the road. "I'm worried, picking that one, it's not very sexy, is it? Should I not pick the T-Rex or something, is that alpha enough for you?"

A blush began to snake its way up his, yes, freakishly long neck, as he said it.

I'm not used to this. Leo actually cares what I think. (Plus, apparently he cares whether I think he's sexy.) Leo's seen me in some absolutely terrible states. And, if you're thinking, so has the whole world, you'd be wrong. There were things we all did in that house that the producers deemed 'unscreenable.' A term me, Madison and Layla have since adopted, messaging each other and saying "shall we get unscreenable tonight?" to describe when we want to go really feral.

Leo's pulled the car over to one side, and has pulled a piece of red fabric out of his pocket. "You trust me, don't you, Angelica?" he says, and I'm strangely transfixed as he's removed his jumper, revealing a tight, burgundy t-shirt. I knew his arms were good, but is that a trace of a six-pack I see?

I nod. "Good," he says, wrapping the fabric around my eyes. As soon as I'm in the dark, it's like my senses have been heightened. I can smell Leo, so clearly. He smells like vanilla and bonfire smoke. He tightens the blindfold, before guiding me, firmly, by the shoulders out of the car. "Watch your feet," he says, in a way that manages to be both caring and commanding all at once. I feel like I could stumble and fall, and he'd catch me. I feel like stumbling and falling so that he *will* catch me. He manoeuvres me so I'm walking in front of him, I can feel his breath on my neck, slow and steady, and, the way we're walking, I can't help but brush my ass against his groin, as we bump along the road. All of a sudden I'm overcome with a desire for him to stop us, dead in our tracks, spin me around and kiss me. To feel his lips against mine, the blindfold still on, to succumb to the tingling of my senses…But then—

"We're here!" he says. He unties the blindfold and the sunshine rushes into my eyes, making me dizzy and confused.

I blink as the world comes back into view. We're…? Where? On some random footpath? Why has Leo brought me here?

"You needed a reminder of the bigger picture, right?"

I nod. "So you thought you'd take me on a hike?"

"Nope, I've brought you to…" He spins me round so I can suddenly see the beautiful hills and trees under the shining blue sky.

"Your namesake!"

The huge Angel of the North dominates the skyline. Even from here, a couple of miles away, it's so impressive. I've seen it before driving past, but I've never stopped to really take it in. When we were travelling between cities for filming, we'd have a mini competition to see who could be the first one to spot it when we were driving north. If we were in the *North Stars* minibus, the first one to see it always did a shot. But I've not seen it from this view before – Leo's managed, as always, to show me a different side to things.

"Angelica, meet the Angel!" Leo says to me. He stretches out his hand and sets off at a rapid pace towards the sculpture. Immediately, I trip on a clump of grass and narrowly avoid faceplanting. A high-pitched giggle escapes me, one that sounded nothing like my normal laugh. I guess I should be thankful that a giggle is the only thing that escaped me, and not a fart.

"It's strong, it's iconic, it's everything you are!" Leo declares.

"What, rusty and left by the side of the road?" I say in mock-outrage, but I can't believe he's actually planned this out.

"No, I mean it, Angelica," Leo continues. "Not everyone likes the Angel of the North – some folks called it an eyesore when it was built. It's not for everyone – some people just don't get it. But those that do, well those people really, *really* like it. And that's what I wanted you to see. Something powerful. Something everyone recognises. And something that means a lot to the people who love it."

I don't know what to say to that. Normally I'd say something stupid, or take a selfie with it in the background while pulling a face. But Leo looks like he really means what he said. And he's walking off in a determined way. I'm wishing I'd not worn my old Converse for this. I'm hardly dressed as a rugged explorer, but I set off after him all the same.

We walk in companionable silence for a while – I know I normally talk non-stop so it's strange finding someone who I feel so comfortable with. I manage to find my stride and stop tripping over, and best of all, I'm not itching to check my phone. There's not a soul about, we could be in another century out here. Leo truly has gifted me an escape from everything. He comes to a halt, and we sit down for a quick rest. He pulls out a water bottle from his backpack. As usual, he's come prepared and all I've got is some inappropriate shoes and half a pack of Fruit Pastilles. I rest my head on his shoulder, soothed by birdsong and the calm of this place. "I so needed this," I tell him. "I know everyone else thinks it's shallow to care so much about fame and how the house burning down is going to impact that," I say. "I do care about it, but not in the way everyone assumes. I want to be able to help out Mam and Dad, I promised them I would, and now I don't know how I'll manage!"

"I know," says Leo. "And I've got a promise for you. I promise that will all work out OK. And Angelica, when I make a promise, I really do keep it. I've got you. But, for now, let's forget all about that world and enjoy this one."

I flop back into the grass and he leans over me, eclipsing the sun, and suddenly he's all I can see, all I can think about. Is he going to kiss me? I can feel the heat rushing through me as he gets closer. It feels like I'm falling into his intense gaze. I blush like I'm sixteen again and instead I focus on his lips. That's no better. I can feel my pulse in my neck and I'm about to reach up and pull his mouth on to me when he moves closer and…flicks me on the forehead.

"Ow!" I yell, sitting up. "What was that for?"

"You had a grasshopper on you," Leo laughs and stands up, setting off again along the path. I follow him, trying to fix my eyes on the statue in the distance, and stop staring at Leo's firm arse as he walks ahead. Why had I never noticed it before now?

Finally we crest a hill then turn a corner and we're in a small hollow tucked off the main path, with a breathtaking view of the Angel. Literally breathtaking – I'm practically panting after the hike. Leo stands behind me, his chest pressed against my back, and I let myself lean into him so I know he can feel me breathing hard against him. Suddenly, the atmosphere flips from calm to sexy. Very, very sexy. He runs his fingers slowly down my neck, pausing where my pulse is racing in the delicate nook of my neck. Then, still with my eyes locked on the horizon, I feel his mouth on my neck. Are we doing this? I don't think I can keep up the 'isn't the view so lovely' act anymore, especially not when I can feel him hard against me now, and so I turn round, lost for words and just bite my lip, looking Leo right in the eye.

Suddenly, he's on me. Pulling me towards him hungrily, kissing me, and running his fingers through my hair. His kisses manage to be both rough and gentle all at once, and I am pulling his t-shirt off, over his head, before I even have time to consider the fact that anyone could see us. Then, at the sight and the feel of him pressed up against my body, my own top now ripped off and tossed on the ground, I couldn't care less. He lies back on the warm ground, his hands roaming my bare body, and I straddle him. I'm just in my bra and old denim mini. I know exactly what I want. I feel as strong as that statue, but come back to myself, my brain not my body, for a second when I feel him pull away, already missing the feel of his lips on mine.

"Is this what you really want, Angelica?" He's asking me as his fingers skim my nipples, sending jolts of electricity through me. "I don't want to be your revenge fuck."

I adjust my position on top of him and pin his arms above his head, knowing this gives him a magnificent view of my boobs. "Does this feel like revenge? Does this feel like I'm thinking about anyone else?" I ask.

"It. Feels. Fucking. Amazing." Leo groans. "It's just us, Angelica, just us."

It was exactly what I needed to hear. "Well, in that case," I say, releasing his hands. I reach behind me and undo my black bra.

"God," he growls. "You are so, so hot." He begins running his hands over the curves of my body, clutching at the dip of my hip, grabbing at the flesh of my thighs. His legs are wide open and I'm straddled across him, I can feel his dick, hard against my leg. I feel so powerful, so sexy in my own skin, seeing the pure lust on Leo's face as he drinks the sight of me in. This is unlike anything I've ever experienced before, it's not a fumble under the cover, a hammering away at me, as if I'm a disposable doll, only good for one thing. This is worship, I think, as Leo sits up and takes one nipple into his mouth, biting gently in a way that has me gasping.

Lucky Break

His fingers are in my pants and they're doing something unidentifiable but delicious, I find I'm panting once again, "please, please don't stop, oh god, don't stop," and he flips me over and I feel his weight on top of me. I want him inside of me now, but he begins to kiss each inch of my body. "Not yet," he says, firmly, taking control. "I'm making this last, savouring every second of you." The ground below me must be rough and dusty but I don't notice. As, his tongue is now where his fingers were, and it's lucky Leo knew this hidden spot as I'm moaning loudly now, as I enter into another orbit, another dimension, dripping with sweat and feeling like the goddamn sexiest woman alive.

* * *

Chapter Twelve

It takes me a while to notice. It's all so normal that, at first, I don't notice that anything is different. But the normalcy *is* the different thing! The cardboard boxes are gone and our sofa, the sofa I've cried on, laughed on, eaten on, been sick on…It's back! All our photos are hanging on the walls, there's me, aged eleven, in my school uniform – teeth so buck I couldn't close my mouth – grinning away. There's us on holiday, me in a big blow-up ring, in the shape of a pink flamingo, and Mam, back when she had her perm.

We'd had a weird drive home from Layla's this morning where neither of us mentioned what happened yesterday – we just turned up the tunes and sang all the way home. And now we're back, and I'd just walked in and sat down on the sofa, while Mam and Dad looked on bemused. "What are you looking at?" I asked, before going. "Oh my god! It's all back! What happened?!"

"Well, you happened, Angelica," Mam says, smiling. "We thought because you're the one who sorted it all, we wouldn't make you do all the unpacking."

I haven't the foggiest what's going on. Leo's standing in the doorway, and chips in, helping me out. "That fucker had no idea what was coming when you waltzed in, telling him you'd pay the next year's rent up front, in cash, if he didn't evict you lot."

Slowly, it begins to register what's happened. Leo! Leo has somehow paid Callum to save us from eviction. How on earth could he afford that? I didn't think cameramen earned that much.

"We're so grateful sweetheart, I was crying when Callum called after you left yesterday. I can't believe you spent your afternoon facing him down and saving this place. We sprung right into action unpacking, didn't we? Wanted to get it all nice and normal for when you came home."

"Because it is your home, Angelica, always was, always will be love," Dad says, squeezing my shoulder. "Wherever you go in the world, whatever you do, you've got a home here. Now, come on in properly, son," he says to Leo. "Stop hovering in doorways, my daughter is looking happier than she has in ages. Whatever you've done to put this grin on her face, I shake your hand for it."

I look at Leo and see that blush is sneaking up his (freakishly long) neck again.

"We went for a hike!" I blurt out.

"What, between going to see Callum and driving all the way to Layla's?" Mam says, confused.

"Er yes..." I say, regaling them with everything we saw on our walk (leaving out a select few parts, admittedly...) "The Angel was stunning, so..."

"Yes, love," says Dad, "It's one of the most impressive erections in the whole of the north east."

I almost swallow my tongue as I'm trying so hard not to laugh. I can't even look at Leo. Or think about what really was the most impressive erection in the north east.

It's hard to concentrate though, even without Dad and his typical foot-in-mouth moment. It's all so confusing, and there's so much to try and wrap my head around while trying to come across as normal to Mam and Dad, and not like someone who's just had three of the most earth-shattering orgasms of her life. With Leo! Someone who until now, I swear, I only thought of as a friend. Of course, I'd admired his looks, his arms and his cyclist's tan, glowing from days spent outdoors, rather than (cough, Damon's) days on the sunbed. I'd also always appreciated his laid-back, friendly and self-assured company. I always feel myself in his presence and I'd assumed that meant we were destined to be mates, after all. Normally when I fancy someone I feel on edge, almost desperate around them. Desperate to impress, to please and to bend myself this way and that, in order to get their attention (sometimes quite literally). I'm used to butterflies in my stomach and the feeling that this person, and the way they feel about me, could be snatched away any minute. But this? Comfort? Being able to laugh after sex and not feel paranoid that my make-up has slid off, and my hair is a mess? This is new.

Maybe Leo doesn't have a million thoughts racing through his mind like I do, considering he's casually chatting away with Mam and Dad, listening intently as Dad lists some facts about coal that are honestly so boring, they blank from my mind as soon as I hear them.

I want to talk to Leo, get him somewhere alone, but I feel like a teenager again. I'm worried if I try and say anything like, "hey Leo, let's go up to my room and chat," it will come out like a squeak and Mam and Dad will think I'm trying to seduce him or something. Maybe I am trying to seduce him? Am I? The sex was obviously incredible but afterwards, we just went back to being us. Angelica and Leo, joking around like pals, racing each other down the hills on the way back. Then, in the car, he could have put his hand on my leg, or given me a kiss but we just drove to Layla's and acted like nothing had happened. I didn't even tell Layla, which is a first for me. It felt too new and special and surprising to share. I can't sense if Mam and Dad can feel the tension in the air but Mam stands up, brushes off crumbs from her toast and says, "I'm meeting the girls for a Chardonnay tonight." She stares at Dad, who then coughs uncomfortably and says, "and I should really go and begin unpacking the boxes in the shed."

Born In Buckinghamshire is on the telly, and that wally Sebastian is dicking around on a horse, and we settle side by side on the sofa for a while, in companionable silence, apart from occasionally bursting into laughter at his expense.

"God he's such a buffoon," I say, before pausing. "That's a posh word for an idiot, right?"

"The perfect word," he says, before adding softly under his breath, in a way that speeds my heart right up, "Angelica, I need to explain a few things to you."

"The house? Was that you? Why?"

"I've got some savings and I hate dickhead landlords," he shrugs. "I particularly hate dickhead landlords who just might have had something to do with the show house fire. I also happen, with the same intensity that I hate dickhead landlords, to like you." He smiles fondly. "I didn't want to see you or your family forced to move out. It seemed simple."

"But savings? Are you sure? I'll pay you back."

"I know you will, 100%. You're going places, Angelica, it's just not showing up in your bank balance yet." He reaches over and squeezes my forearm. "But it will."

"You didn't have to say it was me, you could have taken the glory."

"It's going to be you soon, I was just skipping one step."

He's being so nice I could cry. But, he's also on the far end of the sofa, when he could be closer to me. He could have his leg pressed against mine. Do I even want that? Or am I just so accustomed to wanting men to *want* me, so that's the only relationship I understand? Over the past few months, I've made a few really nice lad friends. I wouldn't dream of getting with Reed, as he feels like a brotherly figure to me or Marc, mostly because of Madison, but even if she wasn't in the picture I don't think I would. He's almost *too* good looking, if that makes sense? Like he wouldn't even have to try in bed because he'd think looking at him was orgasmic enough. And, until twenty-four hours ago, I didn't think I'd have slept with Leo. Sure, there's been a few frissons of electricity, but the smallest amount of electricity isn't enough to ruin a friendship, is it? Because if we keep doing what we did, no matter how fun, or indeed mind-blowing, it might be, we can't go back to friends.

"And...?" I ask. All that's not being said hangs heavy in the air between us. I shift in my seat, look over at him, but I feel almost afraid to look him right in the eye. It feels like this is the moment one of us has to act, to speak, in order for something momentous to happen. I'm too unsure of myself to be the one to do it. I don't know if going from friends to something more is what I really want. But there's also something else there, lingering, in the back of my mind, a small but vicious new feeling. It's doubt about who I am, and whether I'm even desirable to a man like him. What if he rejects me? I didn't used to feel this way about boys, I'd go crazy for them but always feel confident in my own skin. I knew that, no matter what went down, they'd be into me. What's changed? The house. The trolls and their barbed comments but also…one of the unsayable things hovering between us. Damon. What Damon and I have isn't in any way solid, and without actually knowing if he's apologised or not, there may not be a way back from our phone fight. But, that was also only two days ago. So much has happened in the last forty-eight hours – can I really be sure I want to leave him behind? Things are bad at the moment but when they're good…they're so good. I know Damon, I understand him – even the shitty parts of him – but Leo, he's a mystery to me.

It's Leo who breaks the silence.

"I hope you know how much I like you, Angelica," he says, and he's finally shuffled closer to me.

"It's come as a bit of a surprise," I admit. "I thought you saw me as this clumsy idiot friend of yours."

"I do," he says. "Clumsy, yes, but not an idiot. It's all that wildness that makes me, er, like you so much. No one is themselves quite like you. It makes you so…"

"Prone to let themselves get filmed covered in vomit? Bruises?" I point out the scatter of purple marks up my leg, caused by falling over in heels I'm definitely not equipped to walk in.

"No…beautiful. I always wanted to be with someone who would make me laugh as much as you do. Remember the original unscreenable moment?"

I hide my head in my hands. Partly to hide how much I'm blushing, but also because that evening truly was unscreenable. "Yes! Don't remind me!"

That was one of the things that had surprised me. They filmed us round the clock but the bits they cut out weren't always what I thought were the most outrageous – but they were sometimes the most natural. Like the weekend where everyone in the house got food poisoning. That was messy on a whole other level.

Gerald told us later that the TV channel had deemed the scenes too extreme to screen to the public. As if every single viewer at home didn't have the same bodily functions we all do. I'm just glad I can be honest about mine. Still, I hadn't ever imagined that would be what someone said they liked me for...

"I'd noticed I couldn't stop filming you from the very first day. I kept bringing my camera back to you – I convinced myself it was because you were TV gold. But that day, it just became so clear you were so different from anyone else I've ever met before—"

"Because I almost broke a world record sprinting to the loo?" I can almost hear what Madison would have to say about all this, she'd be screeching, "what if he has some sort of weird bathroom fetish?" while cackling.

"No, not that particular element," Leo laughs. "But just the way you responded to it, you don't let the stupid stuff get to you. You laugh it off. You get knocked down but you get back up. You enjoy life. And now, seeing your family, and how hard you love and how loyal you are to the people you care about, I can admit. I wasn't just filming you – I was falling for you."

"Anyone would have done the same given the opportunities I got," I say. "I've just had a lucky break."

"You're not just anyone, Angelica. And it's not all down to luck. It takes a mad, heartfelt kind of courage to be true to yourself, like you are. It may not be rescue-someone-from-an-avalanche or cross-a-waterfall-in-a-barrel brave, but it's brave all the same. You've made your own luck."

I can feel myself melting into the sofa. It's all so perfect. Well, apart from the food poisoning memory, but I guess that's a blessing, after all, because when you love someone they see all sides of you. Poo and all. The amount of times Mam's had some bug and Dad's been there for her, as she sobbed on the toilet. Loving someone, even when they're at their most disgusting, their most feral, that's truly romantic. That's what makes things last.

"There's just one thing though, Angelica," and there's something in the way his tone shifts that's unsettling. When discussing me, it was light as candy-floss, like pink clouds before the sun sets. Now, it's gruffer, heavier, darker. I know what's coming. "Damon. You don't have to pretend you don't still want him because of what I've said just now. I've watched you two from behind the lens for weeks. I know you care about him. A lot. And if you'll forgive me saying it, a lot more than he deserves. But it doesn't matter what he's done. You still have feelings for him."

It's not a question, but a factual statement. Like he's just placed a contract down in front of me, or a maths equation that was already solved.

"No, it's, it's…" I want to deny it but he's shaking his head. I've not said anything yet and already he doesn't believe me. But I don't know what to say. It's complicated? We're not a Facebook status! That feels just so weak. How can I say: *I know* I shouldn't still like Damon. How every cell in my body, knows that the way we're going, the way *he's* going, is not in a good direction. Sometimes I feel like I am just testing how many times he can break my heart, as though I'd rip it out of my own chest, place it in his hands and say 'here you go, do your worst.' But, in some ways, it's all been worth it – every tear shed, the screaming, all of it – for the moment when he does look my way, smile and say "Angelica, there's no one on this earth that can make me laugh like you do."

"Your loyalty to the ones you love is the best thing about you," Leo says, as I still scramble for words. "But some people don't deserve that loyalty, or love. They see it as an opportunity for them to be vile, and cruel, safe in the knowledge you'll still forgive them. They'll suck the sunshine out of you and use it for themselves."

"I know Damon can seem like a bit of prick sometimes. But he doesn't mean a lot of what he does," I say. "He's all bravado, and underneath it all…"

Hurt crosses Leo's face, but I don't know why. After all, isn't this what he expects of me? To defend Damon, at all costs? I'm trying to be honest with Leo – isn't that what he said he liked about me? And if I'm honest with myself, part of me is defending Damon to show that I've not been a total fool, that there's a reason why I've stuck around for so long. I don't want to admit the rest of it to Leo, though. That with all his openness and ability to just say nice things without twisting the knife, well, Leo scares me. I think part of me wants Damon because it's like the producers have known all along: we weren't made for each other, but we were cast for each other. Two party animals, the pair of us not able to believe we'd been given a chance to grab celebrity and get a taste of the high life just by doing what we loved to do anyway – drinking, dancing, shagging and laughing about it all so hard that it feels like nothing else matters. But now the cameras have stopped filming, I've been wondering if Damon and I are on separate paths. It's like the fame is what he craves most of all – I'm just a stepping stone to it. Whereas when I was in the house, when I was falling for him, it was the other way round – all the fame and attention, the nights out and all the rest – they felt like a way to secure what I really wanted, my happy ever after.

And what's worse is I can't tell Leo that, and I definitely can't tell him that I worry he's too nice for me, that for all his caring, honest, chivalrous gestures, he'd wake up one day and grow bored of me and my loud and proud ways. What if I'm just a curiosity to him? He said he's never met anyone like me before…and there's probably a reason why that is: we're from different worlds. As all this whirls through my mind, I realise I've been silent.

"You're going to keep doing this, I know." Once again, Leo sounds so certain. "I'm not sure I can put myself in a situation where I can see the future so clearly. Us being happy and then him clicking his fingers and you running, scampering back."

That annoys me. I've got a weakness for Damon, I'll admit, but I'm not his pet, I don't do everything he says. "That's not true!"

"It is, Angelica, you know it, I know it, Damon knows it and...about a million viewers know it too."

"If I'm such a stupid little doormat then why did you come here? Why did you kiss me? Why did you say all this nice stuff to me only to snatch it back again?"

"Because I..." he falters. "I couldn't not. I knew you'd be hurting and I hated that. I missed you. I wanted to see you. And I was so furious about the prospect of you losing your house that I had to do something. I thought that maybe, that would be enough. But then, at the Angel, when I saw you gazing up at it, away from all this media circus, I knew I wouldn't be leaving this weekend without saying something. But the kiss? And, well, yes the best sex I've ever had? None of that was planned, Angelica. I *had* to kiss you. I *had* to hold you. But this Damon thing. It has to pass before anything else can happen between us. I know it will. I may not look like a TV heart throb but I'm a confident man, I can wait. I just hope, for your sake, you wake up to who he really is, soon. Before he tears your heart, and your glorious self-worth into pieces."

He stands up, kisses me on the forehead and says, "See you soon, pal." Then he's out the door.

I'm left alone, on the sofa, in the house he saved for me, completely head-spun. Should I chase him? Tell him he's wrong? I can't do that. As, despite my protestations, there's something true about what Leo just said. He's right about Damon, I keep swallowing down his lies, again and again, and coming back for more. I'm addicted, even if I know he's poisoning me. But I can't seem to stop.

* * *

Chapter Thirteen

"I was so high, baby, honestly, I had no idea what I was saying or doing..."

I'm in Damon's hotel room in London. No one knows I'm in Damon's hotel room. Madison and Layla think that I've gone to get a spray tan, I've even arrived here in my most stained joggers and a white vest-top, leaving our room with no make-up on but then frantically applying licks of mascara while in the lift up here. We're all down here for a charity event, despite there being no season two, as we're still signed up to our current contracts that say we have to do promotional work for the show. I'm just glad to have the gig. I need to figure out what I'm doing and fast, and there will apparently be a bunch of bigwigs from all different reality TV companies at this event, so if I can just get to them before Samantha, charm their pants off (not literally, of course) then everything will work out fine. Or, at least, that's what I'm telling myself. I'm trying to enter into a state of manifestation. Even if it feels more like delusion right now.

Before I got the train I said to Mam, "I'm off to meet the new producers of my new hit TV show," as I read that if you speak and act as though it's already happened, then the universe does some rejigging, rewards you for your positivity and bam, everything you wished for arrives. But then Mam asked too many questions about what the show would be and was so excited about it all I had to confess it hasn't happened yet and it burst my bubble. Hopefully the universe will understand I wasn't being negative, just trying to please my mam. Something the universe has surely done itself at one point or another.

Then Madison and Layla made me promise on the way here that, no matter how drunk I get, I'm not to sleep with Damon. I pinky-promised them and everything. Technically I've not broken that yet, all I've done is agree to come up and hear what he has to say. And I turned him down twice before doing so! See Leo, I do have willpower!

"Who was it I heard in the background when I called?" I ask, expecting to hear one of his well-worn excuses – it was the window cleaner/the takeaway driver/a faulty line…But instead he says:

"Just some meaningless fling, but that's OK, isn't it? We said we could still sleep with other people, as long as it didn't turn into anything serious."

"Did we?" Did we? I'm pretty certain we didn't. After the telly awards he was sending me all those loved-up messages and I wish I could pull them out right now, but after losing my SIM card in the packing boxes and having to get a new one, all my old messages have been lost.

"Yeah, do you not remember? It was at the after party, just after you showed Ben what's for. Good on you, he's such a dick, you're so strong Angelica, stronger than me…"

He trails off and he's watching me from the big bed, and he does look like he means it. There's a certain look Damon gets in his eyes, when he just softens. All his macho bullshit has been stripped away and I can see him for who he really is: a vulnerable, sweet, funny guy…who also happens to be head-over-heels in love with me.

The thing is, I still don't remember saying anything about us shagging other people. But then I was absolutely wasted at that party, we all were. I have a fuzzy recollection of pulling the duvets from our bedrooms, through to the huge corner sofa, and watching the sun rise over Big Ben, wrapped up warm and safe in Damon's arms. I remember feeling happy, thinking of us on the red carpet and how good we looked together, I remember him kissing my head as I tucked up in his arms and how he murmured, "You're the one for me, you really are." But I don't remember this conversation, agreeing to sleeping with other people. I've been beating myself up about me screwing Leo without being 100% clear whether Damon and I were on a break (although I think him screaming "We're not even a couple" was pretty damn clear now I think about it) – and all this time he's been thinking we each had a free pass to fuck anyone we wanted as long as we didn't catch feelings.

"It's how all the big celebrity couples do it, you know, open relationships?" he's saying, mentioning a few names. I would definitely have remembered this, I may often get very, very drunk and forget certain things, but *never* celebrity gossip.

"So don't let some quick fuck with a girl get in the way of you and me, she's a nobody, I can't even remember her name, I wasn't even looking at her face. But she definitely wasn't as fit as you, look at you, you're in manky joggers and you're still the hottest girl in this hotel." He taps the bed. "Come here, sit beside me. I hate you being so far away from me."

When I arrived, I'd refused to go near him on the bed, knowing full well what could come of being close to that man and his intoxicating scent (and, I'm sure, a penis that has magical powers, I sometimes feel like it's whispering to me, *Angelica, you know you want me*) but now, it's more tempting. I do also hate standing up for long periods. It's like I'm in trouble and have been called in to see a teacher. "Fine," I say, arms crossed and heading over. "But nothing is happening here, no shagging, OK? I'm just sitting down to talk and no, I don't remember agreeing to letting you shag other girls."

I sit down, and damn, I really am close enough to smell him. He's also wearing a pair of grey jogging bottoms, the sort that manage to be both baggy and tight all at the same time. I try not to glance at his crotch, as I know what I'll see. I sneak one look – is that a semi? No! Stop it Angelica! – and focus his forehead instead, surely the least sexy feature of a man, concentrating on staying strong. "Besides, it's not fair to have huge relationship conversations when we're both smashed."

He laughs then, but in a charmed way. "*All* our relationship conversations have been when we're smashed."

"At least then there were cameras to record what you were saying, so I could check if you were being a liar again!"

"It's really hard for me, girls throw themselves at me, every single night," he says and I roll my eyes.

"Oh sure, that sounds really hard, Damon."

"It is," his eyes are wide now, trained directly on mine. "As it's all so shallow, none of the conversations I have with these girls is a patch on how we are, what we talk about. Most of them are so dull, banging on about horoscopes or their make-up or whatever."

"I like horoscopes and make-up," I say. "I don't know what you're getting at? I'm meant to be flattered that you spend time with boring girls and still choose to shag them, knowing it will hurt me?"

"With you, everything you say is funny. *Everything*. I feel like you really know me, that you see who I really am. It's not shallow…it's… deep. I've just been chasing all these highs, since we got out the house. I don't want to but then they're there and the new is just so tempting, you know?"

It's impossible but is that scent of his getting stronger? I feel a little woozy with it all. The hotel bed is so soft beneath me and I know he said some other stuff…but the 'everything' of it all is swimming around my head. I fling myself back, suddenly exhausted, laying on my back and staring up at the spotlights above me. Did they just dim? The light in here feels softer, more golden and much less harsh than it was when I came in, angry and demanding that Damon's explanation "better be good."

"I don't know, Damon. I sometimes think, with you, it'll be new, new, new until you die. I don't want that. I want—"

"You want someone that will be by your side, until you die. Someone solid, dependable, I get it. But I know you, Angelica. You also want someone to have a laugh with." He's lying beside me now, the back of our hands just touching. It's what I told him in the house, how I wanted a relationship like the one my mam and dad had. I'm not sure if they even showed it in the edit in the end, Damon and I, spooned in bed, talking about the things we wanted from our future. The light had felt similar that day, the afternoon sun streaming through the curtains – we'd snuck off for a 3p.m. nap and cuddle, while the others did whatever weird task we'd been assigned to do, our source of entertainment for the day.

"You remember?"

"Course I remember."

He's moved his hand closer to mine and is now, very gently, very tingly, stroking my inner wrist. I didn't know that was a weak spot for me but I don't want him to stop. He doesn't and I shift my body just a little closer. This still isn't breaking my pinky-promise, we're just lying in bed beside one another, and then he grabs my wrist, moves it across to feel that what was once a semi, is now a huge erection. Even his cock is familiar to me. *Fuck me*, I think. And it's as if he's read my mind. Within seconds, he's on top of me, both of our jogging bottoms are down and the soft, gentle, erotic moment is over. He's inside of me in an instant, my legs scissored wide and I'm crying out at the feeling of taking him, and how good he feels inside of me. But then he begins to pound, faster and faster and it's all too quick to appreciate it any more. In the house I could pretend to myself I liked it, because it was fast and sweaty and naughty trying to do the deed before we got discovered, but today it's just *too* fast, *too* sweaty. He hasn't even taken his socks off.

"Damon, Damon," I try to say. "Slow it down, let's make this—" But before I can say "last" he's crying out, shuddering and exploding inside of me. He pulls out and I roll over for a cuddle, but he's up and padding through to the bathroom. "Just a minute, gotta shower. The mobile tanner is coming in fifteen."

I need a wee. I need to wipe the dampness off my leg. He knows I need to wee straight after sex or I'll get a UTI, but he's barged in front of me to use the shower. But maybe that's typical of men, Madison always says how selfish they all are. To his credit, he doesn't take long and when he emerges, towel around his waist, water dripping down his six-pack, I can't help but feel drawn to him, despite the memory of the quite tepid sex that lasted only minutes.

"Can I get in on that tanner?" I ask, looking down at my legs. "I'm *way* too pale for this event tonight."

"Yeah, yeah, sure but after me, yeah? Why don't you have a bubble bath, really take your time in there, I've got all the good products. The Chanel bubble bath, L'Occitane scrubs." He pronounces it "Lockytanny," which I find funny, as I'm certain it's pronounced differently. I'm trying to remember my GCSE French as he hurries me into the bathroom, and begins running the taps. There's a knock on the door.

"That'll be the tanner, you enjoy a soak. I'll call you when she's ready for you." He takes the remote and turns on the mini television in the bathroom, so it's on the music channels. He pumps the volume right up. I'll never get over all the fancy things you get in these hotels that are booked for us, I always take the miniatures home to Mam. I strip off and get in, the bath really is the perfect temperature. I know I'm going to have to confess to the girls what happened, we never lie to each other about boys. But, as I begin to type a text out to them, I'm struggling to frame it in a way that doesn't make me sound like a mug. I decide I'll have to do it in person, later. Perhaps at the event Damon will be all over me like he was at the awards, and his behaviour will help convince them he's a changed man. I let my mind drift while I soak in the bath, before receiving a fright as I am awoken by a woman I've never seen before, prodding my shoulder and hovering over me with a towel.

"Hun," she's smirking at me, in a way that feels slightly over-familiar. "Hun, it's time for your tan. I'm Crystal, I'm Damon's personal tanner. He says you wanted me to do you, too."

"Oh right, um, thanks, I guess…" I gesture to my fully naked body that she's looking at like she's at the butchers. "Um, do you mind?"

She hands me a towel as I clamber out, still not fully getting that I meant, *leave the room.*

"Oh, I've seen it all before, hun, honestly, the bodies I've seen, if you knew, you really wouldn't be ashamed of yours at all." She glances me up and down, flick, flick, with her eyeballs and smirks that smirk again.

"I didn't say I was ashamed," I say. Who is this bitch?

"Oh right, yeaaaah," she drawls. "Body confidence is such a powerful tool. That's brilliant, just brilliant. So…" She pauses for the right word. "Brave."

"Um, right, yeah…" She's such a patronising cow it's left me almost speechless. "Where's Damon?" I finally ask.

"Oh, he had to dash off, see the lads. He told me to tell you…" She pauses. "Wait, no, sorry that's just me being ditzy. He didn't really say much about you at all."

I'm so tempted to throw her out but I really need a tan. The booth has been popped up in the bedroom, her spray tanner plugged in to the side. "Here you go, large paper panties to change into."

"Large? They don't come in sizes."

"Oh, mine do, it's just a little special service I offer. Nasty to have them cut into you."

The pants are so big on me I have to tie them at each side, and I know I should say something and ask for a smaller pair but her barbs are beginning to get to me. I can't face her quizzing me and simpering, "Are you suuure?"

It's only once I step into the booth, naked apart from the pants, that I can admit how pretty she is. She's blonde, a swishy natural-looking blonde that I bet costs a fortune from the hairdressers to keep pristine. Her nose is a cute little button and she's tiny, about five foot, slim but curvy in all the right places. She's wearing a lilac tabbard with matching cropped trousers and the fabric is clingy, it should look unflattering. But it doesn't. The only flaw on her is around her mouth.

"Is that…?" I try to ask, just as she instructs me to turn around, and open my arms out in a T shape. The cold blast of spray tan hits me, like an icy wind.

It's only as I stand there, once it's over, slightly sticky and smelling of old biscuits, that I manage to finish my sentence. "I think you have some fake tan around your mouth." It's like this orange smear, all across her lips and chin and I almost wish I hadn't told her, I should have let it develop and stay like that for days, she's been so nasty. But 'be the change you want to see' or whatever that Gandhi quote is. Though I'm not sure Gandhi ever had to deal with a bitchy self-tanner from Luton.

Crystal dashes through and begins to frantically wipe at her chin, staining one of the hotel's pristine white towels. She's laughing. "Oh this happens sometimes, particularly on certain jobs. It'll come off, I've got a special trick."

It's then that Damon walks in, followed by Marc and Reed. I'm still naked, in the paper thong, my arms out wide and a plastic showercap on my head, to protect my hair from the tan.

"She's full of special tricks," he says, winking at no one in particular.

"Hi Angelica," Reed says, acting as if I'm not naked. "How's it going?"

Marc is less subtle. "Great tits! I'd high-five you but I can't risk getting tan all over me."

"How are you getting a tan done the day of the event?" Reed asks. "Mine always takes at least a day to settle, that's why I got mine on, yesterday, before the train."

"That's one of my special tricks, boys," Crystal says. She's managed to wipe all of the tanner off her face, and emerges from the bathroom looking perfect. "It's my one-hour formula, develops this gorgeous deep colour, no orange streaks, nothing. Your tan's perfect the day you visit me."

"She's the very best," Damon says and this time his wink is definitely directed at her. "And you'll really be doing a lot for charity too, Crystal. When I'm standing up there, all the rich MILFs in the audience are going to go wild in their bidding, *wild*."

"I do really, really care about elephants," Crystal nods. I have no idea why she's talking about elephants. The charity auction tonight is for guide dogs, I'm sure.

As she leaves, Marc whistles after her, before the door has even closed. "Nice work, Damon."

"She's a real pro, Marc." He glances over at me.

"Why was she going on about elephants?" Reed asks.

"Isn't that what we're raising money for, tonight?" Damon says, confused.

"No," I say. "It's guide dogs."

"Oh," he grabs his crotch, like some dodgy Michael Jackson impersonator. At some point he's changed out of his joggers and into a suit that's almost bursting around the groin. He must really want to raise money for the charity. "Must be because I'm packing an elephant's trunk in here."

At that, I scoff and scamper off down the corridor to my room, where I find Madison and Layla sitting on my bed, splitting a bottle of peach schnapps between them.

"You shagged him, didn't you?" They say in unison, almost as soon as I click my key in the door.

"How do you know and how did you get in here? You're like Mystic Meg and Houdini all at once."

"The porter let me have a key-card," Layla shrugs. That girl, she could persuade a dog he didn't want his bone.

"And we knew you'd be off to bang him the moment you claimed you were off for a tan the day of the party," Madison chimed in, before squinting at me. "Though you have changed colour…Did you actually get a tan? Are we wrong?"

"No, I got a tan *and* I shagged Damon. He has a 'personal' tanner now."

"A personal *slam'her* more like," Madison laughs, before admitting, "yep, that wasn't my best work."

"He's doesn't shag every woman he meets!" I say, unconvincingly. "She's very pretty though."

"And clearly shite at tanning!" Layla says. "Have you looked in the mirror?"

I haven't. I dash through and what I'm faced with is… Well, have you seen *Charlie and the Chocolate Factory*? And have you seen that episode of *Friends* with Ross's tan? If the Oompa Loompas had a baby with Ross, that's the colour I am. I'm more orange than an actual orange! I always wanted to be Rachel in *Friends*, why has it turned out actually I'm Ross? I look at myself in the mirror again. How has this happened? Maybe it's just the guide colour. But I rub at my arm and begin to scream. It's absolutely *not* the guide colour. It's sunk so deeply into my skin, it's settled in my pores and I look, well, I look like a creosoted fence. Layla and Madison come rushing in, Madison carrying a bunch of dresses under her arms, in colours she think will 'dilute' the orange. Layla's more practical, she's soon stripping me down, recognising that in my distress I won't be able to think straight, and commanding Madison to put the shower on, *now*. They both bundle me in, and then using the hotel's face cloths they begin scrubbing me, quite viciously. "Owww, that hurts," I cry.

"Do you want to go to the event tonight this colour?" Mads responds. "If we don't keep scrubbing you'll stay so bright they won't need to fundraise for guide dogs…you'll reverse someone's blindness!"

"That's not how it works, Madison," Layla replies.

"Alright, Einstein. Maybe she'll do the opposite and blind people with her orange glow." Madison has abandoned the flannels and is now using the bath mat.

"You're being highly offensive right now," I say, but I'm laughing.

"To you or blind people?"

"Both!" Then we begin to laugh so much we forget about the task at hand.

"Look alive!" Layla suddenly yells, like an army major. "We've got t-minus two hours til we have to leave. And…we've run out of towels."

In the end, Layla calls her favourite porter and he brings us a whole pile of towels. They scrub at me for a full 45-minutes, until we admit defeat. "There's nothing more that can be done," Layla says. "Call off the troops."

I step towards the mirror, afraid of what I will see. It's bad…but it's not *as* bad. I'm less orange but I am more patchy. My face has escaped lightly, there's just a pear-shaped lump of orange under my left cheekbone. My legs can be covered with tights, I suppose, and Layla reckons if we cover my arms in spray-on body glitter it could camouflage the orange dots scattered around my body. And, if I really make my hair high, and my lashes super long, then perhaps everyone will focus on those, instead.

"What would I do without you girls?" I say, pulling them both in for a hug, which they resist in case 'it's catching.'

"And, at least Damon is going to show up all-over orange too. You'll be like his and hers orangutans. After all, it was the same tanner, wasn't it?" Madison asks.

* * *

Chapter Fourteen

The 'red' carpet is actually zebra print, and when we arrive, we're handed a plastic mask that only vaguely resembles a guide dog. There are also people here in elephant masks, including all of the *Born In Buckinghamshire* lot, or at least I think it's the *BiB* lot from what they're wearing waist-down. The lads are flashing red socks, hiked up high, paired with shiny 'formal' shoes and the girls are all wearing pencil skirts so tight they can only wiggle in them, and pointy stiletto court shoes.

"I thought it wasn't about elephants?" I whisper to Layla as we approach the paparazzi pen. I'd forgotten just how bright the flashes actually are and worry they're going to really emphasise my patchy tan.

"It's about both, we're in competition. So we're to raise as much money for the guide dogs and the *BiB* gang are all supporting the elephants," Layla whispers back, as if it's the most normal sentence in the world.

I try looking around for Damon before approaching the mob of photographers but I can't see him, so instead Layla and Madison both grab my hands and we step forward as a trio, with me in the middle.

"Shagged a pumpkin, have we, Angelica? If you think you're Cinderella, it's your carriage that's meant to turn into a pumpkin, not you," the paps begin to shout. It's so tempting to yell "fuck off" but that's exactly what they're trying to do – to get a reaction. A picture of me, going berserk at them, will sell for so much more the next day. Now I know what they're like, I feel guilty for every time I looked at a picture of a celebrity angrily shouting at photographers and thought 'she's crazy'. Now I realise they'll have made her crazy, all for their pay cheque. So, instead, I grit my teeth and smile and laugh until the next person arrives and we can finally step off the 'zebra' carpet and try to have fun.

There's a charity auction later and we're the 'prizes.' On each table sits a catalogue of everything people here can bid for to raise money for the two charities, and we're at the back, after a spa day at Champneys and a helicopter ride over London. My caption reads NO ANGEL: WIN A SINNER and I try not to let it get to me, as, after all, it's all for a good cause. My great uncle had a guide dog that helped him have so much more freedom, so I really do want to help the charity raise as much money as possible. But, admittedly, I'm dreading going up on stage so people can bid on me like I'm a piece of meat. I think of how Crystal eyed me, and glance down at my dodgy tan. I yank my dress down to cover more but it keeps shifting and twisting round when I walk, and Crystal's remarks about the 'large' knickers are on repeat in my mind. That and how pretty and tiny she was, and how much she resembled the girls Damon has been papped with every day of the week. I try and shake all the negative thoughts out of me, remembering how Mam always says comparison is the thief of joy, and she's absolutely right. But then she's never been surrounded by absolute stunners, women whose *job* it is to look hot, while having to deal with a bloated belly and a patchy tan. I grab one of the free drinks that are floating around on trays, a 'Doggy Tini' which, by the taste of it, is just pure gin. I down it in one, just as Samantha approaches, all fake smiles and arms outstretched for a hug. And…is that a new pair of fake tits? When she pulls me in for a hug and I feel their hardness against mine I realise it absolutely is.

"They're great, aren't they?" she says, as I goggle at her chest. They don't feel good but they really do look good. "Ben bought them for me!"

"Your agent bought you new breasts?"

"Yeah, honestly, he's the best. It's a gift he gets all his new VIP clients. Anyway, babe, how are you? You're looking…" she fades out as she realises there are no other words for orange.

It's sometime hard to believe that, for a while in the house, Samantha and I were proper friends. When she wasn't doing the voiceover or calling people to the voting booth to get people's dump day names, she'd come and hang out with us. She really took me under her wing for the first few weeks and I so appreciated her support, she'd always been big on the clubbing scene across Liverpool and Manchester, so knew which bouncers to avoid and which bars would let us stay on past closing time. It was only when she began to notice that I was getting on so well with the lads in the house, especially Reed, that her snaky behaviour began, she'd come over and whisper things like "I'm just telling you this because I care, but Marc said you're a fat slag and I think you deserve to know the truth," or she'd try and meddle with my friendship with Madison and Layla, always under the guise of fake concern. It made it really hard to argue with her because she'd simply retaliate that she was "just trying to help" and that sometimes "the truth is really hard to hear."

It seems, even now, even after making her intentions to me very clear when we last saw each other at the telly awards, that she's still got her eyes on the prize.

I tell her I'm fine, that I'm excited to be in London while also trying not to tell her anything solid about my life, knowing how often she can take even the smallest snippet of information and twist it for her own gain.

"I think it's so great how well you're handling it all, honestly," she simpers. "If I was still living at home, with no real opportunities coming my way, I mean, God, I'd take the house burning down *so* badly. I'm just not upset because Ben's lined up so much for me, you know, he even says that *Celebrity Mountain Cadets* are interested in me!"

When we were in the house we all sat around and spoke about what our dream reality TV show would be. Mine was always *Celebrity Mountain Cadets*, where they take twelve celebrities, from all different backgrounds, a chef alongside an ageing rock star alongside a footballer, and they'd all have to live in a camp up the top of a mountain and do all these crazy survival challenges to win prizes, like ice swimming or camping on a tiny ledge on a cliff. I thought it sounded like such an adventure but Samantha had wrinkled her nose at the prospect of appearing on the show (and me, for wanting to go on it) and said she'd much rather appear on a chat show, or if she was going to 'lower herself' to contestant status like us, it would have to be on one of "the beach ones, so I can just sunbathe all day looking hot" and she'd always maintained that "honestly, I was such a lad for wanting to do *Mountain Cadets*" and had laughed in a way that implied I was idiotic. "No one looks sexy in camo, unless it's a mini skirt," she'd said back then.

"Oh that's brilliant, good for you," I say through gritted teeth. There's no way I'll show her how jealous I am. Unfortunately, it means she just carries on talking, obviously with a mission to get under my skin. "Also, are you here with Damon tonight?" She doesn't stop to give me time to reply. "Babe, I'm telling you this for your own good. Ben's told him it's good for his image to be seen with you, but you need to know he's just doing it for the media. Oh, oh babe, don't cry..."

I am not about to cry. I'm sticking my tongue on the top of my mouth, it's a trick Mam taught me, it stops the tears coming out. Besides, I actually feel more like decking her than crying. And, I remind myself, how can I trust a word Samantha has to say?

Samantha doesn't pause for breath. "I only tell you because I care! Now look who I'm about to introduce you to."

She waves a woman over, who steps up squealing, arms outstretched as if for a hug but when she's within body contact, the pair just do air kisses and begin exclaiming how 'fabulous' they both look. The woman is short, in a crushed velvet suit that's a tad too small for her. But her face is kind, she has a rosy-cheeked insecurity to her that doesn't quite match the way that she's talking. She's bouncing on her toes with a kind of pent-up energy. She says to Samantha, "Can you believe they're not offering champagne tonight? I'm having to drink this hideous sugary cocktail, when I'd much rather a glass of Moet. You'd think they hadn't looked at the guest list before arriving!" Before she notices I'm standing there, and says, "Angelica, so nice to meet you finally. I thought you were an absolute hoot on *North Stars*, you're such a great actress! I don't think I could have pretended to be that obsessed with that himbo, Damon!"

She begins to laugh, and Samantha joins in and I don't know how to explain to her that our reality TV is just that: reality, just with the boring bits edited out. I wasn't faking anything. Now though, outside the house, I am faking things more and more, like right now as I force out a gurgle of a laugh as I'm not sure what else I'm meant to do.

"Nice to meet you too," I say, waiting for her to tell me her name. But she doesn't. Perhaps she's so important she never usually has to. Only I've got no idea who she is. "I think the cocktails are delicious," I say, wishing I had the bravery to also point out the event is for charity, not for providing us lot with free drinks. They've already been generous enough.

"Full of sugar, though," she repeats. "Full of sugar. Speaking of sugar, though," she looks me up and down (what is it with people doing that to me?!) "You know, you should meet Morgan." She beckons over a tall, earnest looking man who is wearing an insanely tight polo neck under his suit. "Morgan McHugh, meet Angelica Clarke."

I smile, but Morgan just frowns at me, looking at me through his heavy-framed glasses like he's trying to solve a theory.

"Morgan has just got over two million dollars funding for his new high-nutrition, low-fuss meal replacements shakes – NuYu."

This seems to stir him up. "They're not 'shakes,' babe," Morgan drawls in his LA tones. "They're the food of the future. Silicon Valley's foodstuff of choice, they're going to revolutionize how we eat. High-fibre, low-calorie, superfood-enriched and brain-stimulating. NuYu is nutrition for the 21st century."

Thankfully, Sam's friend cuts off his advertorial speech. "Anyway, best take my seat for the auction. Lovely to see you, Samantha; and call me, Angelica, if you ever fancy doing a fitness DVD, you know before-and-after?"

"So gorgeous to see you too. You look amazzzzzing, Geraldine," Samantha trills, and the woman toddles away, waving at people as she goes.

"Who was that?" I ask. "And is it not really fucking rude to tell someone they need to do a fitness DVD?!"

"Oh you're not seriously upset by that, are you?" Samantha asks. "That's Geraldine Smith, she's the producer of some of the top-selling fitness DVDs around. Hideous little woman, ugh did you see her outfit? She looked like a magician. But a good person to know. I mean I would never do it, and she's never asked me, as obviously," she moves her hand up and down her body, she's in a wrap dress so tight it's practically mummifying her. "I don't need the transformation they always like in these things. But you, babe, you could kill two birds with one stone. Why not get yourself in shape and make some money from it? God, in fact, I should really charge you commission for introducing you to her!"

"Ladddiiieeesss and gentlemaaaannn," the booming voice over the loud speakers interrupts me before I lose my cool and come close to throwing my cocktail in Sam's face. "It's time for the charity auction to take place, please take your seats and your paddles and get ready to spend generously!"

I'm grateful to be able to escape Samantha and be able to just sit and listen for a while, without having to question whether I'm speaking to the right people or fully utilising this event to boost my career. I hate all that bullshit. I want to be able to just focus on the videos they're playing of the prizes you could 'win' (although I'm not sure why they keep claiming you win the prizes, when you're the one paying for them) and drink my excessively sugary cocktail in peace. But as soon as I sit down, I can't concentrate. I'm just hit with the avalanche of insults that have been hurled my way today, from Crystal to Geraldine to Samantha, and they pile on top of everything I've had to read about myself since the show hit the air. I feel like I am no longer Angelica, but instead have been replaced by a blob of butter, just sitting here all melting and unloveable. I've always felt satisfied with my weight, I've had ups and downs like everyone has, but mostly whenever I've put on a little extra, I've called them my 'fun pounds' knowing it was just because I'd been out having a blast with my friends and, always, finishing my nights off with a kebab. But recently, the fun pounds haven't felt so fun anymore. Not when the trolls are saying things like 'oooft she's got more belly rolls than my dad' and 'no wonder Damon isn't into her, not when she's slowly morphing into the Michelin man.' I know they're just trolls, and those faceless keyboard cowards definitely won't have perfect bodies, as they type furiously from a basement somewhere, but it's really hard not to let them get under my skin. Verity said that, with time, I'll get used to tuning them out. But this fame game is all so new, and the nasty voices keep jabbering away at me, drowning out anything nice I've heard about myself.

"And now for the mega prize of the night! They're hammered, hilarious and horny and…you'll probably get a shag at the end of the night, it's dates with the cast of the hit reality TV show, *North Stars*!"

This is the last thing I want to do. I notice how the *BiB* lot haven't raffled themselves off. Instead they've offered all these 'exclusive' prizes – a ski lesson with Sebastian, pilates with Penelope Titherington-Thomas, clay pigeon shooting with the slightly horse-faced one from the show who claims to be a relation of the Windsors.

But us lot? We're selling fun – a messy night out. So I paste on a smile, preparing myself to do the last thing I feel like – go and stand on the stage, beside Samantha and Layla who are both much skinnier than me and seem unbothered about the fact we're going to have stay up here while people bid for dates with us. It's like being picked for the netball team back in school. I feel so out of place and awkward, but also like I'm being a buzz killer if I complain. As we walk to the stage, Madison accompanies us and Layla can't stop laughing, finding this whole thing so much fun. "A millionaire might bid for us," Layla's saying. "And we'll fall in love, like *Pretty Woman* but the reality TV version."

The lads are walking behind us, pumping their guns at all the old ladies in the crowd and blowing kisses. Damon looks handsome as ever, but also, I realise with dawning horror, he's a completely normal tan colour. How did his end up a subtle golden shade and I look like I've been hosed down with Irn Bru?

We all line up on the stage and the spotlight is so bright I can barely see the audience, or who's bidding for who. The lads have already made it into a contest between them as to who will raise the most, and Samantha's snuck up behind me and whispered, "bet I'll get double how much you get," and, while it's exactly what the lads have been saying to one another, it feels so much bitchier when it's us girls. I want Layla to get lots of bids (and hopefully bag a millionaire as then, surely, I'd get invited to their mansions all the time) but I don't want it to be a competition. But I guess, by nature, it is a competition. Just like the show. Just like this stupid award Sam seems so fixated on.

The lads go first and, unsurprisingly, Marc gets the most bids. And the woman who 'wins' him is actually really hot, she's an older lady but clearly spends a lot of money on herself, everything about her from the tight leather pencil skirt she's wearing, to her swishy blow dry screams expensive. Behind her back, Marc high-fives the lads, mouthing "MIIIILLLFFF" at them. I look over at Madison to see if this has upset her. After all, I know she's just as weak with Marc when he comes calling, as I am with Damon. Damon comes second and Reed comes last, which I think is very unfair, as he's the sweetest of the lot. Damon's bidder, I am relieved to see, is an actual old lady, she must be over seventy, though she's got a wicked glint in her eye. She pulls him in for a massive kiss and he just manages to move his face in time for it to miss his lips. Madison yells, "You get yours, honey" at her, and the old lady comes over and gives all of us high fives. What a legend!

When it's our turn Layla goes first. "She's the size of a pint glass and just as tasty, this little pocket rocket will blow you away!" The bidding races away and soon it's Sam's moment. When the 'winners' come to collect their prizes I realise both Madison and Samatha's dates are older men, both with moustaches. Layla's date is grinning like he's just won the lottery, whereas Samantha's man is much more reserved, and somehow vaguely familiar. It would be typical if Sam had bagged some kind of celeb. I stare at his moustache and try to think why I recognise him. I wonder if the advice of 'never trust a man with a moustache' counts when they're well over sixty and most likely couldn't cause much trouble apart from a run on Viagra.

When it's my turn I try to strut into the spotlight, just like Sam and Layla did. But the strut ends up more robotic than I would have liked, and then, because I realise this, I decide to make a joke of it by doing the actual robot when I get to my spot. The audience looks on, confused.

"We know her moves in the bedroom are much better than her moves on the dancefloor. Could you be the one to tame our little saucepot?" The crowd cheers and I try to smile, rather than wince. I curse myself for ever saying that. I notice Damon out the corner of my eye pumping his arms and grinning. "She's lovely, lively and we all know she's got no inhibitions! Could you be her next conquest? It's Angelica!"

No one else had comments like that. The lads were all about their looks, the man pretended to grate cheese on Damon's abs and compared Marc's biceps to two juicy melons. Then Layla and Sam's were a little more suggestive but they didn't say they'd shag whoever bid for them. I didn't sign up to be auctioned like an escort. I'm fuming and it obviously shows on my face as the auctioneer says, "Smile love, you'll catch more bids with honey." It's then I realise that, so far, no one has raised their paddle to bid for me. That's outrageous! I always thought if I were ever to be a sex worker, I'd be a high-class, expensive one. I, reluctantly, plaster on a smile and try to look like I'm having fun. I notice someone very slowly raising their paddle. This is so humiliating.

"Come on," the auctioneer shouts. "Remember, it's for charity!" It's not clear, at this point, whether he means being charitable to sad old me, or the actual charity. A few more bids come in but I'm struggling to keep this fake grin plastered on my face. Eventually I'm 'sold' to a man who comes up and whispers in my ear, "I bought you as a divorce present to myself, my wife left me for her personal trainer, but you can't leave a date if I've paid for it, eh? Let me get a quick selfie – I want to send it to Susan so she can see what she's missing, leaving me for Carlos, her tennis coach."

I look at him, realising I probably won't have to worry about wandering hands on our date, but I might be in danger of being bored to death. This man is talking so much about his ex and how no one else will perfect *Coq au Vin* like she did, that I almost forget I'm still on stage and meant to be looking delighted. I give him Fliss's number to arrange our date and hope that he loses it.

I step off the stage, feeling deflated and ready to go home as soon as I'm allowed to. We're always told, when we're representing the show, how long it's been agreed we will stay at these parties for. Normally, it's not a problem, as they're parties with free drinks and I always stay way longer than promised. But tonight, I just want to go curl up in bed, hopefully with a cuddle from Damon, and pretend today never happened.

Speaking of the devil, Damon comes up behind me and wraps his arms around my waist, pulling my bum into his crotch. "I'd pay a fortune for you," he whispers in my ear.

"That was so humiliating, Damon."

"At least your date has teeth," he says.

"Aw she's a cute old lady," I reply. "I bet she'll be fun."

"Yeah just what every young stud wants on a date. Varicose veins and a blue rinse. Anyway, I knew you'd need cheering up after you wound up with that guy who's told everyone his sob story about his ex-Mrs, and I've got just the thing to take your mind off it all."

He's read my mind, I think. He's going to come back to the hotel with me, spoon me and stroke my hair until I fall asleep and then, in the morning, we'll order breakfast to the room and have a lazy, Sunday morning shag in the golden light…

"Quickie in the toilets?"

Five minutes later my knees are cold, as I kneel on cool tiles in front of Damon in the disabled loos. From the smell, someone definitely has had a recent curry poo in here.

"Come on, baby, I'm ready for you," he's saying. "No one does it like you, no one."

He thinks this is a compliment but all it does is remind me of just how many blow jobs he's received over the last few months. How many women am I being compared to? Ten? Twenty? One hundred?

I begin grasping his shaft and teasing the head. He's groaning, a guttural sound, his body tensed and I must admit, I do enjoy giving a blow job. And I reckon I'm damn good. But, as I get ready to finish, I notice something. Why is his tan all patchy around his inner thighs? I test him, deep throating, taking all of him in. "Yes, baby, yes" he cries out and he's fucking lucky that I don't, in that very moment, bite down on his cock. Because, going that deep, my chin brushes up against his thighs, right where the tan has been wiped off, leaving white stripes against the mahogany. I remember Crystal's face, from earlier. The tan across her mouth. I open my own mouth and stand up.

"Aw, baby, why did you stop?" he's panting at me, pushing me back down.

"Did you fuck that tanner while I was in the bath?" I yell. The confusion that passes across his face tells me all I need to know. He's not confused by the question but confused as to how I figured it out, I can tell. "What? How?" he splutters.

"Top tip: if you're going to shag your tanner, maybe do it before she sprays you, not after. Your downstairs needs a bit of a tidy up," I say and run out of the cubicle.

Back in the ballroom, the tables have been cleared and a glittery dancefloor has been set up. Layla and Madison are the only ones on it, faux sexy dancing with each other and whooping at the DJ, telling him to put some Britney on. Everything, all of a sudden, seems clear. Like that disabled toilet was actually a magical portal, there to show me how I've been going wrong, up until now, and how to change it. I have to leave Damon behind, the disabled loo is my past and I need to walk towards my glittering future. And there it is, in the form of Morgan McHugh, just stepping onto the dance floor, lit up in purple light, doing a dance move that looks like a cross between the robot and the running man. Never mind, Aladdin's genie was quite odd too and he granted him his wishes. I'm going to have the glow up to end all glow ups and make a million quid doing it. Damon is going to regret ever making a fool of me, he'll be begging me to take him back and all I'll do is laugh in his face.

I walk past Madison and Layla, batting off their requests to join them, and go straight up to Morgan.

"I've got a business proposal for you, and I think you'll want to hear it."

PART TWO
2012

PART TWO

1942

Chapter Fifteen

The beep, beep, beeps are blaring in my head, am I back in the voting booth in the *North Stars* house? "Samantha I'm ready to paaaaartttty," I say, but I don't know who I am speaking to. The words float out of my mouth and into the air. I feel drugged.

I'm interrupted by the sound of my mam's voice. Why is she in the house? Or, I think as I stare at all the blinking lights, am I at a rave? A very bright rave that smells of disinfectant?

"I think you're high enough, sweetheart, you just rest," she says, and I feel her hand land from somewhere, out of the sky, and stroke me gently on my head. It's like I've been switched off and switched back on again. I was lying in bed, chatting away to the nice man in the fetching blue cap, telling him all about how he was eating his kebabs all wrong, you have to separate the meat from the bread to stop going soggy and...then, gone, I was out like a light. Now, I don't know what time it is, or day it is for that matter, or why Mam's at a rave with me. I move my head, from left to right, and slowly, my confused brain must begin to reboot again, as I realise I'm in hospital. I'm also here willingly, I remember, as I decided, after getting sick of people online pointing out that my nose was offensive, that I would get a nose job. Because, guess what? I'm actually rich now. I've sorted Mam and Dad's situation out, I'm even in negotiations to buy a house of my own. Turns out I'm not a bad business woman. The night of the auction, I'd told Morgan McHugh that if he wanted to launch his NuYu shakes over here, then all that Silicon Valley technobabble wouldn't sell it to a normal lass or lad in the UK who just wanted to get healthy and not buy another Meal Deal sad sandwich at lunchtime. I'd offered to be his brand ambassador and things have flown. The first exclusive drop sold out almost instantly online and I knew it was going to go big. I signed off on all the ads, drank gallons of the stuff and signed a contract that mean I got a cut of the very juicy deal when the NuYu range hit supermarkets. The only flaw? It still tasted like fruity mushroom soup, no matter what flavour we launched. I'd filmed endless videos about how plant protein was the future, and I'd never admit to Morgan that his beloved shakes tasted like cardboard and air freshener in a blender, but I was beginning to wonder whether half the secret to their magic weight loss powers was making them taste that weird so no one wanted to drink more than half a serving.

But it hadn't held the brand back. The sleek, minimal packaging was the must-have accessory and I'd even see people pouring other things into their empty NuYu bottles just to be seen carrying our products. And now it's given me enough cash to do this.

I ask Mam to hand me a mirror, I'm desperate to see what my new nose looks like. I didn't really think about it that much before going on the show but it's become a fixation and I want this operation to shut down all the nonsense. Imagine what I can get done if I'm not google searching 'Angelica Clarke + nose' ten times a day. But then again, imagine if it's been botched. If this surgeon has fucked it up, there's really going to be no hiding from it. At least you can hide a dodgy boob job with baggy jumpers, I can't install a set of curtains on my face. Or, maybe I could, and I could rebrand myself as a performance art style pop star, like Gaga with her meat dress. I begin to tell Mam this and she just nods at me, like she's talking to the highest person alive, which, maybe, right at this very moment, I am.

She holds the mirror up and…I can see nothing at all. I'm all wrapped up in dressings. I remind myself of one Halloween where I dressed up like a mummy, buying loads of cheap bandages and just wrapping them all around my naked body. I thought my knot skills were up to scratch, but throughout the night, I came undone, piece by piece, until I was basically completely naked apart from a few loyal bandages that looked more like loo paper than medical equipment.

"Oh, but I can't see what it looks like," I say, stating the obvious.

"It'll be a few days before they take the splints and things off your face," Mam says. "Then, you'll have to be in hiding because of all the bruises. Fliss says the papers have got wind of you being here and they're dying for a shot of you in bandages, or with a swollen, purple face."

"They can't have that! The whole point is I'm going to emerge looking so drop-dead gorgeous that Damon sees me in the papers and regrets ever messing me about."

"No," Mam says sternly. "The whole point is to feel happy and confident in yourself, not for some dickhead who isn't worth your time."

Mam and Dad, for obvious reasons, loathe Damon. They could cope with me getting drunk and being ridiculous on TV, they know what I'm like. But they hated seeing me cry over Damon in the house and, even more so, when they had to see me in real life, sobbing over him. Dad says Damon owes him the money for at least five of his best jumpers, as I've stained them with mascara from all the times I cried on his chest.

I quickly backtrack. "Of course, must be the drugs talking. I'm leaving Damon well in the past." Which is true, the NuYu success has really helped me with my confidence and seeing how much better off I am without him in my life. I always thought when celebs did health deals that they didn't actually use the products, and it involved camera trickery and maybe a dodgy crash diet? But I was shocked when Morgan told me that no, he had no plans to pay for liposuction or that cryo thing where they just deep-freeze all your wobbly bits, and that, instead, I'd have to first go on a fasting retreat for six weeks then work out with a personal trainer for an intense three months while I lived off the shakes with no sugar, no alcohol and no kebabs. When Morgan had told me he was paying me to go and stay at an exclusive Alpine clinic for six weeks to 'eat' only NuYu, do some yoga and take a few treatments, I had pictured a spa hotel, relaxing around a pool and sipping on a shake. Instead, I'd found myself sweating out of places where I'd never sweated before doing hot yoga, drinking NuYu sludge four times a day and then, to top it all off, I had weekly colonic irrigation to 'help kickstart my cleanse'. Nothing I did on *North Stars* compared to the indignity of that, let me tell you.

But I had to admit, when I got back to the UK to start the exercise regime and posting my #NuYuNuMe content, I was looking banging. I had this great idea of getting Anika to train me – maybe even get her famous at the same time. But when I finally got through to her, the ship had just docked in Aruba and she was about to go and lead a circuits class for passengers on the white tropical sand, so I understood why she couldn't quit her job to come and train me in a wet warehouse off the M6. Instead I got given some tall, muscly gay guy called Marshall who worked me to the bone, but made me laugh so much that I've forgiven him.

But writing the text to Anika made me realise I do love exercise now. Even burpees, which is quite sad, but I found a way to make them fun: for every ten burpees I would do a silly, loud, fake burp impression, making them more and more ridiculous each time. In the end I was doing 100 burpees a time and it's actually quite hard to think of ten different inventive burps.

But, just because I'm feeling so much happier with my looks, and that the endorphins have flooded my brain with kind thoughts about myself, and now my new nose is the cherry on this (sugar-free) cake, that doesn't mean I can't also want revenge on Damon. I want him to want me, but I'm not sure I actually want him any more. Maybe I'll find some hot male tanner to shag while he's in the room, and see how he likes it. I fall back asleep picturing Damon on his knees, with a patchy tan, begging me to give him a second chance (or is it a third or fourth chance now? I've lost count.)

Someone has taken two very sharp sticks and stuck them up my nostrils. Whoever it is has now taken to playing the drums, with said sticks, but using my nose as their instrument. I am in so much pain! And

Lucky Break

I still can't even see what my new nose looks like. First, the surgeons have to take out the two plugs that are shoved, like tampons, up each nostril. I know it's going to be worth it, once I can parade my new nose all around town, along with my new, hard-earned body. But at the moment, with the drugs all worn off, the pain stabbing at me now and then, I question, was this worth it? In those moments, I have to look at myself in the mirror and chant – *I am sexy, I am smart, I am a piece of art!* It's something Marshall taught me: positive affirmations. I felt stupid doing them at first and had to come up with a little dance to accompany them, as though trying to make myself feel even more stupid chanting, but it actually made it easier. Now, they're second nature, and it's become this song that I like to sing to myself. Sometimes it gets stuck in my head so badly I have to listen to some Beyonce just to change the track. That way I'm still listening to someone powerful, I'm just not bugging myself with my own self-inflicted earworm.

I'm chanting my song, even while they wheel me off to have my plugs removed. I've been warned it's the worst part of the whole process. I don't know how it works but I think, essentially, these plugs have acted like scaffolding, holding all the bits of my new nose together, until they're all set and ready. But that my new nose has become quite attached to them being there, so won't give them up without a fight and—

"Oooooowwwwwwwwwwwwwwwwwwwwwwwwww!"

I look down, convinced that my brain must be all over the floor. As that's what it felt like, this big gush of… something… just flooding out of my nose, splashing onto my gown and all over the floor. But it's just some blood, and…actually, I don't want to look at it anymore. But I do know it's not my brain. There's not enough there. I like to think I have a lot more brains than that. Despite what the papers say.

The worst part is, even after all that pain (and almost losing my brains) I am still not allowed to see my new nose. Mam drives me home from the hospital, going very slowly over the bumps, as they send shooting pains through my cheeks. I'm to recover at home, staying in hiding (both from the paps and the neighbours, given I look a fright) until it's time for the cast and bandages to come off.

"I'm going to be so bored, Mam. Why can't they just do speed nose jobs, like those flip books I had when I was a kid? One page, flip, boom, brand new nose!"

"Well, they say your nose will keep changing for a whole year until it settles, so maybe life is just going to be slow for a while. Anyway, you won't be bored, as there's a surprise waiting back home for you."

I try not to rush in, desperate to find out what the surprise is, as the new nose demands that I move slowly. That's how I've started to refer to it, saying to Mam, "The new nose needs a Diet Coke, the new nose needs you to change the channel." There's nothing in the living room, apart from Dad who gives me a delicate hug, telling me he didn't want to see me in hospital as he thinks it would make him cry. It's been very hard to explain to Dad that you can be in hospital for positive reasons, too. He just keeps saying, "I couldn't bear to see my baby girl on her deathbed." Which has really made me realise where I inherited my tendency to be over-dramatic.

Upstairs, my room has been decorated with fairy-lights. The bed is covered with big cushions, and blankets and bean-bags are strewn all over the floor. There's even old movie posters hung on the walls, but the movie star faces have all been replaced with mine! There I am as Beetlejuice, with lime green hair in a black-and-white suit, Sandy from *Grease*, hanging off of John Travolta – there's even one of me as Kevin McCallister in *Home Alone*, slapping my cheeks in horror. They're so funny, unfortunately, that it hurts when I laugh so I try to swallow my giggles down my throat. There's also a couple of baskets, bursting with proper movie snacks: popcorn, pick 'n' mix in striped paper bags and chocolate bars. My room has been transformed into the comfiest of cinemas! As there's a projector, transforming one wall into a huge screen, where Pumba and Timon from the *Lion King* are currently singing and dancing to 'Hakuna Matata'.

"This is amazing! Did you do this, Mam?"

"I wish I was this creative! No, it was your Leo, he popped round earlier to get it all set up. Are you sure you're just friends?"

"Yes! I told you Mam, he's not *my* Leo – he rejected me!" I say the last part in a whiny voice. "It's bad enough, without me having to repeatedly remind you."

"I don't think that's quite how it went, love. You said he just wants you to be over Damon and, to be honest, I don't blame him."

"You're taking his side? Even after all this," I flail one arm around the room, pointing out the, admittedly, lovely gesture. But still! I'm angry at him. It might be because over the last few months we've not seen each other. I wanted my transformation to be a proper surprise to the press, so I've turned down almost every invite and launch, and the one time I did venture to one and saw Leo, I found I was clunky and clumsy around him. I'd go in for a hug, and accidentally stand on his toe or we'd speak all at once, overlapping each other with "no, now you go." We very much gave off colleagues-who-once-shagged-and-felt-massively-awkward vibes. I think we both knew it might be easier if we didn't see each other for a while and realistically, we've both been busy anyway. I've been sweating and sipping in the Alps and he's been, well, everywhere. I admit I might have spent a bit more time on his Instagram than is healthy for 'just friends' but since filming season two was canned, he's not been short of work. I cyber-stalked him through the job he had filming a wildlife show at Longleat, then the Hogmanay celebrations up in Edinburgh, and now I thought he was down south doing a show called *Candy Man*, where people make the most incredible looking sweets. But it's been the posts tagged #HomeSweetHome and #BestHousemateEver that have really had me zooming in. I have to tell myself I'm not jealous that it seems his housemate is one of those laid-back, natural beauty, I-woke-up-this-way types. She's called Molly and works in TV too, and I'd be lying if I pretended I'd not asked Madison to find all the inside scoop on her. He's stopped replying to my messages as fast lately and I wonder if whatever we had that day between us in the shadow of the angel has fizzled out.

"This is mixed messages!" I yell, flopping down onto a bean bag. "Also he's got me all these sweet treats when he knows I can't have sugar!"

"I think you might be on a medically-induced comedown," Mam says and it's so annoying when someone tells you why you're feeling the way you're feeling. Like when I'm grumpy and dad says it's PMS. No, it's not, people just happen to be behaving like arseholes coincidentally around the same time I am due my period. This is the same. I was pumped full of painkillers and now I'm not, and Leo is a bastard for doing a really nice thing for me.

I message Madison and Layla. They'll agree with me.

You just only fancy bastards, so you're trying to make him into one. L x

For god's sake let a man do a nice thing for you! You know what Marc got me the other day? THE MORNING AFTER PILL. And I thought it was sweet! M xxxxx

Traitors.

Mam tucks a blanket under my chin and winds the *Lion King* back to the beginning. After a good cry at his dad dying, and singing along to 'I Just Can't Wait To Be King' but tweaking the lyrics to 'I Just Can't Wait To Be Thin' (another one of my songs during training season) I have cheered up. Which is lucky for Leo, as it's just as the credits begin to roll that he appears.

"So," he says, settling down on a bean bag beside me. "Were you fuming at me at first?"

He knows me too well.

"Yeah, yeah I was. I haven't seen you for months, you've cheated on all us North Stars originals by going off filming other shows and now to top it all off, you bring me sweets I can't eat. Marshall can smell a jelly baby at 200 paces!"

"What?" he says. "So I'm not allowed to do nice things for my friend?"

Friend. Well that settles it, then.

Besides, he has a point. I try to make my nod clear under the cast.

"I felt a bit guilty for being a bit of a dick about the nose job," he says. "It's your face so you can do what you want with it. It's just…I liked your old nose. It was cute."

"Cute doesn't make the cover of magazines."

"I thought you'd say that and, actually, it does…"

He pulls out of his bag a pile of magazines. There are none of the usual celeb ones I read. Instead he's got me ones about psychology and puzzles and right at top: *Pup Weekly*. It's a magazine basically full of puppies with the most adorable chihuahua on the cover. "Oh my god, I love dogs. I really want one!" I realise this is doing much more for my mental health than looking at pictures of Kady James' sweat marks or an article about Chad Schmidt's hairline.

We settle against the pillows and begin flicking through the magazine, assigning names and personalities to each pup. "He looks like his name is Edward and he's a really funny gay man, who insists everyone calls him Edway," I say, pointing out a cheeky-looking dalmatian.

"This one looks like a Stewart, and he's a Chelsea fan—"

"who makes up all the rude chants at the matches!"

The puppies, the Disney movies and the fact my face is literally out-of-bounds, so there definitely can't be any kissing, helps disperse the lingering sexual tension that's been hanging between us, ever since *that* afternoon. Leo and I might not have seen each other but we've since found a way to be sort-of friends over text. Behind the safety of the screen we can let our guard down and be mates – no awkwardness, no temptation – and I've been updating Leo on all aspects of my life, sending him selfies of me beetroot-faced and sweaty after workouts, or showing him videos of Mam, Dad and me when we're all a bit drunk and re-enacting famous historical moments (Dad's idea). I just didn't know how to translate that fun, relaxed friendship into real life, until now. Turns out all that was needed was a face cast.

"I am sorry about how much of a dick I was over your nose job," Leo says again.

"I know, you've said. It's fine, I understand."

When Leo first heard about my surgery, he sent me multiple messages stressing what a bad idea he thought it was, and that I was beautiful "just the way I am." He said the same about my fitness journey too, that it was "great" I was enjoying exercise but it should just be about that, my mental health rather than "getting thinner, or whatever."

"I know you were just being nice, but really, you have no idea what it's like to be a woman in this unforgiving world, constantly judged for how you look. I get it, it would be great if I could just 'love myself as I am' but do you have any idea how hard that is, when all the messages around you are telling you to be thinner, to be 'flawless'? When you get notifications, from strangers, telling you how hideous you look?"

"You need to turn off your notifications," he says. Like that's the solution!

"I can turn off my notifications but I can't turn off years of crap, being told I have to be thin, but not skinny, or being told our faces are wonky but if we get Botox or surgery then we're shallow. It's like all that stuff has seeped into me Leo, convincing me I need to look perfect."

"But you are perfect," he says and it's a load of bull. I've seen perfect, mostly draped over Damon's arm in the papers. That's what I need to be. Obviously I can't admit that to Leo, so I just scoff and say, "Whatever loser," and we continue to watch the movie, close enough to be holding hands but not touching. He says he has to go soon and I just want to enjoy the moment.

I've woken up to a national disaster! OK, that's definitely an overexaggeration. But, my mummified face is splashed across the front page of all the papers. The headlines scream:

```
SNIFFER SHOCKER, Angelica NOSE best as she undergoes surprise
surgery.
```

My phone will not stop buzzing.

```
How did these images get out? They look like your
own personal selfies?
```

Lucky Break

```
Are you still asleep? You need to wake up!
Lol, don't really know why I think typing you need
to wake up, would wake you up.
I don't want you thinking I'm mad at you. I'm not
mad at you. I know this isn't your fault.
Unless, this actually is your fault? No. You wouldn't
do that.
```

I ring Fliss back as soon as I see her messages. She sounds out of breath, and tells me this has "totally fucked" the exclusive mag deal she had set up. "They wanted the befores and afters, all the surgery shots and everything!" she's yelping, and I'm gutted as I really wanted to look scorching hot in those afters. I'm trying to think of who I sent the selfies to, but it's only Madison, Layla and Leo. Oh wait…and Samantha! When I was still high after the anaesthetic I thought I'd send her them. "It's Samantha," I say. "It has to be. I sent her them, I'm so sorry, she must have passed them to the papers."

"That snake! Don't worry, I'll sort this…I always do. But, on the plus side, you've been invited to Monaco! *Savage*, the vodka brand, is hosting a party on a yacht to coincide with the Grand Prix and they want you there! I was in the process of arranging your flights before I found out, and really, when you think of it, there's no better place to get papped with your new nose, is there?"

I remember the battered Mini I passed my driving test in (on the third attempt if you must know) and can't believe I'm going to the Grand Prix weekend. I push away thoughts of what Sam's done and decide nothing's going to rain on my parade. I'm off to Monaco and I'm going to be fast, furious and fabulous.

* * *

Chapter Sixteen

The warm air hits my face as soon as I step off the plane and I know that I am exactly where I need to be. Marshall's affirmation: 'I'm in the moment, I am the moment' comes back to me as I disembark the plane, attempting to embody the aura of Grace Kelly (and not trip down the steps). I'm only on the airport tarmac and already I feel more expensive, like the oxygen here consists of particles of gold and I'm just inhaling it all in. I want to yell out "Monaco, are you ready for meeeeeeeee" with arms outstretched, awaiting some hot French man to come running into them, ready to swoop me up off my feet, fling me over his shoulder and feed me oysters. Except they're gross and would make me spew. Maybe some perfectly flaky croissant instead? Though I'd only eat a very small portion, of course. Damn, why am I letting my diet infiltrate my fantasies? That's not how it works. In my fantasy I can eat a whole banquet and my new body would still be as sculpted as it is now.

There's a lovely old man, with a big white moustache (a trustworthy moustache, I decide) waiting for me at arrivals, with my name scrawled on a board. "The beautiful Angelica," he says. "I've been waiting for you," and even though he's pushing seventy and I am slightly worried when he insists on carrying my cases, as he seems close to toppling over, I am charmed, and even a little turned on. I text Madison and Layla.

```
Even the old guys here are hot.
```

My phone pings back straight away. It's Madison.

```
Argh I can't wait to arrive, my clit's tingling just
thinking about all the dick there.
```

Lucky Break

I'm oiled up and ready! (For the sunshine) (and the men) Lx

They've both been invited separately, by different brands. It seems like the entire reality TV circuit is here. Hayley from *Carry on Chelmsford* was on my plane and even said she's going to come over to my hotel room this afternoon and give me a free va-glimmer. I've already shaved down there (it was like battling through jungle bushes, it had been a while, what with the post-op recovery and all) and she's going to apply sparkly gems, which is the latest thing, apparently. I can choose from shapes, like cherries, strawberries or a heart or words. I think I'll go for words. Maybe lucky boy, or even something in French, adjusting to the culture and all that.

Pulling up at my hotel is like pulling up at a palace. Despite it being so central and only a short walk away from the marina, there's this long driveway and the door is framed by two carved pillars, and stepping into the marble lobby I feel like an old-school Hollywood movie star. I'm wearing little black shorts and a vest, and I've already had three proper panics that I've lost my cases, but Antonio my driver has handed everything across to the hotel porters. He blows me a kiss and tells me he will be my personal driver for the whole time I am here, so whenever I need him, I'm just to drop him a text. I've never had a personal driver before! Well, apart from when I nicknamed my dad my personal driver as he collected me and my friends so much from town in the middle of the night, when no taxis would take us because we were too hammered. But I don't think that counts.

I'm absolutely itching to get to my room and see what it's like. No matter where I stay, whether it's a cheapie one (I've paid for myself) or an expensive one (when works books the hotel) I love to get in, run around squealing and then jump up and down on the bed for a while. It's tradition. But it's so fancy here that they sit me on this deep purple sofa with a gold tasseled trim and give me an actual glass of champagne, *not* prosecco, while they check me in. I'm even given a little plate of strawberries to nibble on. I try not to eat them too quickly, so that I look classy and like I am given little plates of strawberries to nibble on all the time. Once I'm all checked in, they give me a tour of the hotel, showing me the cute little secluded courtyard where breakfast will be served and the library, where all these beautiful people are just lounging around reading ginormous newspapers while drinking from teeny tiny coffee cups.

My room, instead of having a key card, has an actual big brass key and as I'm shown around I keep repeating "wow, wow, wow" while swallowing my squeals of delight under my breath. It's the most incredible room I've ever seen, never mind stayed in. Room isn't even the right word, as technically it's four different rooms in one. There's a hallway, with floor-to-ceiling mirrors that magically slide open to reveal a huge wardrobe space and mini bar (I'll be raiding that later) and the hallway leads into my very own living room, complete with a balcony that opens out onto the bustling square below, with a view that stretches all the way to the ocean. The sea just glimmers with possibility, I can't believe I'm here! They've laid out a bottle of champagne for me in an ice bucket, and a cute little card welcoming me to the hotel. Then there's double doors that open, to a – and I kid-you-not – FOUR-POSTER BED. It even has curtains! It is exactly the kind of room little me imagined a palace would look like when I would play dress-up as a girl. "I really am a princess!" I say, unable to hide my excitement which makes the porter smile, he's got these cute sparkling brown eyes and the most incredible tan. "If they bottled your tan, I would buy it," I said to him earlier, but he didn't really understand what I was saying. The bathroom is all marble and the bath, he shows me, has a button that pours water to the exact right temperature alongside jacuzzi jets in four different settings. "Anything you need, Miss Angelica, you call us," he says.

"I can't think of anything else I would possibly need," I say. "This is amazing!"

I'm sure that, from the other side of the door, he hears the excitable scream I let out as soon as he leaves. I throw myself onto the bed, hoping that a man will be the one throwing me on it soon. This new body needs road-testing! And a gorgeous mediterranean man is surely perfect for the job.

It's very, very difficult not to scratch at my crotch-stubble as I stand on the jetty looking at the boats bobbing on the glittering surface a couple of hours later. I forgot all about that freshly-shaved fanny itch, but – hopefully – it'll all be worth it. Hayley's adorned me, I opted for 'hello lover' in cursive font, in fake diamonds, and, surely, there will be someone on this yacht I'm heading to, who will untie my bikini bottoms and have their dirty way with me. That's not too much to ask, is it? But first, to get to the big boat, I have to get into a little speed boat, captained by a lady named Mary who, from the outside, looks not-to-be-messed-with. But as soon as she cracks a smile I know I am in safe hands, plus I swear that's a northern twang in her accent.

"Mary, I don't mean to be rude, but I wouldn't have expected—"

"—a woman my age to be driving a dinghy? I probably wouldn't have either, my love. And yes, normally it's the young lads who are doing these back and forths." Her accent is broad, Mancunian. "Long story short, I fell in love with an Italian man, ooooh many years ago now, then I fell in love with this place, and with the ocean. I swapped Moss Side for Monaco and I've not looked back. The man, well, he left but my love for the sea remained. I said to the captains I'd do anything they needed me to, odd jobs here and there, sometimes it's cooking, sometimes it's cleaning but, when I'm very lucky it's this. Whizzing the beautiful people, like yourself, to the yachts and back."

"That's sad, about the man."

"Did you not listen properly?" she says, revving the engine up. "My life's perfect. Have enough men, as I have," she cackles. "And you'll soon learn they're not worth the heartache."

"I think I'm nearly there on that lesson," I say, thinking of Damon. I'm trying to only remember the bad stuff, and erase all of the good. It's better that way.

"Now, tell me, are you all on your lonesome?"

"I don't actually know," I say, but as soon as I do the boat starts rocking violently from side to side. "Tally ho, watch out," I hear, booming from above us. Then, there's a penis in my face. Well, a penis covered in skintight Kermit-the-frog green speedos. Followed by a toned, tanned stomach, and then there's strong arms holding me. Is this my Italian/French/Greek god? Only the arms aren't holding me as such, more using me for balance as the owner of said arms climbs into the dinghy, and with the boat rocking this much I'm not much of a balancing aid.

"What the fuck are you doing?" Mary asks the figure who has now successfully landed in the boat, after almost knocking me into the water in the process. I'm gripping the side of the boat trying to steady myself as I listen to our skipper address the idiot. "Did you not think to ask for help?"

"I've been in the navy cadets, I don't need help getting into a dinghy," the voice, definitely not Italian, says. It's a cut-glass, up-itself voice that with every word spoken screams "I think I'm better than you." Wait a minute. It's a *Born In Buckinghamshire* voice. It's…Sebastian. Only it's Sebastian not in his standard get-up of cravats and chinos, but Sebastian with hardly any clothes on. A Sebastian, if it wasn't for the voice, and the clumsy, gangly, stupid way he just boarded this boat, I could get on board with. Who knew he had that body under all of his usual tweed?

"You almost killed me!" I yell, determined to focus more on the fact he got into the dinghy like an entitled prick, rather than his washboard stomach with that distracting trail of dark hair leading to his spray-on trunks.

"I did not, you need to get a bit more robust, girl. God, women, why are you such drama queens." That's quite a claim from the bloke standing like Adonis, if Adonis had worn only lime-green Speedos, and flicking his very flickable hair like he's shooting a shampoo ad.

"You did," Mary says. We can both see the sand in the water beneath us, it's waist height at best and not looking very lethal, but still, she backs me. "You can't just be jumping into boats like that, there's protocol to follow."

"If there's protocol to follow, then why weren't *you*, up at the top, waiting to help your guests onto the boat," he says, blustering. His voice becomes even higher and mightier talking to Mary, which I hate. He seems like a man that just expects people to serve him at any given moment. That's my main problem with this Monaco set, they've never worked a day in their life and they think that somehow makes them special. The reality is, it makes them so much weirder as they have no grip on reality, manners, or the fact that if they broke out of their refined, moneyed bubble for even one second then they'd meet some of the nicest people around. Though, maybe that's for the best. The Sebastians of the world don't deserve to meet the Marys.

"You," she says, tapping her watch. "Were ten minutes late. Let me radio to see if there's any more of you due."

I cross my fingers. It can't just be me and *him*. Apparently this trip, being dinghied to the yacht, is only five minutes. I know because when I arrived I had said to Mary, "I thought it would be bigger than this," thinking that this tiny boat was the yacht I'd been promised. I'd still have been happy, considering I can still jump in the ocean from here, but I might have been a little disappointed. Mary had laughed and said, "I think I'm going to like you. Not often I get to ferry normal people."

There's supposed to be a big group of us, guests of the vodka brand who have hired out the yacht for a big promotional party. But when I got a taxi to the meeting point, I was waiting on my own for ages, until Mary decided she would whizz just me across to the yacht and then come back for the others. "No point you missing out on the free drinks," she'd winked.

"OK, so everyone else is running really late," she says. "It's just you two for now. Hold onto your hats."

I do not hold onto my hat (because I don't have one) but I don't hold onto the side either, not realising yet this tiny boat could move so fast. But it does, flinging me back, right into Sebastian's arms. "Steady there, girl," he says, gripping my shoulders. His skin feels warm against mine.

"I'm not a horse," I huff, blowing some hair out of my eye.

"You sure? You seem a fine filly to me."

"I've not a clue what you're talking about," I say but, before I can get him to elaborate on whether this was a compliment, or an insult, Mary says the magic word.

"Dolphins!"

And there they are, gliding alongside us, close enough to reach out and touch, weaving in and out, under and over each other and then... whooosh, one of them jumps in the air, sea water splashing onto my face. I want to squeal but my breath is caught in my throat, the moment is too magical for words. Or squeals. Even Sebastian can't play it cool, whispering "wow" over and over again. I can feel his breath in my ear and, call it biology, I can't help but feel tingly at the sensation. That and the fact I'm still wedged between his thick thighs.

We're so fixated on the dolphins, who stay by our side for most of the journey, that it's only when the yacht's shadow blocks the sun on my face that I notice we've arrived.

I don't know what I expected, but it wasn't the dinghy and it certainly wasn't this. What we've arrived at is less of a boat, and more of a floating hotel. It's this huge, three or maybe four floored thing, looming out of the sea. We pull up at its rear, where three men dressed in navy blue and gold-trim suits are waiting for us. They wave and Mary waves back.

"Two very fine passengers for you, lads."

"Hello, chaps!" Sebastian says, ignoring their outstretched hands as he steps off the boat, which proves to be a mistake, as he slips and falls back into our dinghy.

I, sensibly, took one of their hands. Why wouldn't I, they're handsome and sturdy! So I'm safely on the yacht, watching Sebastian scramble and try a second time, this time taking one of their hands. The annoying thing is, when he fell his Speedos slipped a little and there really is no denying his ass is as firm and tight as the rest of him.

"Did you not pack a shirt?" I ask, as he appears to have come in just the speedos. I'm in my tiniest string bikini, it's hot pink, with a little sheer black sarong tied on top. But I've packed another layer in my beach bag. Despite always going out in tiny dresses and priding myself on never wearing a coat, I'm nervous not knowing the dress code or what's considered on trend. I've got a tiny stretch-lace maxi in my clutch if I need to cover up, even if the lace manages to draw even more attention to what's underneath.

"I had some lovely chaps ferry some things over earlier," he replies.

"Yes, all eight bags arrived safe and sound, sir," says one of the suited men.

"*Eight* bags? For one day?!"

"Oh no, I'm staying on the yacht. Don't tell me you're one of the B-list guests, just onboard for the day?"

B-List! How rude! But then there's no denying it, I didn't know some people were invited to stay on the yacht, and I suspect other people are going to the Grand Prix itself, whereas I'm not going anywhere near the actual race. This is something I've really noticed since I started existing in this mad, fame game world – you'll be invited to drinks at a strange time and then when you get there, realise that a whole other group got dinner first. Or, you'll be leaving and one of the PRs will ask, ever-so-sweetly, who's list were you on? And you reply and it determines which goodie bag you get. Not that it really bothers me. The sign of a good night is that you're more bothered about having a good time than bagging swag. It's stupid though, as it's always the richest, fanciest people who get the best stuff when they could afford it already. Though, now, I have to keep reminding myself – I am one of those people. And it means that when I'm lucky enough to get gifts, I love it the next morning when my hangover finally clears and I can root through the goodie bag with Mam or Madison and share it all out. The NuYu range sold so well and there are loads more deals in the pipeline, including my dream: a clothing range. But it's surreal, suddenly having money. Unlike Sebastian, I didn't grow up in this world so I don't know the appropriate etiquette. Should I have tipped Mary? She's whizzed away now. Should I tip these men? I don't want to seem rude but I also don't want anyone to act as though I'm above them. We're being guided through some narrow carpeted corridors and upstairs, and I keep seeing glimpses of the ocean through the port-holes, which are gilded and polished so smoothly, I can see my face in them. Although I keep having to double check – it *is* my face, I'm just still adjusting to how it looks these days.

"The event is this way," one of the men says, and gestures to the deck. I feel like I've landed on another planet. There are all these white benches, tables laid out with buckets of ice, heaving with bottles of vodka and all sorts of mixers. There are more men in cute suits, holding silver trays, brandishing drinks. I grab one that's the exact same colour as the ocean, and look around, hoping that Madison and Layla might have arrived on an earlier dinghy. No such luck. I don't know anyone. And everyone on this boat looks like they belong here. The girls are all in white bikinis, or white swimsuits with legs cut so high I don't know how they don't have a permanent wedgie. The men are either in Speedos, so Sebastian clearly knew what he was doing, or navy blue shorts, with white shirts buttoned open to reveal tanned six-packs. There's not one ounce of fat on anyone in this boat and I feel grateful for my new, gym-honed frame. And yet, a part of me still wishes my sarong was that little bit bigger. It's funny, isn't it? Even when we've hardly any clothes on you can tell who was born rich, and who wasn't. Their tans are from summers in Ibiza, winters catching the rays off the snow, mine is from a bottle. Their bodies are pilates-toned, sleek and chic, with maybe a bit of chemical assistance, mine is from kettlebells and shakes and while it may be toned, it certainly isn't that supposed heroin-chic that some of the models draped around the yacht seem to be going for.

I look at Sebastian nodding hello to everyone, and concentrate on just soaking it all in. I try to stay cool, not goggling at the two hot tubs overlooking the ocean that are full of proper bona fide stars, or the people very openly scoping out the guests for whoever they think is the most famous or influential. I don't like him but I realise, after scanning all the faces and returning to Sebastian, he's all I've got.

Where are you girls, I think. I need you to liven the place up with me, I very much doubt any of these ladies have diamantes in their bikini bottoms. Plus they all seem to be trying incredibly hard to look incredibly bored, like it's not cool to have fun or admit you're impressed by anything. If Mads was with me, she'd be grinning from ear to ear and nabbing the best hot-tub. I feel my phone vibrate. It's Layla.

I'm shitting myself.

I text back quickly.

Don't be nervous. Yacht is amazing. You'll love it.

I snap a quick pic and send it over and Layla replies instantly.

No, I'm ACTUALLY shitting myself. I should have known not to have prawns. There's no way I can make it to the yacht. Sorry babes.

As I wonder when Mads is going to show my phone pings again.

Oh my god, I won't make it either, I know, I'm sorry but, argh can't type right now, it'll be worth it when I tell you. Mxxx

Damn, I look at Sebastian, who grins at me. "First time on a yacht?"

"No, I'm on them all the time."

"Oh really? Didn't think they had many yachts up..." He struggles to remember where I'm from and wrinkles his nose. "North."

I won't give him the satisfaction of correcting him, or tell him that when I was tiny, I thought I wanted to be a marine biologist (before a crab pinched my toe in the sea at Whitby and I changed my mind). For all I care, he can assume I've never seen the sea before, I don't need to impress him. "No, no I've never been on a yacht before."

I'm being spiky. I know I am. Normally, if a man with such a fine body was talking to me, I'd be nicer. *A lot* nicer. But this is Sebastian. From *Born In Buckinghamshire*. He's the enemy. Any minute now his comrades with their swishy hair and old money will arrive and begin making barbed comments about how they've seen my vagina on TV. Which wasn't even my fault. The producers should have blurred it out in editing, but someone forgot. Anyway, it's a damn nice vagina.

"None of your lot coming, then?"

He shakes his head. "They were meant to, but they were invited on another yacht. Something to do with Chad Schmidt apparently."

"There I was thinking there was no way anything could top this!" I say.

"Don't be sarcastic, it doesn't suit you."

"I wasn't being sarcastic! Look around, this boat is incredible!"

"Oh right, I would have thought being alone with me, stranded at sea, would be your worst nightmare."

"It would be…but there's vodka here." I down my blue drink. "Another?"

Five blue things later and Sebastian and I can't stop laughing, though I have no idea what at. Everyone else on the boat talks about posh things, like investments or polo, and every now and then one of them will come over to speak to Sebastian and I have to just zone them out, as really it's like listening to another language. Also, the more blue things I have, the better Sebastian looks in those Speedos. His body really is *carved*. I've also checked out his bulge, quite a few times (hopefully subtly but, to be honest, I'm not sure). I also have a feeling he might be into me, too. A few times our legs have touched and he's not recoiled. Also, his friends did eventually arrive, and they keep waving him over so he easily could have abandoned me for them ages ago, but he's still here.

"It's dead nice of you to stay with me, you know, you didn't have to do that," I say quietly, and he has to move closer to hear me. Our bodies are now touching. He grabs one shoulder, pulling me even closer.

"I'm loving this, you're so much fun, Angelica." I sense we might kiss in that moment, but when we look up, one of the girls from *Born In Buckinghamshire* is standing above us. "Uhh umm," she clears her throat loudly and Sebastian jumps away from me. I'm trying to remember her name and whether she's ever been involved with Sebastian before. Confession time: I've not really watched much of BiB, I just find it hard to invest in any of their antics as they don't seem to have fun like we do, but I have seen headlines about Sebastian, and everything I've seen or heard about him, I don't like.

"Angelica, this is Arabella," Sebastian says, and even though I tap the seat beside me, inviting her to sit down, she remains standing and quite literally looking down on us. "Ara," she says. "For short."

I want to ask her, why not Bella, but decide against it in case it would sound rude. I really shouldn't have bothered, as with her entire body angled towards Sebastian, resting herself in between his open legs, she whispers something in his ear: "I see you found cattle class."

"Excuse me, I heard that," I say, tapping her on the shoulder.

She turns around and casts me a withering look. "Well, you weren't meant to."

"I did and that's not an apology." I glare at Sebastian, expecting him to take my side. He just remains quiet. Absolute pussy!

"Now ladies, no need to get antsy," he simply says.

"Who's getting antsy?" I say, admittedly louder than normal.

Our (very minor) altercation has attracted a crowd and a few more of Sebastian's friends come over, hovering within earshot. Not all of them are from *Born In Buckinghamshire* but I know when I've been outnumbered. Both the lads and the girls are giggling and saying things to each other behind their hands. I'd already felt left out on this yacht but now I feel completely isolated. I know I have a couple of options, I could burst into tears (tempting but I don't want to look pathetic), grab 'Ara' by her hair and drag her into the pool (even more tempting, but I know I'd be giving them what they wanted…Thank goodness I've not drunk any whiskey, that's my anger juice) or I could storm off. I decide the last one gives me the most dignity, but where to? I'm in the middle of the ocean.

I stand up. "I thought you were all meant to have been raised with manners, it's horrible to treat someone like this," I say, before stabbing my finger in Sebastian's chest. To think I was this close to kissing him. "And you should be ashamed of yourself, you called all of this lot boring See You Next Tuesdays earlier and now look at you."

With that I wobble off in my wedges, only stumbling a few times. As far as dignity goes, I think I've maintained it. Now, I just need to not look back and head to my failsafe napping place. The loos. I can sleep off the vodka there until the boat docks again.

* * *

Chapter Seventeen

I wake up angry and determined. This will *not* be remembered as the holiday where Sebastian and a bunch of his dickhead mates made me feel like shit, and I had to, once again, sleep in a toilet. Thank goodness I could wash off the arrogance and general *eau de posh wanker* under a hot shower when I got back to my hotel, and then starfish onto the superking bed with its zillion thread-count sheets. I'm in a luxury resort, the sun is shining and I'm determined to prove Sebastian wrong: I am made for this life and I do belong here. Something is going to happen today and it is going to be magical. I'm just not yet sure what.

Luckily, Layla's feeling better and Madison's called an emergency group lunch at some fancy restaurant on the marina. So, I don my classiest dress and strut down to meet them, a pair of shades hiding my puffy, tired eyes. I won't admit it to anyone, but I did miss Damon yesterday. Yes, he's treated me horribly but he's always fun and he always stands up for me, there's no way 'Ara' would have got away with that behaviour had Damon been on the yacht with me. But I don't know if I can share that with the girls. Layla and Madison are already at the restaurant when I arrive, they've bagged the most amazing table overlooking the sparkling water, the masts of the boat stretching into the azure skies.

"White wine, chips and Caesar salad," Madison says, pointing to everything she's already ordered for us, knowing exactly what we would need.

I don't say but I know I'll just pick at the chips, and choose to drink my calories instead. Madison is radiating a smug glow. I squint at her.

"Did you get laid last night?"

"Last night, this morning, in the car on the way here…I've been shagging non-stop. Girls, lean in, I have to whisper this next part as it can't get out to the press. Actually, let's fill your wine up first."

She reaches for the bottle but a waiter comes rushing over, insisting he will pour, then takes far too long doing so. I mean, he actually probably only took two minutes but when you're awaiting what appears to be the gossip of the century, every minute feels like an hour.

"So, I was walking past this restaurant yesterday, really feeling myself, you know, the sun was shining, I'm looking good. Sure everyone looks classy here but I look sexy, I mean you don't need to fit in when you stand out…And clearly someone agrees with me, as I just get to that boat over there when this cute little man taps me on the shoulder. He's in this white linen suit, dead expensive looking, and he tells me that his boss really wants to meet me!"

"Was the boss a creepy old man?" Layla says. "It always is, that's why they send their handsome assistants, to lure you in."

"No, his boss was…" She mouths the name. Neither Layla nor I understand what she's saying.

She mouths again and I try to lip-read.

"Short and wide?" I say, confused.

"No, you numpty!" She mouths again until Layla shouts, "just spit it out!"

"CHAD SCHMIDT!" Madison yells in frustration, and a table of girls next to us turn around and say, "where?!"

"Oh, sorry, we thought we saw him but it was just that try-hard Marc from *North Stars*," Layla says, expertly batting them away. They don't know who he is, and turn away from us, disappointed. We all lower our voices.

"What? So you went on a date with Chad Schmidt?"

"Better than that, I've literally just come from shagging him and… this whole lunch is on him."

"In that case," I say, giving the waiter a little wave. "Can we have a bottle of champagne, please?" I don't even particularly like champagne, but it feels like the sort of thing you order after discovering your best friend has just shagged a movie star.

Layla just sits with her mouth wide open. "You'll catch flies," Madison says, shutting it for her. "Or better yet, a cock."

"Are you serious?"

"I wouldn't have just let Angelica order a bottle of champers if I was kidding you on, would I?"

"How was he?"

"I want to say amazing but—"

"But…"

"He was bang on average. Literally. Like, I don't know, it was fine? He knew what to do, in, out, shake it all about etc."

"I don't think I know that move!" Layla giggles.

"Will you two stop it, it's distracting from the shagging story!" I love a good fairytale, and the runner and the Hollywood star is exactly that.

"I think we did it like seven times last night and this morning, I'm exhausted. He was…obsessed by my tits."

"Who isn't?"

"Yeah your average lad from Wetherspoons is into them but he's been with, well, basically every hot celebrity around. He's seen LA tits."

"He's not seen a rack like yours," I say, suddenly very proud of my best friend. "What's Hollywood got that Liverpool hasn't?"

"Anyway, he wanted to do all the tricks, and I let him because, well, he's Chad Schmidt. But it wasn't really rocking my world. He only went down on me for, like, ten seconds at best and only because I asked him to."

"This is the problem," Layla nods, just as the champagne arrives and we instruct the waiter that yes, we do want a glass of champagne *alongside* our wine and could he top up both, pretty please. "Because he's always had that face on him, he's never had to get good at sex.

Ugly guys, they're the best sex I've had, because they actually had to try. I once had sex with this guy, he was no oil painting but…wow do I think about what he could do."

"Tell me more?"

"You don't want to ask," Madison says, before lowering her voice even further and whispering, "when Layla woke up the next day she realised he was missing his front two teeth. He had dentures!"

Layla lightly punches Madison's arm. "That was a secret! He'd lost them in a fight, it wasn't like he was a crack-head or anything. Anyway, when he did oral it was earth shattering."

"Well lucky for you," Madison chimes in. "When we're all old and wrinkly and all the guys we pull have false teeth, you can look forward to some great head!" she says, waving her arms out wide. "But anyway, back to meeeeeeeee. So…after his assistant chased me down, I came to the private back-room of this restaurant and it was down this big long corridor. I was walking down it thinking, god, maybe I'm being lured to be murdered…"

"Glamorous way to get killed though, unexpected," I say.

"That's exactly what I thought! Everyone thinks I'm going to die—"

"As part of a botched bum job in Turkey, so, why not opt for this more glamorous way instead, so I kept going."

When she reached the room, apparently Chad Schmidt was just sitting there, at the end of one long, gold table, with a bottle of champagne in front of him and he just drawls, "Good to meet ya honey, pull up a chair."

"We chatted for hours, but his chat was pretty tame and he refused to tell me anything interesting as I hadn't signed an NDA yet, so I said 'Chad, mate, you don't have to sign anything to hear my stories,' and told him all about us…"

"Does that mean…?"

"Yes, that means Chad Schmidt knows about the times you were caught short, Angelica."

It's then I hear that dreaded voice.

"I definitely don't ever want to hear those stories," he says, disdain almost dripping off the figure suddenly blocking our harbour view. It's Sebastian, and despite it being over thirty degrees and blazing sunshine, he's decked out in a tweed jacket, worn over a pair of salmon-pink shorts and those sludge-brown boat shoes him and his mates insist on wearing to all occasions. It is suddenly very baffling to me that I ever found him attractive. I have to take another sip of wine to stop myself from saying something I'll regret.

"Not in your Speedos today then?" I mutter instead.

"No, that wouldn't be the correct attire, would it?" he says, deadly serious. At what point are budgie smugglers so tight you're worried they're going to be deemed inappropriate attire? "Anyway, ladies," he pulls up a chair and sits beside us, even though no one invited him to join. "I wanted to steal Angelica away for a minute, my manager has had a rather splendid idea."

"We're kind of in the middle of something," I say.

"And we're kind of on the front-page of every red-top newspaper in Blighty," he says, pulling a folded tabloid out of the inner pocket of his jacket, and there we are: huge, colour pics of us...I'm lounging in my bikini, laughing, with shots of Sebastian and I looking like we're about to kiss, the headline declaring:

THE PRINCE AND HIS PAUPER
Why is TV's richest rascal romancing our favourite good-time girl?

"Skinny bitch," Madison says, grabbing the paper for a closer look. "You look gooooood, Angelica."

I shrug, she is right. I know these photos are all about angles but it's true, I look banging. Which almost makes up for the headline.

"Good-time girl? That makes me sound like a slag."

"But at least they call you our *favourite* slag," Layla corrects.

"Indeed, and that's what my manager wants to talk to you about, people are loving us together. He thinks we should make this an official pairing."

"Are you asking me out via your manager?" I ask, while Sebastian helps himself to a glass of wine. I snatch the glass off him and down it in one. "The answer is no."

"Don't be so arrogant," he snatches the glass back again, while Madison and Layla watch on, their eyes darting like it's a tennis match. "It's only a business proposal, you know, for publicity, a showmance type thing. He thinks it would get us great press coverage and…let's face it, you need it."

"Errrm, so do you," Madison interjects. "Otherwise you wouldn't be asking her."

"What are you, her manager?" he fires back.

"I do have a manager, and your manager should be asking mine, rather than whatever this is," I say. "So go tell him to call her, the fabulous Fliss Evans, and let us get back to our lunch." I say, yanking the bottle out of his hands before he can pour another glass.

"Fine," he shrugs, standing up. "Angelica, believe me, I know how to treat a lady, just ask, well, all of my 100+ body count. Being seen on my arm really means you've arrived." With that, he swaggers off.

"Ugh," I mime vomiting. "He's so sleazy."

"Great ass, though," Layla says, watching him walk off. "And into you."

"No he's not, he's just into attention from the papers, that's all he wants from me."

"That's never stopped you before," Madison says, in a not-so-sly dig at Damon.

"I just hate that Damon gets away with it, you know, all the guys do," I say. "So smug about having shagged over a hundred women, I've only got with a fraction of that, and yet he's a legend in the papers and I'm a slut."

"Hey, there's nothing wrong with being a sexually confident woman. We're getting ours, everyone else is just wound up and bitter."

"I'd rather it wasn't the first thing people think of me, when they hear my name: Angelica equals easy."

"Well stop being so easy then," Madison says, but with a sweet grin on her face. "Stop doing everything you can to lure Damon back and bin him once and for all. Oh and I know it sucks, the double standards. There needs to be a name for a male slut."

"There is: hero, legend, lothario, stud, player…" Layla lists them off on her fingers.

"But an offensive one."

"OK, let's brainstorm then," Madison pulls her eyeliner pencil out of her bag and begins writing words on a napkin.

PENIS PUMPER. DIRTY DICK. GIRL GRINDER. HUMAN DOORKNOB. THE WALKING STD. THE ROMANCE ROACH.

We're cackling at our suggestions, while messages from Fliss are flooding my screen, asking me what I think of Sebastian and his manager's plan. Clearly he hasn't wasted any time trying to seal the deal. Fliss doesn't pressure me either way, just says it's my decision and whatever I want, she'll help me. It's sweet but I almost wish she'd just tell me exactly what to do.

"What do you guys think? Should I follow through with this Sebastian plan?" I don't tell them that a part of me isn't just considering what Damon would think, it's wondering if Leo has seen the pictures.

The girls both vote yes to the #Sebgelica scheme. Madison's answer is always "do it for the memoirs, it'll make a funny story one day" and she reckons I'll get to see his parent's legendary mansion, which is known for having an actual ballroom which the cast used as a roller disco rink in one episode, three swimming pools (indoor, outdoor and a spa pool) and even exotic animals in the grounds, according to rumours. "Their parties are said to be off the charts, just think, you could get us all on the list. The *North Stars* lot take on the toffs!"

"No party with the *BiB* lot is ever fun, even if there is a tiger there," says Layla, who's way more pragmatic. She always says she'd rather be in the shittiest of pubs with the nicest people than a nice place full of shit-heads, and she sticks to her word. Her friends are all lovely…but they're rarely found in posh places. Her last birthday party she genuinely held in her local working men's club so everyone could afford to come. It was a banging night, to be fair. "I still think you should do it, though Angelica, without series two our chance of a career could be short-lived and this could really boost your profile. You would only have to hang out with him long enough for the photos to be taken then you could bugger off and come hang with us."

I'm still not sure. We drink some more wine, and just as the sun is setting, turning us all into golden, shimmering beings, I get a text.

Is that your new boyfriend then?

It's Damon. He's clearly seen the pictures and is Shrek-green with jealousy. It wasn't my intention but, if it rubs him up the wrong way, or makes him feel even the slightest fraction of the pain he caused me, well, then…I message Fliss.

Sebastian and me? It's on.

* * *

Chapter Eighteen

I have something big and strong between my thighs, something sturdy and hard clenched in my hands, and I'm ready to take control. I squeeze my legs together, mutter "let's go" and I'm off, but – wait, I'm actually kinda scared? The horse below me definitely has a mind of her own as she sets off trotting and I begin to screech, dropping the polo stick while I'm at it, gripping on to the horse for dear life. After all, her tail is all wrapped up pretty, which I thought was for the photos but have since been told this is apparently to stop accidents. How dangerous is this game?

"Steady on, steady on," Sebastian chases after me and Winnie, that's the horse's name, and grabs a hold of her. "Angelica, you can't be screeching like that, you'll scare the mare."

"You should have warned me she was going to go that fast," I yell, but my words are lost to the wind. I'm very, very high up on this absolutely massive horse and very out of my depth. I've come to Sebastian's parents' house in the country, and much to their dismay, there's a bunch of paps (leaked to and let in by Sebastian's management) hiding in the bushes. And considering that display of Winnie being a rebellious, wild thing, much like myself, they've probably already snagged their shot.

This is mine and Sebastian's first 'date.'

"You've got to go slow, we're practising, you can't just run off and be waving your mallet around." That's the official term for the hammer thing I'm meant to be holding. It's this long, thin stick with what looks like a miniature beer barrel at the end. We're meant to hit the little white balls which are dotted all over the ground, and whack one in the goals. Sebastian said it was like hockey so I confidently said I would be absolutely fine as we played that in school, but then I remembered I spent most of my time bunking off PE and trying (and failing) to learn how to smoke. Also, hockey is played running on my own reliable feet that I control, not at the mercy of a horse with a mean streak.

"She's a polo pony, she doesn't understand when you use two hands on the reins, you're only meant to use one, your left hand, I told you this."

"And I told you I think it's offensive to left-handed people to not be able to switch hands." Apparently in polo, you have to swing the mallet with your right hand, no exceptions. Sebastian said his father would "have a heart attack" if he saw me holding a mallet with my left hand. What can I say? Rich people care about the daftest things. "Anyway, that did look a little scary, do you want to get down?"

But I'm no quitter. I've agreed to play polo, for the photo opportunity, and also "for the memoirs" so I'll keep playing. "It's only been five minutes, I'll get better."

One hour later and guess what? I've not got any better. Winnie, who I thought was once my comrade, I believe now has a vendetta against me. She doesn't listen to any of my cues, she keeps running off without me telling her to and I've not managed to hit even one ball. But, I am laughing. A lot. And that's the key thing. Everything I do in life is mostly just to have a laugh and have some fun. Sebastian clearly disagrees. The worse I am, the more I laugh and as a result, the more pissed off Sebastian becomes. He's huffing and puffing about how I'm "just not listening" when the most gorgeous older man I've ever seen comes swaggering onto the lawn. He's well over six foot, with salt and pepper hair, these big strong eyebrows and the most captivating smile.

"Can't you see the girl's trying, son, also it's time for a break, it's G&T o'clock. Sweetheart, let me get you down from there."

Then, with a magician's touch, this man walks straight over to Winnie, who stops dead in her tracks, as he then pats her murmuring, "there, there, good girl" (and, I can't lie, I was fluttering down there as he said it, *lucky* Winnie.)

"Now gently ease your feet out of the stirrups, one foot at a time. That's right." I do exactly as this silver fox says and manage, miracle of miracles, to elegantly pull my feet out of the stirrups and gingerly step down from Winnie, directly into this man's very large, very capable hands. As I slide down the horse, his hands graze my hips, pulling me close to him. I feel his breath in my hair, as he whispers, "you're trembling, don't worry, you're safe now." I can smell the leather from Winnie's saddle, and feel the warmth of the just-setting evening sun on my face and, oh my god, I'm so horny for this sixty-year-old.

"I'm Thomas," he says, shaking my hand. Did I mention his hands were firm? "But you can call me Tommy. I'm this reprobate's father."

Sebastian shrinks in his dad's presence. He's also well over six foot with a taut well-proportioned frame, but he becomes flustered around his father. "Daddy," he coughs. "I mean, Dad, this is Angelica, she's my..." He pauses. "Girlfriend."

"I heard from your mother (who's not happy by the way, you have some groveling to do, I'm afraid) that none of this is real. I'm sorry if you were under a different impression Angelica, but you're not his genuine girlfriend, are you? Even if he's told you otherwise, my son is quite the scandalmonger."

"Oh don't worry, sir, I know exactly what I am getting myself into, I can assure you of that." I don't know where the sir came from, it just slipped out, such is this man's power over me.

"I got the impression you were a smart girl, now," he clicks his fingers and some men appear, guiding Winnie and Sebastian's horse back to their stables. "Let's go for a G&T and you can tell me all about your upbringing. I've got a feeling you've been quite naughty in the past..."

"Oh Tommy," I say. "You've no idea. And it's definitely not in the past."

Four very strong gin and tonics later, which we swig while overlooking the "grounds", and I've gone from sensing that Sebastian's dad is being a tiny bit flirty, to being almost 100% sure that he definitely wants to fuck me. His suggestive comments are getting more and more direct with each drink and, about two G&Ts in, I realised that the knee touching mine under the table wasn't Sebastian's but Tommy's. Tommy, it turns out, is a self-made millionaire, he grew up in Yorkshire, his dad was a miner and his mam died very young, which fuelled his determination to make enough money to care for his two younger brothers. After moving down to London to work as a hotel porter ("and sending money home every week") he learned the tricks of the trade, eventually ensuring he was in a position to take over management of the hotel. Now? He owns a whole chain of them ("which you, Angelica, are welcome to stay in whenever you want…")

"Dad, we've all heard your rags to riches story about a million times before," Sebastian says, in a very whiny, unsexy voice.

"I haven't," I say. "That's so inspirational."

"I imagine you and I are cut from the same cloth, Angelica." He constantly says my name, and I know it's a trick to make me feel special but, even so, it's working. "You really know the graft, the power of grit and hard work."

"Angelica knows the power of a good job, alright," Sebastian says, rolling his tongue around his mouth.

Tommy glowers at him. "Son, that's a crude choice of words. Your mother and I raised you better than that. With that said, I've no doubt she's acquired skills in all sorts of areas," he then actually *winks* at me. "I was talking about how you were born with that silver spoon in your mouth and now consider tarting about on television to be laborious, whereas Angelica and I have had to earn our money the hard way."

"Thank you," I say. "I did always have part-time jobs growing up, all throughout school." I don't mention that until the old people's home, they were mostly shop jobs where generally I sat on a stool and read magazines, apart from an awful stint in a bakery which I quit as the hair net really didn't suit me. "Now, if you'll excuse me, I need to go to the bathroom… where is it?"

It takes walking down one set of stairs and through three different heavy wooden doors while I mutter to myself "this is some *Alice In Wonderland* shit" before I end up in their bathroom. It's like stepping inside my old jewellery box. It's big enough to fit a dusty pink velvet chaise longue and there are porcelain figurines of ballerinas and tiny vases of fresh flowers. The wallpaper is rose coloured and there are Diptyque candles burning, creating the softest, muskiest of scents. There's a full length gilt mirror by the sinks, and I check myself out in it, just for a second (I don't want Tommy to think I'm doing a poo, there's something about him that makes me want to be all ladylike) when there's a knock on the door.

"Angelica?" I jump. It's Tommy. He speaks through the door. "I wondered if you fancied another drink?"

"You came all the way down here to ask me that?" I open the door and instead of stepping aside to let me pass, Tommy joins me in the velvety room. It suddenly doesn't feel so large with both of us in here.

"Well…" He steps closer, now just a few centimetres away from me. "I did wonder about this…"

That's when he leans in to kiss me and it's rough and tender all at once, the bristle of his neat beard against my cheeks. "God, you're so sexy," he growls in my ear, and part of me really wants him to push me back onto the sofa behind me.

But in that same moment a thought crosses my mind, an unwanted one, like a pesky fly that's just flown into my vision and now I can't get rid of, no matter how much I swat it away. "Aren't you married?" He pauses, stops, turns around.

"Oh Angelica, why would you ruin the moment like that? But yes, yes I am. My wife is currently knocked out upstairs on Diazepam, she had to pop two the moment she saw who her son had arrived with."

"Charming."

"Only because she finds youth so repulsive, she hates seeing all she has lost. She'd inject your blood into her veins if she could."

"Still," I say, "I'm not interested in getting with married men, no matter what the press says about me."

There's a slight shift in his body language, visible even from the back, when he says, "it's not real any more, it's like you and my son. A façade we maintain for the sake of 'society' and 'family' but, truthfully, we haven't been a legitimate couple in years. She has her precious pills and I have my, well, I have my own relief…"

Already I can feel myself being turned-off by the whole thing. I can suddenly see Tommy a little clearer now. Earlier, I thought he was this sexy, self-made charming man-of-the-people genius, but now I think he's more of a manipulator who plans on seducing his son's girlfriends when he brings them home. As if he could read my mind he says, "I don't try it on with all of my son's girlfriends you know…" Then he turns to me. "Just the sexy ones." And, damn, I realise I've had a lucky escape here.

* * *

Chapter Nineteen

I'm sitting in the nail salon with admiring the mini works of art Selina, the nail technician, has crafted on my fingernails. A whirl of tiny stars, a little tribute to the show, glitters across my fingers against a backdrop of twinkly, inky blue. Selina has moved on to my pedicure now and I text the girls a quick pic of my mani.

Layla's reply is lightning fast.

Gorgeous, babe. But we want to know where your hands have really been? What's happening with Sebastian?

Madison is not far behind her.

Does Loverboy Leo know about Sebby? I wanna know who's the best in the sack, and don't pretend you're going to keep it all official with your Bonking in Buckinghamshire boyfriend!!!

I pause. I've not seen Leo since that day watching Disney together and he's not even texted back to the last thing I sent. I guess that means he has seen my romance with Sebastian. I need to tell him it's not real, but what if he just blanks me again?

"Selina," I ask, deciding that a manicurist is basically like a priest. They must hear all sorts of confessions and I could do with some advice from someone who doesn't know these guys that are messing with my mind. "What do you look for in a guy?"

She laughs. "Me? Nothing. I'm strictly ladies-only, sweetheart. But I'll tell you this for nothing – men, women, straight, gay or anywhere in the middle, we all get distracted by that mad rush of lust. If you're looking for more than that, then it's easy – who could you imagine getting old with?"

I shudder, thinking how Damon once told me he was never going to shag anyone over a day over thirty-five, whatever age he was because "old birds were not his scene." But then I can't exactly picture growing old with Sebastian. Not if he was going to grow up into his father – trying to bed girls half his age while his wife was in the house. It's not like Leo's any better though – he never really talks about his family, apart from dropping hints that his parents were a bit crap. Whereas I can't imagine not introducing anyone I'm seeing to my mam and dad. Although I've told my mam to stop looking at wedding hats every time I tell her I want to bring someone home. Which is why tonight is going to be mad. I pick my phone up again.

`Well, you two can see if Seb and I put on a good show tonight. We're getting the train up north as soon as I'm done in the salon. Are you ready for a seriously big night out, girls?`

Layla doesn't even type a reply, just sends a picture of her on the train – the little table in front of her full of already-drunk gins-in-tins. Madison is clearly on a mission, too.

`Marc won't know what's hit him. I've packed leather, lube and love-cuffs. But my mum's just made me a packed lunch for the trip and saw what was in my bag so I've told her they're presents for you.`

Thanks, Mads. I must remember never to look her mam in the eye again.

"Do *not* flirt with my mam," I'm saying, as we wait in the wind tunnel that is Manchester Piccadilly station for my parents to come and pick us up. Sebastian scowls at me and crosses his arms.

"You mean like you flirted with my dad?" He looks so out of place in his gilet, with his aubergine-purple drainpipe trousers and stupid pointed shoes that make his feet look three times longer than they actually are.

His hair is in a posh-boy's quiff and he's wearing Ray Bans even though it's grey, windy and drizzling. I hate him. Things have not been going well in our showmance since we attempted polo. Funnily enough, he did not take kindly to the clearly fizzing energy between me and Tommy, and was huffy when the car came to collect us to take us home, shortly after the almost-incident with Tommy in the bathroom. I don't think he actually knows what nearly happened but still, I'm allowed, I'm a free woman.

"And? He's a good-looking man. I don't know how often I have to remind you, but *this*," I gesture to the pair of us. "Isn't real."

The photos of us playing polo went down a treat in the papers, they were splashed across all the major ones and my insider intel (Madison and Layla) have reliably informed me that Samantha is absolutely fuming about how much attention I'm getting. Her antics have slowed down considerably, I'm not sure whether that's because she's not actually shagging anyone famous or because the papers have grown bored of her, but either way I'm delighted she's stopped sending me texts about how she's got the award in the bag. Now I've got the money from NuYu I don't need to obsess about trophies anymore. I just need to focus on what's best for my career. Unfortunately, because everyone seems so into the #Sebgelica 'romance', the whole 'from two different worlds' angle, our managers have agreed it should continue a bit longer and it would make a great 'photo op' if we're now spotted in my world. So I've planned a big night out, up North. What's even better is the whole gang are coming, it's going to be a proper reunion! Even Damon said yes. A fact that makes me want to run to the bathroom and vomit if I dwell on it too much, so I'm trying to push it to the back of my mind. Particularly as I can't figure out if the nerves are down to me wanting to see him, or to punch him. One person I definitely want to punch is Sebastian, who is now over-the-top shivering. What a pussy! I'm not even wearing a coat.

"I don't see why we couldn't stay in a hotel," he whines. "Look there's one there, one there and one there." He points at the various chain hotels lining the street outside the station. "Obvious shit-holes, but preferable to where we're going."

"Excuse me? We're going to my parents' house. As my mam wants to host you! And that's how you act? God, your rudeness astounds me."

When Mam heard that Sebastian was coming, she insisted that he stay at ours. I kept saying we could book a hotel, that his management would foot the bill, or even that he could stay in one and I could sleep in my own bed. But Mam insisted it would be "criminal" for her not to host and "what if word gets back to his mother that we didn't offer," and no matter how much I tried to explain that people in Sebastian's world don't think the same way we do, her mind would not be budged. Still, despite my hatred for the man, I am excited to show him my city, my people and how, up here, we're actually *nice* to each other. Shop keepers say "hello" and call you "love" and make silly little jokes that aren't that funny but you laugh at them anyway. There's no airs and graces but when I think of home, it's a happy place where we don't take ourselves too seriously, but also a place where strangers smile at each other and where, even if you're down to the last pennies in your bank account, you'll still offer someone a pint and they'll do the same in return.

"Toot, toot," Mam yells out the window, she just needs to circle round to collect us. When we hurry over to the car she rushes out to give Sebastian a bear hug, while Dad takes his bag off of him. Sebastian is, admittedly, a gentleman and shakes Dad's hand, before telling Mam he's looking forward to seeing her home and agrees that, yes, he is absolutely gagging for a brew. (Even though I know he's not actually the biggest tea drinker. He's more of an oat latte man.)

We pile in the back and begin the drive through the streets to my home. *Torn* by Natalie Imbruglia is blasting on the radio and Mam is singing along, and I feel oddly happy. When we get back to ours, Dad and Sebastian are ahead of us (Sebastian can actually talk for England about the war, so Dad is chuffed) and Mam whispers, "I don't know why everyone calls him such a hunk, even Damien was more friendly, and this lad, he's not a patch on your Leo."

How many ways can Mam drive me nuts in one sentence? She has taken to deliberately not saying Damon's name correctly. "He's not my Leo, Mam, and Sebastian's not mine either, remember? It's fake."

"It sure looked real in those polo pictures," she says. "Believe me, I know when my daughter is smiling her true smile. That was your real self. Unlike those gooey grins you wasted on you know who."

I pretend to her I don't know what she's talking about, that I am just a really good actress, when inside I secretly do understand what she means. There were a few moments on that day, when Sebastian was slagging me off for not knowing the polo rules, and messing up and making fun of me, where I'd laugh and he'd grab me, knowing the cameras were nearby, and fling me back, movie-star style before kissing me. And, even though I knew why he was doing it, there was no denying that his lips felt good against mine, and that he really could make me laugh. But a few staged kisses and the odd actually funny joke does not make up for the fact that the majority of the time he's a snobby, arrogant knobhead with questionable taste in clothes.

We settle in the living room and Mam makes cups of tea that she brings through with biscuits, and she frowns at me, noticing I've not taken one. "I'm all for being healthy, love, but it's healthy to enjoy a biscuit or two," she says.

"Can't be without life's little pleasures," Dad agrees, shoving a whole jammy dodger in his gob.

"I've got to be in the tiniest of dresses tonight, and be photographed Mam, so I can't be having biscuits." I say.

"Fine," she says. "I'll leave it but you're getting too thin, my love."

I sigh, biting my lip to stifle a scream. I know she's my mam and she's not the hordes of people on the internet, who always have something to say about my appearance, but it's frustrating. Before I did NuYu there were people picking apart my belly rolls, shouting in capital letters from their keyboards that I NEED TO PUT THE KEBABS DOWN and now? They're all saying the opposite. NO MAN WANTS TO BE WITH SKIN

AND BONES. It's not just the randoms on the internet either, the press keep sticking their nose into my new nose! Headlines keep asking **HAS ANGELICA GONE TOO FAR WITH THE SURGERY AND WEIGHT LOSS?**

Do they think I'll never see this stuff? That I don't have to walk into my local newsagent and see my face plastered all over every magazine? I always say hello to Sami, who runs our nearest corner shop, gather my bits and try to make a joke to him and he smiles, sympathetically, and says "I love my most famous customer, she's beautiful, don't listen to them." I don't know why, but it's his kindness that makes me feel the most humiliated by the headlines. Mostly, I try to live by Verity's advice and shrug it off, after all it's my face, my body, I should be allowed to do what I want with my own skin and bones so I feel good, but every now and then, the hypocrisy of it all makes me want to scream. But I won't scream at Mam, I think she'd always be like this about me, after all, that's what mams do, don't they? They worry about their daughters.

But it makes me remember what Anika texted me the other day. Clearly the papers broadcasting my new revenge body, as they're calling it, have reached the cruise ship, or at least the Dominican Republic where they've docked now.

```
Looking hot, babes. But how are you feeling? I remem-
ber what you were like when Robbie broke up with
you. You can't eat, drink or exercise your way out of
heartbreak, Angel-face. You've clearly been working out
hard - but don't forget you do it to be strong and step
up - not to waste away! Can't wait to see you when I'm
next home. I'm taking you out for a pie and pint! XXX
```

I know she's just looking out for me, but I want to tell her that I'm not too thin, it's just the camera angles. Also, I've been so busy recently, I've barely had time to eat, and I've found it's easy enough if I just convince whoever I'm with that I ate at my last meeting or on my way over, so no one really checks up on me. And it's showing. Half the dresses in my wardrobe are baggy on me now.

Lucky Break

The dress I'm wearing tonight is hot, *hot* pink, and I'm wearing it with black, wedge platform heels, teasing my hair into a bump-it, so my hair looks almost bigger than my body. We're hitting all of our fave bars, Velvet, Common, the lot, and I'm so grateful that the girls arranged for this to be a reunion, so I won't have to deal with Sebastian's sneering alone. I can just down Jägers, dance on the booths, and wing-woman the girls so they can find someone to neck on with. I know Madison's main mission tonight is to make Marc as jealous as possible. Unfortunately, because she was NDA'd to excess when she was with Chad Schmidt none of their fling has made the papers, and when she told Marc he laughed in her face and told her to stop being a fantasist. Which is awful for her considering that she told me that being with the real Chad Schmidt only made her miss her Poundland version even more. Usually, I'd be joining her on her mission and trying to make Damon jealous, but for once it seems like I don't even have to try! The messages he's been sending are increasingly attentive and bordering on desperate, the more my romance with Sebastian makes the papers. And, if you'll believe it, I've been IGNORING every single message from him. He keeps asking if it's real or not, and whether he actually is my boyfriend and I need him to keep feeling this jealous, I hope he's sick with it. But I also have never been able to lie to Damon, so I can't reply because then his jealousy would evaporate in an instant, which I definitely don't want to happen yet. I have made it clear to Leo though, that it's not real. Despite everything, he's my friend, I want him to see me as I really am. Well, that and I was hoping he'd text back and tell me if he's still single or if perfect-Molly-from-his-Instagram is more than just a flatmate.

When we arrive at the bars (Dad insisted on driving us into town) it immediately feels just like old times. Even Samantha's being nice to me, hugging me and telling me how amazing I look, without any of the usual barbed insults wrapped in niceties. Damon isn't here yet, but I'm insisting on being all over Sebastian, grabbing his bum and pulling him in for big snogs, as I need that to be the first thing Damon sees when he walks in.

"Why you being so…handsy?" Sebastian says, as I pull him in again. I run my hands over his abs. Polo clearly is a good workout if you actually know what you're doing.

"The cameras, silly, we need to give them a good show."

"And someone else, I reckon," he whispers in my ear. How is it he always seems to have my number?

Sebastian has, annoyingly, gone for a wee when Damon does eventually walk in, so it's the one moment when I'm standing on my own. Madison and Marc are sitting in a corner together, furiously whisper-yelling in each other's ears, Samantha's gone to the bathroom and Layla's being Layla and just bending the ear of one of the bouncers.

Damon comes up behind me, and whispers in my ear. "Looking good, Angelica," but I'm not expecting it and yelp out loud. We hug, and then, it's just like old times all over again. This is the problem. As much as I know Damon is no good for me, when we're together, we just work. I can be in the loudest of nightclubs, music blaring, even foam pumping out onto the dance floor, and I'll still feel like it's just the pair of us, like we're communicating just with our minds. I can think something and I somehow know he's on the same wavelength. And now, I know I'm not meant to wonder, but I can't help it: what does he see when he looks at me? Because right now, in this very moment – after months and months of hard work and an operation that made me feel like my brains were about to fall out – I look like his dream girl. My hair is blonde, my tan is that perfect Australian golden colour and my legs look like they stretch up to my armpits. The girls used to say I was being paranoid, but I always thought that Damon felt like he was hotter than me and could do better. But now, as I stand in the club where we first kissed, I am an entirely new person. I'm not the girl who'd follow him home, even after watching him kiss three other girls, and give his number to plenty more. I'm not the girl who would crawl into bed with him, drunkenly flipping between crying and wanting to kiss him, letting him climb on top just to pump away for a few half-hearted thrusts. No, I'm hot, I've got money in my bank account and I've got a 'boyfriend' who's heir to billions. Damon should be in my rearview mirror. I'm doing everything I thought I wanted, so why doesn't this feel good? Why does it still feel like he's the one in control?

"So, tell me," he says, wrapping his arm around my waist, so as to whisper in my ear. "How did that horse feel between your legs?"

I want to say something flirty and disparaging, something to put him in his place. But, all of a sudden, I find it impossible to get my words out. It's that familiar feeling, that intoxicating sense of having him so near, I want to just grab his face and kiss him, in front of all of these people, in front of the cameras that I know are hovering nearby, in front of Sebastian who I know would report me for breach of agreement. It's all too much to bear, and far too tempting. I still don't trust myself around this man. So, I simply say: "I need the loo," and run off.

In the toilet cubicle, I try to take deep breaths. But someone's clearly vommed in here, quite recently, so the deep breathing is nowhere near as soothing as it was in the yoga studios when I was on retreat. So instead, I just put the lid down, hold my nose, and sit for a little while, trying to contemplate how on earth I can get through this night without falling prey to the temptation of Damon. I know if I made a move he'd definitely respond. But is that because he fancies me, or because he can't stand Sebastian and would love to get one-over on him?

It's then I hear the clatter of heels, and a sharp, but very loud *sniiiffffffffff*. I'm about to leave the cubicle when I hear my name. "She honestly thinks she's it now she's lost all that weight." It's Samantha. "But you can't shed being an airhead, you know," Samantha carries on to her unknown companion. "She followed Damon around like a puppy, waiting for him while he screwed endless women in front of her, and now she thinks she can bleach her hair and everyone will forget she was spellbound by him. But they won't. My agent, Ben, says she's got no career without him. And as for Damon, he's literally been advised by Ben to keep her sweet as the audience like them together so much. It's nowt to do with him actually fancying her. I feel sorry for her, actually," Samantha says. "Some of us are working on long-term goals and she's just flailing about, with no clue what she's doing, getting taken advantage of by anything with a dick."

"But that Sebastian is quite hot..." the other voice ventures.

"That low-grade aristo?" There's a pause and Samantha lowers her voice, so I have to shuffle closer to the door to hear. "It's not even real. He loathes her. All that flirting and groping? It's just for publicity."

"Noooo."

"Yes! Even more sad, right? I'd never do that. I'm tactical, discreet and exclusive when I choose who to date."

I'm tempted to storm out and tell whoever it is Samantha is sniping to that her last three photo ops were all set-ups, but I don't know if I can face blowing my cover and making it clear I just heard everything they said. Particularly as I can't exactly deny it, can I? I did follow Damon around on television like a puppy dog, and my relationship with Sebastian is weird but I can't deny I'm getting into where it's going. But, at the same time, I don't believe he hates me and, while publicity is always in the forefront of Damon's mind (like it is for Samantha) I refuse to believe that's the only reason he likes me. But how do you explain to a couple of bathroom bitches what it's like to be stared at by those eyes? What it's like when Damon laughs at something I said, then looks at me in surprise, like he's just discovering who I am for the first time? It's true that men can be full of bullshit but it's also true that they can be afraid of their feelings, burying them deep inside.

"Anyway, we need to get back out there and work the room," Samantha says, and I hear them clatter out, so I can finally escape. Back out in the club, thankfully, Madison and Layla have lined up the shots for me, and Sebastian is waiting with a glass of fizz. I slam down three shots, and gulp the prosecco despite Sebastian telling me to "steady on."

"I'm not your horse," I say to him. "And you're in my world now. Get ready to cling on for dear life."

* * *

Chapter Twenty

I wake up with a familiar taste in my mouth. Garlic sauce. I am in my childhood bedroom and I can hear snoring beside me. God, how many times now have I woken up and had to do detective work to find out who's asleep in my bed? I edge over to see that the man in question is Sebastian, and breathe a sigh of relief. Mam made up the spare bed for nothing, she folded her best towels and everything. I also spot that he's fully clothed. As am I. Well, my dress has rolled up to above my stomach, exposing my black thong. Last night turned out to be a lot of fun. There was no way I was going to let Samantha's bitchiness spoil the mood. As Layla pointed out, she only sees a quarter of my life and it's through the tinted lens of her own bitterness. Her point of view is not to be trusted.

I search around for my phone, seeing that it's only got 5% battery left. There are several messages from Damon.

```
Where did you go?
Did you go off with him?
You can do better you know.
C'mon... I've got needs.
Gel, sorry, Idnt mean dat.Just come bak.
```

The thrill of his jealousy and my plan working rushes through me. Because no matter how hard I deny it to the girls, the truth sits deep in my bones. There was a big part of me that worked so hard, endured all those burpees and sprints, the burn of exercise (and bleach on my scalp) for him. For Damon to see what he was missing. What I have to keep reminding myself is it was for him to want me, badly, and not be able to have me. Giving myself to him, climbing back into his bed and into his life, would be a mistake and undermine all my efforts. I know that. But still, why can't I stop fantasising about it? How much I miss that first moment, when his cock enters me, feeling all of him fill me up. I try to remind myself that the rest, after those delicious few minutes, is always a rushed disappointment but I can't. My fanny is already fluttering. I glance over at Sebastian, he's still fast asleep, so I let my own fingers snake into my underwear, touching myself how I wish Damon would. How Tommy might have. How Leo did. My brain gets cloudy, and I shut my eyes, seeing Damon's abs, the tattoo that rests just above his hipbone. I think of how he looked at me, that first moment he saw me, the hunger in his eyes. I remember his hand around my waist last night. I think of the way he looks when he winks. I imagine him holding my hands above my head, pinning me down, and…I shudder, biting my lip from crying out. Sebastian remains sound asleep. Flushed and only vaguely satisfied, I crawl out of bed, looking for my phone charger. I find it tangled in one corner of the room and bend over to retrieve it when I hear Sebastian's plummy tones from the bed.

"Nice ass, you know what I've been thinking?" I dart up, press my ass to the wall so he can no longer see it.

"What?" Though I think I can guess, from the tent he's erecting using my duvet covers.

"Why don't we road test this in real life? You know, try the humpy-pumpy…"

His use of the words 'humpy-pumpy' immediately turns me off.

"It's not in the plan, Sebastian," I say, my eye trained on my phone which, now happily plugged into the wall, is firing up again.

"Precisely, we take it off paper, see if this thing works in real life."

"You don't even like me," I remind him, opening up the *Daily Wail* website.

"That's just not true, we clash but…isn't it delicious to clash? Don't opposites attract? There's something between us, Angelica, I can feel it."

"You can feel your morning horn, that's what you can feel."

He laughs. "See this is what I like about you, you're funny, a straight talker. You're not…" He pauses for the right words. "Afraid of me."

"Why would I be afraid of you? Mr seven-step-skincare-routine and Just For Men."

He sits up, looks at me. The tent is still there, in fact, it may have got bigger. What was once a two-man is now a safari. "I'm a very powerful man, and that will only with grow with everything I am due to inherit. And there's not much money can't buy you."

"Love," I suggest. "Manners. People's respect, the common sense to realise not everyone reads *Horse & Hound*. There's plenty money can't get you."

"Keep going," he says, in an almost growl. A threat? Or something else?

"Fine. You've come here to my home town, you're under my mam's roof and you've had this poncy, judgy look on your face the whole time. I didn't mention it because you're often not worth the fight, Seb…" I know he hates it when I call him Seb. "But yeah, you could buy everyone in the North a drink but you will never be able to make them like you, no one here likes you. They all think you're a jumped-up posh boy with no dress sense."

I maybe took it too far, I'm feeling a little guilty, when I glance down at the tent. Then I look at his face, all flushed and hungry. He's turned on!

"Oh my god, of course," I say. "You're one of those, a man with power who gets off on being insulted! God, Seb, you're such a cliché!" I'm not annoyed, more amused. Why didn't I realise this before?

"You sussed me," he grins. "I like being knocked down a peg or two, and you are more than up to the task."

"Let's get this straight," I say. "I'm not your dominatrix. If you want that, you can pay for it. In real life, sex is not in our deal, this is all fake. Fake!" I throw my arms up in the air.

"If this is all fake then why am I in your bed?"

That I cannot answer. I don't remember much of last night. I know it was fun, but that's it.

"I dunno, why are you here?"

"Because you begged me, you were all over me in the club, and then later, you came on to me, all doe-eyed in your tiny-little dress saying 'please Seb, please' but I knew you were too drunk. And besides, I'm not a fan of whimpering girls begging me for sex…"

"No, you like to be the whimperer," I say, trying to wrack my brains for the version of myself he's relaying back. It really doesn't sound like me. But then, I was desperate to make Damon jealous and I was using Sebastian as a means to an end. I also needed to be on good form for the photographers. It's tough pretending to fancy someone so much, even tougher when they actually are, on paper, good looking. Throw a few drinks into the mix and my brain and body probably got confused and I thought I actually wanted Sebastian. Something which, in the cold hard light of day, I tell myself was simply a mistake, my heart (and other areas) confused by all the acting. How do actual actors manage it? I guess that's why they so often end up actually banging each other.

The other thing I don't remember is now also being reflected back to me. Not from Sebastian but in pictures when I automatically check my phone and the tabloid homepages, as there I am, all over the gossip sections with an absolutely massive kebab in my hand. Please tell me I didn't eat that! I click through to the story, and sure enough, it's like a picture-book of my own horror! The first pics are me, Sebastian, Madison, Layla and Samantha all standing outside MeatMizzle kebabs, lit up by the orange and blue lights. They're quite cute shots, actually. I'm hanging off of Sebastian's arm, laughing at something Madison is saying while Layla is dropping chips into Madison's mouth. But then they get progressively worse, as all of a sudden, I have a kebab in my hand and in the next shot my face is literally in it. Like I stick my face into the kebab, and there's garlic sauce all over my nose, cheeks and chin.

"You look like you've seen a ghost," Sebastian says.

"I have," I say. "The ghost of Angelica's past." I crawl over to him. "Look at these pictures! They're disgusting!"

He takes my phone out of my hand and scrolls through, his laugh getting louder and louder.

"Don't laugh!"

"Come on, you can always laugh at yourself, these really aren't that bad."

I know he's right, I would never have been bothered by pics like these in the past. But new body, new nose Angelica is annoyed. I think of how Samantha said that no one is taking me seriously in London's media circuit, and I can feel all of that late night takeaway, heavy in my stomach. It's churning around in there and I can almost picture it, morphing into evil little fat cells that are swimming, right for my belly and thighs, laughing and rubbing their hands together.

"I look so fat!"

"Everyone looks fat in pap pictures, Angelica, that's their aim, to take the least flattering shot possible."

"I don't know why you're being nice to me, I was just horrible to you," I say, feeling my lip begin to shake slightly and my throat get sore. My throat always gets sore just before I'm about to cry and, is this really happening? Am I really going to cry over a greasy kebab and some mean photos of myself? I'm stronger than that, come on! But, despite the kebab swishing about in my belly, I'm also hungry, sad and feeling weak. Hangovers used to be cured with macaroni cheese, a full-fat Coke and some trash TV. Now all I've got is the trash TV and I have to be very careful not to pick anything where they're eating, as that's just miserable viewing these days. But then, I remember something! Sometimes when I'm hungover, I'm sick. My body rejects all that I put in it the night before, and it comes tumbling out into the toilet bowl.

"I'm just going to the loo," I say, and scamper through, turning the tap on to mask the noise. I kneel in front of the bowl, hoping that just the smell of Toilet Duck will remind my stomach that it doesn't want to keep this kebab inside, that it wants it out. I take a deep sniff of the bowl but…nothing. Am I really going to do this? I hesitate. I recall what Anika said about getting fit not famished, about me being strong not invisible. But this isn't something I'm going to make a habit of, I tell myself. It's just a hangover cure. I think of Damon seeing the pictures, how he'll be reminded of the old Angelica and there will be no more desperate messaging, no more compliments whispered in my ear. I'll just go back to being his backstop, the one he only kinda wants if there's no one else. I need to be desired fully, I need to be wanted 100%. If I keep looking like this, keep fitting into the smaller sizes the stylists pick out for me, that's what's going to happen, I'll be his first choice instead of his reserve. I'll be the one chased, instead of the one chasing. I look around for a toothbrush, something, anything to use other than my long, acrylic nails which I know will scratch my throat. But Mam cleaned everything out of here so it would feel more like a guest bathroom for Sebastian. Honestly, I don't know why she was trying to impress him so much. So, fingers it is then. God, considering I've just got myself off with them and now they're going down my throat, it's already been quite the day. I don't get them down far enough the first time and just slightly gag, but the second and third times I manage, the splatter and shame of last night coming out and hitting the toilet bowl. I peer in. What's happened to me, I think. I can't do this again.

I pad downstairs, looking for some mouthwash or to find where Mam has hidden all our toothbrushes, eager to scrub the smell of garlicky sick off my tongue.

"Here she is," Dad says, flicking the kettle on. "Let's get a cup of tea down our fuzzy-headed girl."

"Have you seen where Mam put the toothbrushes?"

"Ah yes, she's kidnapped them all. Worried his nibs upstairs would see the presence of the toothbrush and think we're actual normal people."

"As if the 'live, laugh, love' signs don't do that already."

"Or the *ssssh there's wine* fridge magnets."

"It's wine-o-clock somewhere!"
"A meal without wine is called breakfast!"

That's when Mam walks in and starts laughing. That's one of the nicest things about Mam, she laughs at the same jokes time and again.

"Where have you hidden the toothbrushes?" I ask and she opens the cupboard under the kitchen sink, where all three of our brushes sit in a mug. "They're here, put them back when you finish."

"Sebastian is leaving soon!"

"That's not the point," Dad says. "The point is why were you hiding the toothbrushes from the lad in the first place? Surely it's worse for him to think we don't brush our teeth?"

"I just think it's unsightly, to see something you put in your mouth, in private," she's saying, as I begin to brush my teeth over the kitchen sink.

"But," I say, my mouth full of foaming paste. "I don't put anything that dodgy in my mouth, in private or not," I add, just as Sebastian walks in.

"Cheeky girl, your daughter," he says as he taps Dad on the shoulder. "Right, you," he points at me. "We need to start getting ready, we've got that shoot in a couple of hours."

"A shoot!" Mam yells. "But Angelica, you were out last night. You're all puffy."

I am, I'm red and puffy, most likely aggravated by the vomiting. I'm never doing this again. I know I'm on dangerous ground.

"Verity will work her magic, don't worry."

The whole crew are heading up on the train, one of the glossy mags thought it would be fun to shoot Sebastian and me in one of the nightclubs, accompanied by an interview. That way they have 'official' shots of us, alongside an interview discussing these last few nights together, just as the public's interest has been piqued by the pap ones. However, this has obviously sent Mam into a spin as she's wrapping a bag of frozen peas in one of her tea towels and lunging at me, pressing them hard against my cheeks.

"What on earth are you doing?" I ask, dodging the peas.

"I read that ice helps with puffiness, only someone..." she glares at Dad. "Didn't refill the tray last night."

"Someone," he glares back. "Was necking so many gin and lemonades that I didn't get the chance."

"Fine," I say. "If there's a scientific reason for it." I hold my hands out for the Birdseye.

"No science that I'm aware of, but Kylie Minogue does it."

"I'm sure Kylie's dabbing Captain Birdseye all over her face," Dad says, while Sebastian looks on, laughing in a baffled way.

"Welcome to the family," I say, holding the tea-towel to my closed eyes.

* * *

Chapter Twenty-One

It's strange being in this club during the day. It feels flatter, like some of the life has been sucked out of it. Dust rises in clouds from the golden tables, and the harsher light reveals the velvet booths are ripped and stained. I tiptoe across the sticky floor and notice that by day, everything looks more like a shabby stage set than a neon pleasure palace.

"I wish I hadn't seen this," I say to Sebastian as we enter. "It spoils the magic."

He smiles. "You see magic in the most unusual places, don't lose that special talent." It turns out to be the nicest thing he says to me all day, because as soon as the photographer enters the club with his camera swinging round his neck, Sebastian morphs into someone else. Someone I don't know. Or, actually, I do know: his television persona. They're high-fiving each other over the lamest of jokes, and practically comparing penis sizes as they exchange pictures of each other's cars on their phones. It's gross. Verity agrees.

"There's a certain type of man who thinks their greatest qualities lie not in what they do, or even in what they own but in who they can prove they're above. All they care about is status," she whispers to me, eyeing the pair, while she applies my blusher. "At this age, it seems all well and good. They attract the string of girls, they reap the perks of looking a certain way and falling for the false promise. But, trust me, I've met their type when they're older and they've never learned the true value of life, of friendship, of fun…And, once the looks are gone and the money begins to feel a little sleazy, they pretend they're still living it large but, on the inside, they're crying."

"How do you know? They could genuinely be happy," I say.

"Because a make-up artist sees it all, hun, once the door to the trailer is closed, the men let it all out, sobbing to me about being all alone. No real friends, no solid relationship. Your Sebastian needs to be careful, as they're all nice, underneath it all, they've just been sold the lie that bravado and being as manly as possible is how they're meant to behave."

"He's not my Sebastian," I correct.

"Sure, he isn't," she winks. "But it's the same with your Damon, in fact all the men you fall for seem to share those same qualities. And they view you as a prize, a shiny trophy to show off…"

"It's good to be a prize though, isn't it?" I'm trying not to sneeze as she dusts even more powder on my cheeks.

"You are a prize, the greatest there is. But what I mean is, men like that see women as raffle prizes, disposable things to show off and discard. You want someone who will treasure you for who you are, not how many front pages you're on. Someone that can look at you and think 'there she is, my one who shines.'"

"Do you have that?"

Verity chuckles. "I realised long ago that I can do that for myself, I can tell myself in the mirror, smile and shine, baby! And this world – for all its fun and sparkle – this is my work. My real life? That's with my husband and kids. They keep me sane."

"Can you really have both - a life like this and a family?"

"It's not easy," Verity says. "Life's a juggle and sometimes it means working out what my priorities really are. Sometimes I feel pulled in different directions. But so do my single friends, so do my friends without kids. It's about carving the life you want, hun, not the life anyone else tells you to want." With that, she spritzes my face with a setting spray and yells to the stylist that I'm ready. Shoots are so much easier now, I've obviously adjusted to them but also, there's no more struggling into clothes, or having to awkwardly ask for different sizes or help with the zip. They just glide up and, most of the time, the outfits look good on me. Today I'm trying an array of bandeau dresses in metallic colours – copper, gunmetal and burnished gold. The shoes, as is always the case, are platform wedges which I wobble on. The television creates an impression that I am always dressed like this but, truthfully, I much prefer to be casual – in shorts, trainer pumps and t-shirts. I only really started dressing this way in the house, often borrowing Samantha's stuff (back when I mistook her for a friend) as I saw that was what Damon seemed to like in girls. His head was always turned by the glammest, most tanned girl in the club.

"Whit whoo," Sebastian wolf-whistles as I wobble onto the set. He then whispers something to the photographer, who gives him this wicked grin and a high five. What did he say? They're doing solo shots with me first, and, as always, I move between different poses, trying my best not to look too startled by how bright the flash is. Photographers tend to coach you through it, telling you what to do, complimenting you and generally trying to get the best angle possible. The shoot begins how it normally does, a few casual instructions: "hand on your hip, that's right, babe" and "lean forward a little, nope, too far, back a bit" – that sort of thing. I'm used to it, this is my job now so I just do as the photographer, stylist and art director say and trust that they will capture the best shot for their story. But, as the solo shots with me continue, I begin to feel more and more uncomfortable. He asks me to get down on the floor so he can take shots from above. I'm close enough that I can smell his sweat and feel the heat radiating off his crotch. I look up at the camera, and the photographer says, "oh, she does look good from this angle." I look over at Sebastian, quizzically, a sort of 'what the fuck' look, hoping he'll tell the photographer to stop dicking about and that it's time for our couples shots. But he doesn't.

"Um, I'm not sure…" I say to the photographer but my head is swimming, I've not eaten anything since that kebab last night, and most of that ended up, deliberately, in the toilet. Maybe this was part of the plan? Is it supposed to be an edgy shoot? I've never known the weekly mags to be particularly edgy before but perhaps this is all part of a grand plan. I begin to crawl.

"That's it, girl," the photographer growls, and I hate the way his voice sounds. Ever since I arrived he's treated me like I don't matter, that I only exist as a public spectacle to be ogled. I think of Verity's words, and try to picture him in ten or twenty years, all alone and sobbing in a trailer. But it doesn't work. As that's in the future, and this is now. "Has anyone got a tie? I'm thinking maybe we could use it like a lead?"

That's it. "I don't like this," I say, trying to assert authority from where I am, low on the ground. "I don't think I was told about this." Fliss usually attends shoots with me, but as this one is near home, I told her not to bother, as it would be so far to come and I knew what I was doing. If she was here, there's no way I'd ever have ended up on the floor.

"What?" he sneers. "You're happy to cavort in bed on TV but you're not willing to do this? This is art, sweetheart. Don't fuck with the vision."

I look around for the art director of the magazine but he's nowhere to be seen. Neither is Verity. It's just me and this jerk of a photographer, even Sebastian seems to have scarpered to the loo. No one is on my team. I need to stand up, face this man eye to eye and tell him "no" but these damn platforms and the tightness of the dress mean that every single time I try, I wobble back down to earth again. "You had some wine already, have you?" he smirks, as I try to get up one more time. I want to call out for Sebastian to come and help me up but I just know, given the way he's acting today, he won't come to my rescue. God I hate him! Who behaves like this? I find myself hungry and cold on the floor, suddenly desperate for Leo to be here. He'd know exactly what to do. But, I'm on my own. I have to muster my inner strength. With a roly-poly ninja move, I roll onto my side and manage, with only one near-miss tumble, to make it to my feet.

"I don't think this is very arty," I say to him. "And I'm sorry, but I'm not doing it."

"You've got nothing to be sorry about," Verity's stormed in, the art director trailing behind her, looking sheepish. "Found this one getting stoned round the back, and I've got the mood board." She brandishes it in the photographer's face. "Where on here does it have her crawling around on all fours?"

"I don't have to follow that to the letter, I have my creative freedom."

"There's creative freedom and then there's being a DICK," Verity says as Sebastian slopes back in, now he doesn't have to save the day. "I've worked with you before, I know exactly what you're like and, believe me, this power trip you're on won't last much longer. Word's spreading and it's spreading fast. So, if I were you, I'd take some nice shots of this gorgeous couple, as you've been asked and paid to do, and then get us all a very welcome early finish time. Understood?"

The art director is swaying from side-to-side at the back. He just nods and says, "ermm yeah just do what the ladies say."

That's how Verity and I end up art directing and co-ordinating the whole shoot. Verity's been on so many shoots she knows exactly what to do, but the hardest part for me is being convincing with Sebastian, pretending I'm in love with him, when the cameras flash. Every time the camera is off us my smile falters. I'm just praying for this day to be over. But then, on a break, I check my phone.

```
Don't forget, limo comes for you at 6. Photo-op at
Giovanni's. F x
```

Fuck! I *had* forgotten. This was something I'd set up as well. I've known the owners of Giovanni's, my favourite Italian restaurant, for years. I figured if I was going to have to fake this relationship for column inches I could, at the very least, help out a few of my friends along the way. I knew that if I was papped with Sebastian at Giovanni's, that could promote his business. If it wasn't for Gio, and the dreamy look in his eye when he speaks wistfully of his retirement and how hard he's worked all his life, I would definitely sack the whole thing off. But Gio's been kind to me since I was a kid, he deserves to make as much money as he possibly can before he goes off to live his beachside hut dream. I can do this. The shoot rounds off around 4p.m., and Verity and I give each other a victory hug as Sebastian buggers off with the art director for a pint down the road.

"I'm sorry I wasn't there for you sooner," Verity says. "I clocked what was happening straight away and went hunting for Tom, for back-up. That lazy stylist had already packed her cases, so he was my only option and there he was, useless sod, getting stoned! Still," she pulls me in for a hug. "You should be so proud of what we achieved today – it's going to look incredible in print." She massages the knots in her shoulder. "I'm going to have the best night tonight when I get home! Glass of wine, deep bath, pop on a *Real Housewives*... bliss."

"You deserve it. You truly had my back," I say. "I should have stood up to him sooner, I just hate not looking professional."

"Something that dickhead clearly never worries about. Now, here, you're tired, the studio is booked til six, have a nap and chill for a bit. You should recharge your batteries before tonight."

"I'm so tired!" I smile, as she tucks a blanket she found under my chin.

"I'm sure it's very tiring pretending to shag that fine specimen of a man," Verity says.

"Don't forget his personality," I mutter, my eyes already closing.

"You're right, you savour that rest. You deserve an Oscar."

With that, she's gone, and I drift into the deepest of naps. When I come to, with creases from the sofa cushions all over my face, I feel Sebastian gently shaking me awake while whispering my name. "Angelica, the limo's outside, come on, gorgeous, it'll only be a few hours." He's back to nice Sebastian again but I am not falling for it.

"Where were you when that pervy photographer was being creepy earlier. Does all that crawling around on all fours do it for you? It's the only explanation I can come up with as to why you were so far up his ass."

"I'm sorry you felt that way, I thought we were all just kidding around," he says.

"Everyone knows 'sorry you felt that way' is a shitty apology," I say, standing up and pulling my dress down. I catch sight of myself in the mirror, not bad actually. That setting spray Verity uses must be like super glue.

Waiting for us outside the studio is the biggest limo I've ever seen. I told Giovanni that I'd transform the photo op into every little girl's dream of the perfect date: limo, flowers, shoes I can't walk more than two metres in. I even requested the company send their hottest driver and they delivered, a guy called Ravi with the cheekiest grin. He opens the door for me, and I step inside. "It's like a flat in here!" I say, looking up at the ceiling, which is covered in twinkling fairy-lights. There's enough floor space to move around, there's even a strippers' pole in the centre. Plus, a giant cooler full of drinks. It's not even that long a journey so even though I don't want to spend even one more second with Sebastian, I ask Ravi if he can stretch out the journey, just so I can get stuck into the drinks. I may as well enjoy some of tonight, even if the company is dreadful.

At first, we don't speak at all. What's the point if he's just going to say it was all a joke? Sebastian might not know me but anyone who does, knows that's my sore spot, that I value being funny – you've got to laugh to survive this harsh world. But, eventually, the silence becomes unbearable and I have to say something.

"You were a real prick back there, you know that?" I start, before launching into a tirade about how he only cares what a certain type of man thinks, how he should have had my back in there and that if it were the other way round and he was a woman forced to crawl around a photo studio on his knees I'd have called it out. "Do you think it's fair, all of this?" I'm demanding. "Do you? Do you?"

"No, no I don't," he's saying, in a pathetic whimper. It's then that I notice something: he has a hard on again. Of course. This is his kink. What do I do? Do I carry on, knowing that he's getting off on this? Or just return to the stony silence? The partition between us and Ravi is firmly closed, he'd told us that he can't hear a thing, so if we need him we're just to press a button. In a split-second decision, I decide that I'm enjoying this too. I have total freedom to let loose.

"You're just like so many men, thinking you're all macho and powerful when underneath it all, you're just spineless, aren't you?"

He nods. I've never done anything like this before but he's smiling.

"Look me in the eye while you address me!"

Oooh this is fun. He looks at me. He's got this glazed, grateful but sorry look in his eyes. I carry on.

"You think that you've got what it takes to impress a woman, don't you?"

"I do," he says.

I laugh. Louder than I usually would, seeing his erection growing. "You don't, you think that's going to impress me? I've had so, so much bigger."

I have absolutely no idea if I'm doing this right. After all, I know this is what he's into and I am aware of the shift, from me just naturally telling him off, to becoming this character. His mistress. The boss. We probably should have set a safe word or something, or I should have got more guidance on what he likes and doesn't like. I may not respect Sebastian but, at the same time, I don't want to hurt him. I'm just enjoying this release. For so long, so many men have held power over me. They've told me to jump and I've asked how high. I've seen myself as weaker, as not hot enough…I've felt as if I need their attention in order to feel good about myself. As I sit here, in my stiletto heels, a man hanging off my every word in the seat beside me, I realise I have never needed them. I've always been hot and funny and enough, I just needed to see it myself. Still, for one second, I break out of it, give Sebastian a tiny nod, and he nods back, he's OK. Plus, I can still see from his pants that he's enjoying this. A lot.

I decide to take it further. "Get on your knees." There's plenty of space in the limo, so Sebastian does as I say. It's at this point I realise that this isn't just turning him on, I'm aroused too. At first, it was just fun, a little like when I do boxercise and release all the pent-up aggression. But, as I look at him on the floor, I realise how sexy it is to feel this wanted, this worshipped. He will do anything I say.

"You want me, don't you?"

He nods.

"Look at me."

He looks up.

I open my legs. "Kiss my feet," I instruct. He does as I say, slowly kissing from my ankles all the way up my thighs, until I'm desperate for him to take it further and put his tongue where it counts. The soft vibration of the car moving through traffic, knowing there's people outside of these blacked-out windows that we can't see, that have no idea what's going on, makes the whole thing so much hotter.

"Now...Lick it."

He does as I say and I feel the tingling all over, he really knows what he's doing. Damon barely ever went down on me – wait, why am I thinking about Damon in this moment? Concentrate Angelica! So I do, and even while knowing that Ravi could hear, that actually I have no idea how soundproof the doors are and if the people walking by on the street can hear, I find I am gasping, moaning and yelling. Finally, fireworks! And Sebastian looks up at me, a devilish grin on his face. I pull him up to face me, I can feel his hard cock pressing against my thigh and I'm desperate to feel him inside of me but it's then that the car stops, and we hear Ravi's voice over the speaker.

"Giovanni's, we're here."

Sebastian and I look at each other and laugh, we begin to vaguely sort ourselves out so that we look presentable for the paps that I know are waiting just beyond the limo door. Still, emerging from the vehicle looking freshly shagged can't be a bad thing, can it?

* * *

Chapter Twenty-Two

I rush to the shops to grab a copy of *Flair* so early that I'm still in my pyjama bottoms and old school leaver's hoodie with my Uggs hurriedly squashed onto my feet. My greasy hair is scrunched in a top-knot on my head and my lashes are about three days old. I'm praying no one recognises me, but when I see the pictures I realise they definitely won't. Talk about a catfish! The Angelica in the magazine is the total opposite of the Angelica standing in the newsagents, with a pint of milk in one hand and four magazines in the other (Mam wanted me to buy the whole shop, to give to relatives, but we settled on four. I want other people to read it, not just my family!) Magazine Angelica is so fit! I think this is the best I've ever looked in a shoot, my hair is so long and blonde, and my legs are tanned and shimmering and seem to stretch for miles in the mini dress. Also, none of the shots taken before Verity and I took over have been chosen, so we've really proven ourselves to be the best art directors around. There are six double spreads, with me and Sebastian draped all over each other. Considering I was fully hating him in that moment, I've done a brilliant job of looking loved up. I'm gazing at him like I want to devour him. Which now, well, maybe I do...

After Giovanni's, in which we played footsie under the table for the whole meal while eating our food way, way too quickly (Gio wasn't happy with me as I ordered a salad, he's used to me tucking into all my favourites) we rushed out of the restaurant and straight to a hotel, which Sebastian gladly paid for on his gold card. The sex was incredible.

We'd had all that build-up in the car, plus I realised all these months of switching between absolutely hating each other whilst being pretend lovers was the most delicious foreplay. As soon as we stepped foot in the room we were tearing each other's clothes off. I lost count of the number of orgasms I had, I didn't remain in dominatrix mode the whole time but I was, by the time we got to the hotel room, incredibly confident in being able to ask for what I wanted. It made such a difference. I'm so used to just lying back and thinking of England, letting Damon use my body for a quick thrill, that I had forgotten that I also have needs to fulfil. And when they're met, wow, it certainly does give you a taste for ensuring they *keep* being met. I must be grinning at the memories as our local newsagent, Sami, asks, "What's got you smiling? You look like the cat that's got the cream, Angelica."

Instead of telling him the truth (imagine!) I open the magazine and show him the pictures.

"Aw, you look beautiful," he says.

"Unlike now!"

"No, you always look beautiful but perhaps especially beautiful in these shots," he says, slightly blushing. I know he'd hate to ever come across sleazy and he absolutely doesn't. Just sweet. He begins to read the article, "'I've never been treated this way before, Sebastian is a true gentleman, always picking up the bill, and holding doors open for me.' Ah, that's exactly what you deserve, I'm happy for you."

He carries on reading and I can tell from the blush snaking up his neck when he reaches the section where I am claiming Sebastian is the best I've ever had. At the time it was all rubbish, I said it simply hoping that Damon would read it and be absolutely fuming. But now, it might just be the truth…It's definitely a toss-up between Sebastian and Leo. But considering Leo hasn't exactly been chasing me down, I think I'll bump Sebastian to the top of the list. I'm certainly willing to have another go, and see where this takes us. They always say that hate and love are closely connected and I'm beginning to believe it. But it's at that moment that I notice a strange look spreading all over Sami's face. I know I got a little raunchy in the interview, but not that raunchy.

"What's shocked you?"

He shakes his head. "Nothing, nothing," while trying to rearrange his stock, spreading Mars Bars, Dairy Milks and packets of Ginger Nuts across the pile of papers resting on his counter.

"You can't trick me! What you covering up?" I begin to swipe the chocolate bars away while he swipes them back on again, the pair of us are in this frantic, strange chocolate bar war and I have absolutely no idea why. And then I see it.

BONKING IN BUCKINGHAMSHIRE, SEBASTIAN CAUGHT IN TEN-WOMAN ORGY

And there he is, exiting what is allegedly a very exclusive dungeon, his shirt ripped open, a glazed look in his eyes and wearing the same contented grin he gave me, after going down on me in the limo.

Of course, I know this isn't an actual betrayal, it's only the breaking of an agreement. Even though it was an agreement I was beginning to enjoy. Originally, we had both committed that, for three whole months, we wouldn't be spotted with anyone else, that we would do all we could to ensure that, according to the press and the public, we were really in love. If I'd known we'd be having to plan a break-up too, I'd have put some thought into that. Even if 'dungeon paparazzi' hadn't been on my list, it might have been fun sitting around a business table and brain-storming ways to dump someone. Might try it with the girls next time we actually need to do the deed.

But now, clearly, all our plans are off. I'm amazed – relieved even – to discover that though I feel surprised, I don't feel devastated or jealous. It's not like those awful mornings waking up to Damon eating face with some new arm candy. Even after our non-stop, all-night sex session the other week I don't see this as cheating from Seb. It's not my heart that feels like it's missing out as I realise #Sebgelica is over – only my VJ. I could have happily had a couple more nights of hot, domineering sex with Sebastian. But this hook-up has run its course. Still, I know Sami will be expecting me to break down or, at least, offer some emotion other than just shrugging and buying the paper.

"Oh no!" I manage, quite half-heartedly. "That scoundrel! I best go phone him, demand some answers."

Maybe I wouldn't win an Oscar after all.

"Take care of yourself Angelica," Sami shakes his head. "You deserve better than this. I won't put these papers on display, for your dignity."

"Don't worry, you need that money," I say. "Let's show the world what he's done!"

Back home I have to quickly get ready as Fliss is on the train up for our regular catch-up, she's going to dial-in Sebastian and his manager as they keep spamming us with endless texts and voicemails saying they're in 'crisis mode'. I can't admit it to Fliss, or anyone, but inside I'm finding it all funny. My mam's a nurse, crisis mode is when people are actually dying in front of you, not when someone with enough money to last several lifetimes is caught with their pants down. Maybe I should be worried as to how it makes me look, but it wasn't me caught doing the dirty. If he wants to have an orgy in his own time, spending his own money (dungeons don't come cheap I bet), I don't see what the problem is. But then, I forget that everyone else thinks that he's "so in love" and that he's "found the girl I could marry." Admittedly, the pictures dropping the same day as the *Flair* shoot was unfortunate timing, that observation can be my contribution to the meeting.

I head to Fliss' hotel room where she's set up an online meeting, and I see Sebastian on screen and god, does he look rough. He has bags the size of a Birkin underneath his eyes, his skin looks pasty and yellow-ish and he looks very sorry indeed.

"Was it at least a good shag? Or shags?" I ask, to lighten the mood.

His manager, Ben (who else?!) does not take kindly to that. "Angelica, this is not a laughing matter. We're losing brand deals left, right and centre here."

"We?" questions Fliss, quite rightly.

"OK, just Sebastian."

"Angelica, all you need to do here is carry on with your head held high. Your fans will just want to know you're OK. After all, everyone's been heartbroken and wronged by men but we keep surviving and thriving. You're moving on!"

It's at this point that Sebastian looks like he might be about to cry, welling up, saying how sorry he is and how he wishes he could take it all back. A little part of me wonders if he had really started to like me? Obviously not enough to say no to whatever he got up to in that dungeon, but we were hot together. I know I didn't imagine that. I do really feel sorry for him but, at the same time, he'll bounce back from it within a month. Famous, rich men always do.

Fliss and Ben begin to debate the best way to handle this. Ben would prefer it if we carried on with the agreement and arrange some damage-control "I'm standing by my man" photos but Fliss absolutely disagrees. "And make her look spineless? Absolutely not. No, Angelica's going to elegantly break-up with him then, go out on the town looking absolutely fabulous and show all the girls out there that they don't need to take this sort of cheating from anyone, even trust-fund horndogs who haven't made a penny of their own money."

"Hey, that's not true, I—" Sebastian tries to interject but Fliss simply "sssshs" him.

"You still made an agreement," Ben says, his face resembling a tomato more with each passing second.

"An agreement your client broke," Fliss reminds him. "We don't owe you anything. This whole call is a courtesy, given my client has developed – god knows why – a certain amount of empathy for your client and wants to work with him on this, so he can come out of this as best he possibly can, so I can guarantee you Angelica won't do any kiss and tells or trash-talking. Instead, she's just going to embrace her single era and maintain a graceful silence if anyone asks her about your client's S&M interests. Right now, she's got bigger fish to fry."

Lucky Break

After about forty-five-minutes of Ben trying to persuade us that we should repackage the whole scandal as me and Sebastian having an open relationship, and me being totally approving and delighted with the whole thing (at one point Ben even wanted me to agree to a leather-clad photoshoot), we eventually settle on the light touch approach Fliss originally suggested. I'm not to say anything at all, but be seen, non-stop, out on the town, looking fucking amazing and when the paps ask, I'm simply to say, "I'm single now, and I don't give a damn where or what Sebastian is up to." After all, Fliss was right, I've got other things I need to be doing. I'm going to throw a huge housewarming, as my new house is almost ready, host a private tour for the biggest celeb monthly mag and generally just show the world that Angelica doesn't need a man and is thriving as a single liberated woman.

"You handled that brilliantly," Fliss says, once we're off the call. "I know you've got a soft-spot for Seb, and he's not a bad lad, but sometimes your heart is too open, and you can't look after everyone, Angelica. You need to show you're resilient enough to keep smiling through this adversity, that's how the public fell in love with you in the first place, as a girl who wears her heart on her sleeve, falls hard and then dusts herself off again. You always believe in true love."

"I do believe in true love," I say, agreeing. It's funny now, being famous simply for being myself. Sometimes it can feel like I am a caricature of myself, like I'm not even real. When I did the NuYu promotion I had to pose with this huge cardboard cut-out of myself, standing beside her in the most unflattering lime-green bikini. I kept looking at this fake version of myself and feeling out-of-body, like all versions of me were now cardboard cut-outs, just different iterations of Angelica and that I'd ceased actually being real. I'd spent months looking at before and after shots…but without knowing what happens next.

* * *

Chapter Twenty-Three

My new house is incredible. I keep wandering around it just letting it sink in that this is my home. It has this big sweeping staircase, as you enter, that leads you up to the bedrooms. It reminds me of a fairy-tale tower or something, I can just imagine gliding down the stairs in a butter-yellow ballgown, a prince waiting for me at the bottom. That's what I keep reiterating to the press, "My Prince Charming is out there, I know it," and with this house I can definitely believe it. Although do I really want a man in here, ruining the vibe and leaving wet towels and balled up socks all over my perfect palace?

The living room has floor to ceiling windows that open out onto this huge garden that stretches so far I can't even see where my "land" ends and the neighbour's "land" begins. I love calling my garden my "land," it makes me feel posher than anyone on *Born In Buckinghamshire*! My kitchen has one of those 'islands' – I'd said to the builder I wanted one of those things that you see on crime dramas, where the wronged woman pours herself a huge glass of wine, dramatically wraps her cardigan around herself and ponders who's really doing the murders. He's definitely delivered on that. I even have a wine fridge, which, at the moment, is full of sugar-free Red Bulls. It's been work non-stop since Sebastian was caught with his cock out. Fliss was right (she always is) – sometimes the way to stop worrying about other people and what they think or what they're saying is just to keep busy. I've done so many different magazine shoots and interviews, I have been invited to so many parties and have been up-and-down to London more than ever. I've been papped flirting with a male model, an up-and-coming actor and four of the *Carry on Chelmsford* lads. The best thing is none of these have been set-ups, I actually was flirting with them all. It's like I have this glow radiating off me, or maybe even a sexy scent, men just can't keep away. It's just a pity I'm only existing on the Red Bulls at the moment, and they may give you wings but I still don't have enough energy for any actual shagging. The press are absolutely loving it too, they're calling me Queen of Revenge:

> *Angelica's on a one-woman mission to prove that the best revenge truly is never looking back. After her Born In Buckinghamshire scoundrel boyfriend, Sebastian, was caught in a filthy ten-woman orgy in one of the UK's seediest (and priciest) dungeons, Angelica has been showing us all how to handle a break-up in style. Everyone's keen to work with her and her thriving in the face of heartbreak has even been dubbed by girls all across social media as "doing an Angelica" with them posting themselves looking hot, in the wake of splitting up.*

Meanwhile, the others aren't all thriving so well. Samantha was secretly filmed being a cow to a shop assistant and since then she's been laying low, apparently Ben said she's not to say yes to any party invites for the next two months. Which is great for me as I won't bump into her anytime soon, and also, I think she got what she deserved. Samantha's always acted like people who work in hospitality are beneath her, she rarely says "thank you" when ordering a drink or even looks at the waiting staff when ordering at a restaurant, I've always hated it. As for Damon, it's not that he's been caught doing anything particularly bad, it's just he's mostly only mentioned in conjunction with me, with some papers speculating that, now Sebastian's out the way, the pair of us might reconcile. I have, and I'm sorry to admit this, snipped those clippings out as souvenirs. I'm beginning to lose sight of my original mission, was it to get revenge on Damon by being this hot, unattainable girl? Or was it to get him back? I just don't know. What I do know is that most of the time I'm too hungry to properly think about it. The other night, to stop me from ordering a McDonalds I indulged in one of my other vices: him. I messaged Damon and invited him to the housewarming tonight. He replied straight away, and said he "wouldn't miss it for the world."

I've invited Leo too, who says he'll be there but his message had no kiss at the end. Does this mean I should tell him to bring Molly along too? I'd toyed with the idea the party might be the chance to finally show Leo that I'm over Damon and that, if he still thinks about that time we spent together at the Angel of the North, maybe we could take a chance on us. But for the first time since I was crying my heart out over Robbie Thompson, there's a voice inside that's telling me not to rush into anything new; that maybe, for a while, I should be OK with just being me, not half of a couple.

Either way, I will enjoy flaunting this gorgeous house. Not that it's quite the reveal I'd intended. Alongside all the usual appearances and pap shots the papers run, other tidbits keep making their way into the press too. None of them are necessarily *bad* things or anything very controversial, but I don't understand how they're leaking out. The cost of my house, for example, and how much I've spent on the redecoration. Or the fact that I've hired magicians for the party tonight. The thing is, neither me, nor Fliss, are the ones giving these little nuggets to the press, as they're always things that make me look like some spoilt princess or as if I'm losing touch with reality. One article even said that...

> As reports come in that Angelica has dropped a whopping £10,000 on her housewarming party, including hiring three magicians who will perform tricks, alongside a litter of puppies who will entertain guests in cute outfits, insiders are saying that the once-down-to-earth

Lucky Break

North Stars fave is losing touch with her audience. Animal charities have questioned her decision to use "puppies as props" and say that Angelica should be setting an example that puppies are for life, and not party favours.

It's all hugely over-exaggerated, I have hired a magician for the party, but just one and he's my cousin. He wanted to practise his new hobby. And the closest I've been to puppies is meeting my mum's newly-adopted dog, Frankie, and she's definitely not a party favour! Mam won't even bring her over to mine in case she chews my new furniture. The thing that's confusing me is I've been trying to keep all of this stuff a secret, as I wanted it to be a surprise for my guests. So how did the papers get hold of it? I will get to the bottom of this. I'm trying to rise above it all but I don't like the slightly malicious tone creeping into the articles. Whoever is leaking these stories to the press doesn't have much to go off now, but what happens when they do? I know I signed up for fame but I didn't think it would involve having to second guess the closest people in my life and whom I share my secrets with. The only people who knew about the magician were Leo, Madison and Layla. I know it can't be those three. When anyone dropped stories on me before the obvious suspect was Samantha. She has, as they say in my crime dramas, a motive. She wants to come out victorious and win Reality TV Star Of The Year and so sabotaging me with unflattering stories would be the perfect crime. But these latest things she definitely didn't know and would have no access to.

I down one more Red Bull, then begin to assess how I'm going to prepare for the house party. Fliss said I should have hired party planners, considering it's going to be such a big press moment for me, but that felt far too indulgent. We threw parties, well mostly after-parties, in the *North Stars* house all the time, I can do it alone. See! Sell that to the press! But they wouldn't run that as it makes me look far too chill and laid back and doesn't fit with this diva Angelica image they're clearly trying to push. I've not got fancy caterers in, just the same local firm that did the vol au vent buffet at all our family occasions growing up, and there's a big supermarket order arriving any minute, with plenty of emergency booze, multipack crisps and the ingredients for a lethal punch I found online. It's not like I'm going to touch the food anyway – eating is cheating, I remind myself when my stomach rumbles. And the house speaks for itself, I don't need fancy food and drink on top of this pad to impress people. Everyone is going to get a shot of tequila rose on arrival and then they can just help themselves to the buffet. We can always order pizzas later if people seem too hammered. I'm mostly hoping that everyone strips off and piles into the swimming pool. And I texted Madison and Layla some strict instructions earlier:

Be ready to cause chaos, girls. It's not a party without gossip.

It's officially off again with Marc so I hope you've provided some fit lads for me to climb like a tree. Mxx

I've made 300 vodka jelly shots, reckon that's enough? Lx

Layla, 40 people have been invited.

You're right. I'll make 100 more.

As for what I'm wearing, I've decided to opt for classy in a glittery LBD. It's my tightest, sexiest one, the first thing I bought with my NuYu pay cheque, but when I put it on I find that it's hanging off me. It used to fit me like a second skin, now it drapes off of me, like ballsack skin. This won't do! I can't be a sparkly ballsack when Damon sees me, finally, after all of this teasing of my new dignified era in the press. I frantically begin to raid through my boxes of clothes, I've not unpacked my bedroom or upstairs yet as I reasoned all my energy should be channelled towards downstairs. I threw my all into making it look incredible in the living room, kitchen, garden and swimming pool. Upstairs on the other hand, well, it's chaos. And I feel quite wobbly looking at it, I can't really remember when I last ate and I really don't have the time now to focus on that. I need something to wear! Except, much like the black dress, everything is hanging off of me. Eventually I settle on an old sky-blue dress of mine, pulled in at the waist by a black studded belt. I bump my hair high and line my eyes with Kohl in the hope it looks a bit rock chick and indie. Of course, I'm the last person anyone thinks of when of the word 'indie' springs to mind but I can say I like the Killers or Maroon Five, they're indie, right? I hear the doorbell and go rushing down the stairs. It's Madison and Layla. Madison is in a micro latex dress that's more like a tube top. "Wow," I say. "You're even sluttier than usual, what has Marc done this time? It must be pretty bad."

"He's done a...Sebastian," Layla says. She's in cut-off denim shorts and a white vest. It would all look very casual if her make-up and tan hadn't been layered on about ten times.

"How many? More than ten?"

"No, less orgy, more..." Layla mimes whipping.

"I had no idea he wanted that kind of thing!" Madison says, storming through to the kitchen and cracking open a vodka which she begins to mix with orange squash. Her signature drink. "I'd happily have kicked the bastard in the balls."

"Wouldn't we all," Layla says. She's trying to stack all of her vodka jellies into a tower but keeps getting the proportions all wrong. "Argh, can you help? I'm no mathematician."

"Who is? Just lay them out normally, that thing will topple anyway."

"So, who's coming tonight?"

"Some of the *COC* cast, obviously no one from *Born In Buckinghamshire*," I say "All the *North Stars* lot, including, sorry, Marc."

"I want him to be here, he needs to see me in this."

She gestures up and down and I realise the outfit is a vague nod to dominatrix style, and obviously a ploy at either revenge or them snogging at the end of the night. Except, as it's Madison, and she likes to wear as few clothes as possible, the only difference between this outfit and her regular ones is the dress is made of a material so shiny you can practically see your reflection in it.

"You could have at least gone for real leather," Layla says.

"I tried that but it just made the sound of farting whenever I walked and I didn't want to have to stand beside Angelica all night and blame all the noises on her."

"Does that also mean Damon is going to be here?"

I nod, sheepishly. "I could hardly invite all the others and not him."

"Or someone's looking to fill a Sebastian shaped hole in their life."

"Hey, that's not fair. Sebastian and I weren't even real, I've been successfully single for months now!"

"Precisely, and needing that hole filled."

I don't have time to continue defending how much I don't want to shag Damon, as the doorbell goes and then it's pretty much like that consistently for the next two hours, as I greet people, eventually giving up on the tequila rose shot glasses and just pouring the stuff directly into mouths. The party seems to be a success, not that I've had a chance to speak to anyone beyond a hello. I've not even seen a magic trick! The photographer I invited is happy though, he's already snapped two girls from COC kissing in my pool. I'll have to make sure he goes soon, as I want things to get even wilder later and I know, with him sniffing around, there's certain people who really won't let loose. Leo arrived on time and I'd be lying if my heart didn't jump when I saw him. But there was no hug at the door, barely even a smile, then he just handed me a pot plant (a pot plant!), said happy housewarming then walked off. Suddenly, all the things I'd been planning to say to him - to tell him that Damon and I were finally in the past, that I needed to know if that spark between us was something we could explore, all those questions died on my lips. Instead, I watched him launch into the crowds, laughing and joking with all the other crew members I'd invited. Marc and the lads arrived about an hour in, but there was no Damon with them, and Marc was predictably vague when I asked him where he was. I know I protect my girls and would lie about anything for them (yes, even to cover up a botched boob job) but I do find it annoying how much the *North Stars* lads cover up for each other. I *would* lie for my girls but I don't have to very often, as they're mostly behaving decently, or at least, behaving indecently in a way we're all proud of.

Except, actually, right now. I can hear yelling from the swimming pool and I go outside to find that Madison has got in between the two COC girls, attempting to be part of a three-way kiss that's gone wrong. Marc is yelling "cat fight" from the side of the pool, showing it's not really having the desired effect of making him jealous (it was either that, or a threesome was her intention, or perhaps inviting him into the threesome and then throwing him out again, I don't know what she was really thinking). Reed comes and stands beside me and together we observe the unfolding scene.

"I can break this up for you, if you like?" he suggests, which makes me laugh as Reed does not have 'bouncer' energy. In fact, the opposite. He has panda energy. He's soft and smiley, although I've heard pandas are absolutely useless at sex.

"I'm sure you'd absolutely love that," I say, as we watch Madison rip the top off one of the girls. Is this really fighting? Or foreplay? "It's fine, I asked for drama, I got drama. The only thing I don't want is sperm in my pool—"

"I think that's a bit ambitious," he says, as Marc has now piled in, under the guise of 'breaking up' the fight but now him and Madison are snogging furiously, all tongues and anger. The doorbell goes and I move through the crowds to answer the door only to spot Leo in the hall checking his phone. It's the first time I've seen him alone all night and the first time I've seen even a bit of the old Leo in the smile he gives me. I've had more tequila roses than I can count, and the punch is a lot more lethal than I intended, particularly as I'm beginning to think someone's spiked it… but I feel a wave of courage hit me. I need to say something. "Leo," I start and he looks at me, with a hard to read expression. But then the shrill buzz of the doorbell goes again. Someone is ringing and ringing. "Keep your hair on," I yell and fling open the door, keen to get back to Leo before I lose my nerve. But there, in a vest so tight it might be cutting off his circulation, is Damon.

"Err, hi," I say lamely before Leo leaps in and tells him he's three hours late.

"It's a party, mate," Damon says. "Chill out, I can arrive when I want." I have to agree, I would have liked Damon here earlier, mostly because my make-up is melting off a bit now and it would have been nice if he'd seen me looking my very best. But everyone knows that a party start time isn't the actual start time, it's a loose promise. I smile at Leo, "Shall we get Damon some special punch?" But the smiles he was giving me earlier are completely gone and he just stares at me and says, "If Damon wants punch he can get it himself."

"Alright, alright, I know when I'm not wanted. Come find me later Angelica, I want the full tour," Damon says, bouncing into the party. I just hope he doesn't find the mini swimming pool orgy and join in. I may be over him but that doesn't mean I want him shagging in *my* brand new pool.

"Why did you invite him?" Leo asks.

"Because he's my friend."

"He's not your friend, you still think that arsehole gives a shit about you?"

"I know he does, and besides, why is it any of your business who I invite to my party or not? This isn't your party, or your house, and I'm certainly not your girl, so you have no right to tell me who I can or can't invite."

"I didn't say you couldn't invite him," Leo fires back. "I said you were stupid to."

"I know what I am doing."

"Yeah, jumping back to his dick, clearly."

"Jealous?"

He stumbles then and just looks at me, dead in the eye and it's suddenly as if the rest of the party has had the volume muted and I will him to continue.

But just then I see Damon reappear over his shoulder, a drink now in his hand. "Oi, oi!" he hollers and Leo spins round. The pair of them look at me and it's as though I'm in some kind of freeze-frame. I don't know what to say - to either of them - and so I take the only safe option. I turn on my heel and go and search for Layla.

Finally, I find her by the huge bifold doors in the main room, looking transfixed by something going on on what I've decided will be the dance-floor. "You OK, Angelica?" she says, seeing the anxiety written on my face.

I nod, quietly, dumbly. What else is there to say? That I just ran off and left who I used to think was the love of my life standing with the man I thought might be my future, and now I'm not sure either of them want me? But Layla breaks my reverie.

"I reckon your mam is off her face on the punch." She gestures to the crowd she was looking at before and sure enough, there in the middle of it all, is my mam, apparently doing the worm. To be fair, she's still got it. She's giving the younger ones a run for their money, and half the guests are now copying her. The music changes and soon she's busting a move to 'I've Got A Feeling' and screaming about how she'd absolutely love to shag will.i.am. "Layla laughs and asks, "I wondered if you wanted to rescue her? Send her home?"

"Is she having a nice time?"

"The best, by the looks of it."

"And has she got, ugh, I don't really want to say this aloud, involved in the swimming pool orgy?"

"No, she's staying well clear, I've intercepted her each time she's tried to go to the pool."

"Thank you. You're a good friend." And as I say it I realise that's why I didn't say anything to Damon or Leo. I really am just at the start of working out who I am by myself, no man, no cameras, no expectations. And the people that I need round me right now are my friends. Forget this fancy house – I'm richer than most when it comes to having solid gold mates.

"So, do we stop her?" Layla carries on. "Your dad said he'd come collect her whenever, before he left."

"Nah, my mam never gets the chance to let loose. If she's having a good time, let her." By now, Mam has really got the party started. The dance floor is heaving, everyone's having a good time and I have a moment to think I've done it - I've thrown a good party, on my own, and I'm going to have the best night.

We wander through to the kitchen where I find Damon, alone, despite the fact that there's three girls, in sopping wet t-shirts, looking over his way and giggling.

"There you are!" he says, offering me a glass of punch. "I was worried you'd gone off with whatshisface."

"His name is Leo," I say, taking the drink. "But I think he's gone," I won't give Damon the satisfaction of knowing how much that bothers me. "So, how are you? Still living the high life?"

"I guess…I dunno, Angelica, I've been to some pretty amazing places recently, met some pretty amazing people. But I keep finding myself, at five in the morning, in some soulless hotel, boozed up, girls waiting for me and—"

"Sounds torturous."

"Let me finish. And…well, thinking of you. How we were in the house. We had fun, didn't we?"

I can't believe it. That's two men basically opening up to me in the space of thirty minutes. What was put in this punch?

"We did, Damon. But do you ever think it was just fun because it was all new? Because it was exciting? The beginning of something."

"It *was* the beginning of something," he reaches for my hand. "Me and you. Seriously Angelica, it's all so shallow, the party scene, but we could have fun anywhere. We have had fun in the weirdest, shittiest of places."

"Quite literally," I say, thinking of the night Damon and I decided we hated the club we were in so settled on the floor of the disabled loos and just chatted for hours. Time stopped then, just like how it's stopped now. The house around me feels fuzzy, like everyone else is caught in a haze and only Damon and I are the solid, real people who exist.

"So," he says, eyeing me up and down. "You gonna give me the full tour?"

"You can see most of it," I say. "There's a swimming pool through there, then that's my telly area, there's a pool table over there and…"

"I meant the *full* tour, the bedrooms and that…"

He's just as gorgeous as he always was. Standing there in a tight white vest, and loose jeans, his hair falling over one eye. I can see the outline of his abs underneath his top, and I know what treasure his jeans contain. He's also just been the nicest he's ever, ever been to me, so, of course it's tempting to think 'fuck it' and grab his hand and lead him upstairs. The boxes aren't unpacked but the bed certainly is. But, I can't let him win that easily. I *have* to be strong. For one, the photographer I hired is still here and I know me leading Damon to the bedroom would be front-page news tomorrow and I'd let down all of those #doinganAngelica girls. They might go running back to their exes if they see me do it! I shake my head. "Sorry Damo. I gotta be here for my guests."

"Maybe later?"

"Maybe later."

* * *

Chapter Twenty-Four

I wake up to the strangest of noises. Floating up the stairs, from my kitchen, I can hear Damon alternating between whistling and singing along to Magic radio. Currently he's belting out 'Total Eclipse Of The Heart' and I pad down the stairs, in just a grey-marl t-shirt, to find him, sporting my daisy-covered apron wiping down the surfaces. All the loose bottles have been bagged up, he's lit about a thousand scented candles (including my really expensive Diptyque ones which I was saving for a special occasion, but I won't start whining now) and the house looks almost like it did yesterday morning, before chaos descended.

"Did you have to clear sperm out of my pool?" I ask, as I go over to give him a big hug of gratitude.

"I didn't..."

"Phew. I'd quite like to have kids one day, I can see them playing in that pool."

"But Marc did. He was still up, off his head, at like 10a.m. this morning."

He grins at me. Back in the house we used to spoon each other, gossiping about everyone else's romances, completely ignoring the fact that both in and out of the house, ours was the main focal point. It was so much easier to talk about everyone else than it was to discuss our ever-confusing situation. I don't want to do that anymore. So, even though I'm in my manky tee, with only what's left of last night's make-up on my face, I decide to be straight with him.

"Damon, all that stuff you said yesterday, was that the punch talking?"

"It was a powerful punch—"

"Oh, never mind then." I begin to turn around, walk back up the stairs. He grabs my hand.

"You didn't let me finish. It was a powerful punch but it wasn't what led me to say the things I said. I meant every word. Why do you think I'm here? I even put out all your recycling! For you. To show you how much of a changed man I am. How much I want a future with you. Not a clubs-and-paps-and-headlines future, but these kind of everyday, simple pleasures – sunny mornings and slow breakfasts and…"

His hand feels so good holding my arm. I feel the pull towards him, yearning for his body against mine, to feel his breath catching with his lust for me. His words are more powerful than the punch, they're making me dizzy. I know I should challenge him more, insist that he can't just show up here, say a few nice things and assume all is forgiven. The amount of tears I've cried over him, Mam has had to comfort me far too many times, and I know she wouldn't be happy to hear that I am still feeling this weak for him, this willing to drop everything I've learned about myself over the past few months to fall back into bed with him. But last night, when Dad had eventually come to bundle her in the back of the car, and while she was still high on punch, she'd gripped Damon's face and said, "Gosh you are handsome, I can see why my Angelica fell for you," before very lightly slapping him and adding, "but your looks don't excuse your behaviour, sort it out young man." He'd grinned that winning grin at her and said, "of course, I'd never hurt Angelica again," before spinning her around, with the pair having what I've now decided was a forgiveness dance.

"What are you thinking, Angelica?" he asks, his blue eyes wide with desire. I decide to succumb. After all, I am different from who I was before. I'm stronger, I know what I want and deserve and, besides, I look so good. I want to show off this new body to the man who encouraged me to get it in the first place. We begin to kiss, at first softly and then hungrily. His hands are roaming my body and he mutters, "Oh Angelica, when we get upstairs you are in serious trouble. I'm going to make love to you til you see stars, I'm going to take my sweet, sweet time and make you scream my name." He kisses down my neck, his tongue in my collarbone and then he scoops me up, into his arms and begins to carry me upstairs, only accidentally knocking my head on a beam once.

In my bedroom, he lays me down on my bed, on top of the crumple of discarded dresses from yesterday and the general chaos of my life that I tossed and turned in last night. He begins to, torturously slowly, kiss me from top to toe, pulling my t-shirt over my head and gazing at me.

"Wow, you're stunning, you truly are."

I'm tingling, desperate to feel him inside of me but, at the same time, wanting this to last forever. Then…he begins to clumsily finger me. Stabbing at me down below, as if he's frantically pushing a button to call a lift. And, let me tell you, the lift is *not* arriving. I've felt more aroused by a smear test! But despite learning how to ask for what I want, having experienced it with Leo and demanding it from Sebastian, I find that I can't with Damon. I may be in this new, banging body but the girl on the inside is still the same old Angelica, the one who only wanted to impress Damon and lost herself in the process. I begin to fake moan, hoping that will encourage him to stop and climb on top of me. It doesn't. It only spurs him on further as he says, "oh you like that, do you?" I say, "yes, yes" when really I'm thinking that I could tolerate this mediocre sex, if it meant that Damon finally wanted to be with me, and only me. If it meant that I won this race, one that I've been in for far too long and which is exhausting me.

I decide to distract him with a blow job and he repositions himself so that I'm kneeling before him. At first, I like it. But then he starts pounding away at my throat. I take as much as I can before gagging and pulling myself up to face him. Eventually (finally) he throws me down, climbs on top and I gasp, for real, at the feeling of him inside of me. It truly feels spectacular, nothing, not even my favourite vibrator can match how perfectly he fits me. But, as always, it's two to three pumps and then…done. He collapses sweatily on top of me, "that was amazing, just amazing. God I've missed you."

What happened to taking his time and me screaming his name? He's all done in less time than it takes to heat a microwave curry – and less spicy. Rather than feeling ravished, I feel raw.

We have a nap, and I'm grateful it means I can skip the small talk, before, to my dismay, he wakes and wants to go again. This early on in us getting back together (if that's what this is) I don't want to reject him, I want him to see how great life could be with me, so we have a repeat performance, only even shorter this time. I roll off him wondering if he'd notice if I went to the loo and finished myself off but he's just lying there grinning asking if he's the best I've ever had. I check my phone to avoid talking. I have so many new messages! Mostly people thanking me and saying what an amazing time they had at the party, Fliss saying the photos look great and will be in a spread in the paper tomorrow and then a message from Layla and Madison calling for a: PPP. This was one of our many traditions in the house, we'd have a Post Party Pampering, reasoning that there was nothing that couldn't be solved with a face mask and a gossip. They both say they're going to be over in an hour or so, which means I have to get Damon the hell out of here (I can't rely on the 'or so' – that could mean anything from five to fifty minutes). Unfortunately, he proves quite hard to get rid of. As he lies on my chest he says, "I could just stay here forever, couldn't you?" and I say, "mmmhmm, yes that would be bliss but…" I tap his head. "We both have things to do."

"Do we? It's a Sunday. Let's get a takeaway and watch telly."

In the house, Damon couldn't leave my bed fast enough. I'd want him to stay for at least a cuddle and he'd deem me "demanding" and say "I thought you were different from other girls, Angelica, that you didn't need all that girly, stupid, desperate shit," and I'd quickly change my tune to impress him and be like, "I only meant a five minute one, calm down, then I'm off with the girls."

Sensing that he isn't getting the hint, I decide I have to be straightforward. I tap his head again.

"Damon, seriously, you'll have to get off soon. The girls are coming round."

"You don't need to do that anymore," he says, thinking I'm playing it 'cool' like before. "I told you I'm all in, we can cuddle all day if you want to. Anyway, you don't need the girls, you've got me."

Now that I'll never agree with. "Madison and Layla are coming round for a debrief…this is sacred girl time and it's starting any minute now."

A look of sheer panic crosses his face. He knows what a cross-examination from the pair of them will be like. Definitely not fun. (For him, I mean, I'd probably quite enjoy it.) He's up, quicker than Usain Bolt, and getting his trousers on so fast he misses the leg and falls over. He pulls his jumper over his head, and, with a quick kiss on my head, he's gone.

Just five minutes later, my doorbell rings and in comes Layla, closely followed by Madison. They've already got their own keys, of course, and when I shout that I'm upstairs they race up to join me.

"It smells like sex in here," Layla proclaims.

"You know who to blame for that," I say. "My swimming pool certainly was not prepared for a good old porno orgy. This isn't the Playboy mansion."

Madison smirks. "It practically was last night, that girl, god she was good with her tongue. And Marc? I don't think he knew what hit him…"

"We've not even had a drink yet," Layla says. "And besides, what I'm smelling here isn't that, it's…fresh sex. Angelica's had someone here, I know it. Perhaps they're still here," she begins walking through to the kitchen yelling names. "Damon! Leo! Sebastiaaaaaaan!"

"See!" I say, triumphant, "there's no one here." Then, she spots it. The used condom in my bedside bin, resting there, betraying my secret with its presence, on top of bundles of tissues, used ear-buds and make-up wipes. "Aha! I knew it!"

"Knew what?" Madison peers into the bin. "Angelica, you're not meant to stick the ear-bud all the way into your ear, you'll go deaf."

"Not that," Layla says and Madison spots it.

"That's Damon's."

"What? How do you know? That's so creepy! Seriously, how can you tell?"

She laughs. "I can't. I was taking a guess, I knew Leo left, Sebastian didn't come so there was only really one prime suspect, it was either Damon or that fit Domino's guy who delivered the pizzas at 3a.m."

"Nah, I got with him," Layla says. We're then temporarily distracted as she fills us in on what it was like to have sex in the back of a pizza van, and are dismayed to discover that the pair poured garlic and herb sauce off of each other and licked it off.

"That'll help with the diet," I say. "I can never have a tub of that ever again now I know where you've put it…"

"But now we know where you've put it, or rather Damon has! God, are we really going back there again?"

"He's changed this time, he really has."

Madison downs the rest of the white wine she'd poured for herself. "Bingo, I win."

Turns out the pair have an ongoing game where whenever I insist Damon has changed, Madison drinks, and when I insist that the girls he's got with mean nothing, or that it didn't happen, Layla drinks.

"If you're going to be pathetic, we may as well be drunk," explains Layla. I can't fault the logic.

"Honestly, though," I say, beginning to pull out all the face-masks I own and spreading them out on the floor for us to take our pick. "It does feel different this time. He said so many nice things. If you'd heard him I swear you'd be convinced."

"Except he didn't have the balls to stick around and convince us, did he?"

I remember how quickly he shoved his clothes on, there's practically skid marks in my hallway he got out so speedily. "No," I shake my head. "But you'll see one day."

"We hope the same for you," Madison says, smearing a chocolate mask on her face that looks revolting. "That one day you'll see."

"We only tell you all of this because we love you," Layla says. She's stripped off and is just in her thong. She wants us to top up her tan on the back, which I dutifully do, shaking the can of peach-scented tan and getting ready to spray.

"His career's tanking, his agent has said you're his best bet to get his fame back on track, or he'll drop him." Layla tells me.

I begin to spray.

"Ohhh, don't shoot the messenger," Layla squeals, the tan is cold against her skin and I assure her it isn't intentional. What they are saying matches what I overheard Samantha saying in the toilet. It does also make sense, there's no denying my career is soaring right now and Damon's isn't.

"Can't it be both?" I ask, only slightly aware how needy I sound. "That he's realised he likes me just at the exact same time his agent wants him to get back with me?"

"Oh, sweet, sweet Angelica," Madison shakes her masked face. "That would be nice but I don't think that's what's happening here."

"I'll ask him, that's what I'll do."

"He'll only come up with an elaborate lie," Layla says. "He may be between jobs, but he really should take up acting. The man can lie for England."

"Is the sex, *at least*, good?"

"It's got to be, the man must practically have chocolate for a willy, the amount she lets him get away with."

I pause. I want to be able to tell them that it's mind-blowing, addictive and that I can't get enough. The strange thing is it does seem to be addictive and I can't get enough, I always want more but…it's not mind blowing. I can't figure out why this is the man who has super-glued himself into my thoughts. Maybe I just need to prove something to him, to myself, to everyone. And the only way to do that is to make him obsessed with me.

"It's…fine."

"*Fine?*" Madison yells. "Good god, woman. The sex with Marc throws me into orbit, the man has me screaming words that have not yet been invented, it's never boring and there's always something new. Last night—"

Layla cuts her off and squeezes my knee. "Not all sex has to be stratospheric, after all my mam always said, 'don't marry the man who you have the most insane sex with, that man is a psychopath.' But if you're going to end up with Damon and, boo for us, it does seem that's what you want, then it should at least be good – the kind of sex you can imagine having for years. You should definitely be getting yours."

"Yes! Are you getting yours?" Madison asks intently.

I shake my head. "But I don't think it's his fault, I should be more assertive with what I want. I've managed with all the others. But Damon, I just…let him do what he wants. And what he wants is a BJ and three thrusts." I clutch my neck. "My throat is sore!" I'm beginning to feel really sorry for myself. A hangover comedown, blended with the reality of my situation: why am I like this with Damon? He's got me loopy, for no good reason.

"Deep-throated?" Layla nods sympathetically. "I hate it when they do that."

"Oh I like it!" Madison winks. "If I'm ever short of work in telly, I reckon I could get a job as a sword swallower."

"Can you like, damage yourself from it? He wasn't at it for long." I croak for exaggeration. "Imagine I end up not being able to speak, all because of Damon and his stupid willy."

"You won't lose your actual voice," Layla comforts. "But make sure you don't lose your true voice, Angelica, if you know what I mean. You're loved by so many people, us, your family. You don't exist on this planet to please Damon. If it's real love, as you say it is, then he'll love you for who you are – who you were back in the house, who you are now and who you'll be in the future. It won't be dependent on you staying one size or always having this swishy blonde hair, or being popular with the press, or putting up with crappy sex. He'll love you, for *you*. Just like we do."

I squeeze both of their hands. "You're the best girls, you really are. Now, let's talk about something other than me and Damon. Tell me, *please*, about the orgy! And I've not checked the headlines for a day! What's going on, gossip-wise?"

Madison gives us all the details of the pool orgy, how it ended with her and two of the girls tangled in each other, kissing, with Marc 'enjoying' watching them. "I think I might still have something my hair!" she confessed, and Layla swiftly sent her into the bathroom with one of those purple shampoos that are good for blonde hair and which, we reasoned, might also be good for getting sperm out. It was such 'us' logic: couldn't be explained to anyone outside of the three of us, but made perfect sense in this room.

While she was showering and singing Pitbull to herself, loudly and out of tune, Layla and I opened up our phones and took part in our favourite hobby: scrolling and analysing what we were seeing. Working our way through all the different social media apps, and then each of the websites. I knew it was juicy when Layla's eyes rolled to the back of her head and she exclaimed, "Oh for fuck's sake, no one's falling for that, are they?" She then instructed me to open up

Samantha's page, where she was standing, vat of soup in front of her and ladle in hand, in full glam, grinning at the camera. The caption read:

> Until now, I've kept quiet about my ongoing charity work, but I've decided to let the world know about my favourite way to spend an afternoon: serving up soup to those a lot less fortunate than I am. I hope this will inspire others to go out into their own community and make change. The people who come to this project I visited in Liverpool recently are some of the nicest humans you've ever met, they've just fallen on hard times and need someone like me to smile and hear about their day. Now, tell me in the comments, what will you do today to make someone smile?

We scroll through the comments, it's all, *you're an inspiration* and *gorgeous and kind, are you the perfect person?*

"My mam volunteers there sometimes," Madison says. "She'll know what actually happened." She rings her, putting her on speaker.

"Mam, you're on loudspeaker, the girls are here."

"Hi girls, miss you, make sure you come round for wine soon. I've cut every little bit of press out about you, I'm making a folder. Angelica, you make sure you're eating something won't you?"

Madison cuts her off.

"Yeah, I'll get them round but Mam, have you seen Samantha's meant to have been down the soup kitchen?"

"Oh it's been absurd, we've all been talking about it. But we're so low on volunteers at the moment she's hoping it'll help us attract some more."

"Did she make a donation?" At least if this is Samantha's charity of choice, it'll be going to a worthy cause if she wins the donation that comes with the TV award, I think.

"Yeah, and she asked for one of those big cheques! That's when Joan said, politely, that we don't get those big cheques out for donations under £500."

"Angelica, I know you're wise to it all, but people seem to really like what Samantha's done here…"

"Roger that, don't you worry Lynn, I'm on it." Maybe she's right – maybe I should get back in this vote if I want to make sure my charity is in with a chance. After all, it's close to my heart.

We hang up the phone and, along with my girls, I begin to hatch a plan.

* * *

Chapter Twenty-Five

"Ugh, it absolutely stinks in here."

"Well, breathe through your mouth then, and *smile*. Remember there's a photographer here. Besides, it's not even that bad."

The smell *is* certainly peculiar, Damon is right. It's a mixture of over-boiled cabbage, TCP and, well, farts. But I was used to it when I worked here and at least it's stopped my hunger in its tracks, I had to take Damon's cock in my mouth again this morning, quite simply to give it something to do, before my hunger took a over and walked me to KFC. He said it was the best blow-job he's had in ages. I must be *really* hungry.

Following Samantha's soup kitchen visit, I'd been persuaded I should share my cause more publicly. It makes me feel slightly icky, I think charity work shouldn't be done to get one-up on someone and it certainly shouldn't be done to help win you an award. But, I reasoned, if I do win the award, the £10K the prize brings could really change things here. And anyway, it's nice to be back at Oakdene. Without the backing of my guys and gals here, I'd have never done the *North Stars* audition. So coming back to visit with Damon, even just for a day, feels right.

A curly-haired, smiley woman called Deborah ("you can call me Deb") who started after my time is showing us around, forgetting I used to work here. She keeps stopping to talk every few minutes to the various nurses, staff members and porters, explaining who we are, as if we aren't standing right beside her. "They're from that show, *North Stars*, you know with all the drinking and the shagging, yeaaah, that one, yeah that was probably her, yeah, you probably did see her do that."

I'd find it annoying if Damon wasn't beside me, taking the piss, making faces and impersonating Deb. He's been holding my hand the whole time, showering me with little kisses, basically behaving how I always dreamed that he would. If only Layla and Madison could see him now! Except there is one little niggle: they will be able to see him, as we've had a photographer trail us this whole time. It's been a week since the party and Damon has practically been living at mine, playing the perfect boyfriend and plotting out our future together. He's even mentioned a wedding (without actually proposing, of course), although I don't know if that's because he really wants to get married or because he knows the coverage would be wild. "I reckon brands would even fork out and pay for the most mental stag-do, for me and the lads," he'd said and, despite myself, I'd got excited at the thought of Damon and me getting married, imagining all the sweet things he'd say to me in the speech.

It's this whole 'wholesome content' thing that helped persuade Damon to come to this old people's home (except apparently we're not meant to call them that anymore, and instead it's recently rebranded as a 'retirement village') as he was dead against the idea at first. "I've got a bad boy image, you know," he'd said, sitting on my cream sofa, hugging a pink fluffy cushion and wearing a face mask. "I can't be seen with old, stinky people. Can't we do cooler charity work?" I'd asked him to name 'cool' charity work, and he hadn't been able to come up with a single suggestion, and besides, as I explained to him, we'd been able to care for my beloved nana at home, up until her death, and she was so funny and wise, my favourite person ever. That was what had made me so good at working here. I hated to think of the people whose family couldn't take them in, or those who didn't have many people to visit them or take care of them. Yes, the work had been messy and hard at times, heartbreaking at others, but I used to have a genuine laugh with some of the residents, sneaking in a bit of Beyonce among the Vera Lynn and Nancy Sinatra numbers I used to perform in our Tuesday afternoon singalong sessions.

Lucky Break

Annoyingly, it was Ben that managed to convince Damon to fully agree to come with me today. I overheard snippets of their conversation, Ben saying things like "overhauling image" and "family man" and then something that mentioned my name multiple times, but I couldn't properly hear in what context. So now we're here, photographer in tow, and I'm so excited to get chatting to people. Sadly, not all my favourites are still here but I make my way to the communal living area hoping to see some of the old crew. Deb says to make the most of our time we should split up and spend time with different groups, and she introduces Damon to an old man sitting in the corner who I don't recognise. He's wearing brown corduroys and his face is moon-shaped, with a permanent smile stamped across it. I notice that Damon doesn't shake his hand, he just sits down beside him and asks for a selfie. But I don't have enough time to watch what Damon is doing as I spot three ladies all huddled together in the corner. One has a ball of wool on her lap and is knitting away, nodding every now and then, another has her hair dyed an icy blue and is wearing hot pink lipstick, while the third is drinking tea out of a mug that says THANK GOD I'M FABULOUS on it. This legend is Mavis. She'd not long moved into Oakdene when I quit to go on the show but even in the few weeks I'd met her, I could tell she was a firecracker.

I love this girl gang straight away. Deb pulls up a seat and does her usual introduction which pretty much implies I've been shagging a queue of men on national TV.

Mavis smiles at me and says, "that sounds a lot of fun, was it?"

"Oh the best time, honestly, we were just being so silly and wild."

"Fun is what matters most," her friend with the knitting nods. "I'm Carla," she gives a little wave and then introduces the others. "I hear you already know this wildcard, our Mavis, and then this," she says, pointing to the woman with the blue hair, who extends her hand for a kiss, "is Beryl."

Beryl grins and tells me I'm pretty and that she loves my hair.

"Deb," Carla asks. "Will you be a dear and fetch us a pot of tea?"

"And maybe some vodka," Mavis adds, before whispering to me and saying, "oh she's a right judgy madam that one, your replacement, but don't let her get under your skin. I can't stand her but Carla has her wrapped around her finger so she's always getting us the best stuff."

"You have to know who to make friends with," Beryl says, tapping her nose. "That one treats us like pathetic, frail old ladies, when we're nothing of the sort, but I like to play it to my advantage."

"Oh you should see it," Carla says. "We'll be walking down the corridor, on our way back from Zumba—"

"—in chairs but still, Zumba."

"You should *see* the instructor…"

"And Beryl will see Deb coming and straight away hunch herself over and begin saying 'owww, owww', and when Deb comes rushing over she somehow manages to persuade her that the thing that will help her most is a cigarette! Deb then goes into her own stash—"

"—as we all know she's got a secret stash, they're not Vogues but they'll do…"

"And we all get to go for a cheeky ciggie!"

They all want to know about life in the *North Stars* house and what I've been up to since.

"A TV star!" exclaims Mavis. "Oh, I'd have loved that! When we were younger there weren't that many options for women, you could be a secretary, or a teacher. I wanted to be an actress and, you might not believe it now, but I had the face for it—"

"And the body!" says Beryl. "She was like a Mancunian Marilyn Monroe."

I learn then that they've been friends since they were 21, as their husbands worked together. "My first, of course," Mavis says, and Beryl whispers to me, "she's had four."

"Looking back, he was maybe the best one," Mavis says, her eyes going misty. "But I was so young, I thought I deserved richer, more handsome. I had an affair and, let me tell you, the shunning you got back then for having an affair. But this new fella, Richard, he had it all – a yacht in France, a house in Mallorca. He was my passport to adventure."

"If you wanted adventure, back then you had to have a man really, for the money, the means, you know, it was so hard any other way," Beryl explains. "I married the love of my life early, had my kids, had a content life but Mavis and Carla, they craved adventure and they both found it, in different ways."

"We were all rebels, in our own ways," says Carla, telling me how she also left her first husband, and went off to be a nanny for a rich family in San Francisco right after the war. "It's what bonded us."

"I wasn't that much of a rebel," Beryl says.

"Maybe not, but you kept us two grounded—"

"And you stuck by us when everyone else didn't."

"I remember, now, was it my second, or was it my third husband, anyway," Mavis says. "I can't remember which husband but what I do remember is he left, and I was devastated. I'd thought we were going to have a child together, that he was my happy-ever-after. Beryl was living miles and miles away and I'd been crying all day and all night, and then there she was, on my doorstep with a bag of homegrown vegetables from her garden and three bottles of white wine. That's friendship. Some people will say to you, after you've suffered serious heartbreak, 'is there anything you need' but my best friends, these girls, they know what I need, without me even having to say it."

I think of Anika, halfway across the world, and feel a pang. She'd get on so well with Mads and Layla. And she'd not let Damon get away with any of his bullshit. I look over at him now and the ladies follow my glance. He has looked up from his phone and is at least talking to the old bloke now. I'm pleased Damon is finally engaging but then I notice in the corner, the photographer is here.

"So, tell us about him…" Carla says. "He's certainly a handsome lad, isn't he."

"Handsome often spells trouble, but I didn't learn that until the fourth – and last – of my men..." Mavis says, plucking the knitting out of Beryl's hands to help her with an awkward stitch.

I could lie and tell them that Damon is nothing but loyal but, just like how I hate to lie to Madison and Layla, I find, sitting with these three ladies, that I can't lie to them. I tell them the whole story, all the ups and downs and back and forths, and where we are now.

"Do you think I'm a fool?"

Carla squeezes my knee and says: "You're not a fool, the heart wants what it wants and sometimes you have to make mistakes to learn the lessons. Your friends can tell you until they're blue in the face—"

"Bluer than Beryl's hair! Oh how we told her..." Mavis says.

"But you have to experience it for yourself, to truly learn. I used to go for the bad boys, the rollercoaster...But did you know that people fall more in love when they're in life-threatening situations, or they feel in danger? Apparently our brains can't tell the difference between the fluttery feeling of falling in love and the pitter-patter of our hearts when we're at risk. It's why, so often, we get what love is confused. I thought it had to be fireworks, arguments, on-off, lust, lust, lust, and that can all be fun...But it's not love. No, my husband was very solid, if he was going to meet me at a certain time, he met me at that certain time, he didn't play games and I felt safe with him."

As she says this, I realise that the only man who's made me feel safe lately isn't the one currently preening himself in the corner. It's Leo.

"At first she thought he was boring," Beryl says, signalling for more tea. "But I had a feeling there was more to him than that, I told her to persevere."

"Thank God I listened to her! He made me feel so loved, every single day. 47 years we were together. It's impossible to get over a love like that, and I wouldn't want to. I miss him so much."

"We all do," Beryl says. "He was a great, great man."

I say sorry for making them talk about all this sad stuff and they insist that they're used to it, and that they like doling out their life lessons. "Makes all the heartbreak seem worth it somehow," Mavis says, just as a tray of scones with cream and jam arrive. She grabs one and begins layering on the clotted cream, until the jam just wobbles unsteadily on top. "I'm maybe not the best role model for love…"

"I don't know, it sounds like you've been romanced all across the world."

"And fucked all across the world too!" Mavis adds and I try not to look too shocked at her language or the thought of her having sex, after all, I'll probably want to be banging in my eighties, too.

"But, I guess I have learned a thing or two from all my strings of failed relationships, and that is you should never be afraid to get out, or worry about what's on the other side. If you think something isn't right, trust your instincts. Now that's not me saying that you and your Damon aren't for the long haul, but instead saying short haul isn't a failure either. Just have fun, don't put pressure on him being 'the one' or anything stupid like that. The moment it stops being fun, or he stops making you feel good about yourself, get out."

"Now for something almost as good as sex," Beryl says. "Scones!"

They hand me one but I shake my head. "I'm on this strict diet, see? I'd love to but I can't."

Usually, when I tell other women I'm on a diet they'll begin to tell me about their own, along with how much weight they're trying to lose. We'll then spend at least an hour discussing the merits of the South Beach Diet versus Special K, filling each other in on the different ones we've tried. But these ladies just gasp at the thought of a diet. "No! Oh my love, you're missing out," says Carla. "We're not telling you to have twenty scones, I understand the importance of keeping healthy, as you get older you realise that more than ever, but have one. Savour it. Enjoy it. Your mental health is as important as your physical health."

"And there's no point living to be 100 if you have to give up everything that makes you actually want to live to 100!" Beryl chimes in. I notice she's tucking into her second scone. My stomach twinges.

"If only you could see how marvellous you look," Mavis says, eyes shining. "How individual and beautiful you are. I worry about you young girls, sculpting and moulding yourself into some unattainable ideal"

"Usually a man's," Beryl adds.

"When you don't need to, gosh you're so pretty, make sure you tell yourself that every single day." Mavis squeezes my hand.

I am assuring them I absolutely will, when Damon comes over and taps me on the shoulder, not even bothering to say hello to my new friends. "Can we go now? We've been here well over an hour. I need to have my protein shake before the gym."

"Give you terrible stinking farts, that will," Carla says, and the other two crack up laughing. I introduce them and Damon just nods. "So? Angelica, can we make a move?"

"OK," I say. "Just give me a minute to say goodbye."

I give them all a big hug and tell them how much this conversation has meant to me, and promise that I'll be back to visit soon. I want to bring Layla and Madison next time, I just know they'll adore them! We're on our way out, Damon looking at his phone as if his life depends on it, when I see someone who looks like Leo. I do a double take, my chest squeezes tight. It is Leo! It's like I've summoned him by thinking of him while I was talking to the girl gang. What on earth is he doing here? He's just left a room and is clutching some papers in one hand.

"Angelica!" he says, and pulls me in for a big hug, as if the other night never happened. I'm baffled but can't pretend I'm not delighted to see him. "Are you visiting someone?"

He gives Damon a terse nod, who exchanges an equally terse nod, and I explain and begin to tell him about the ladies I met.

"They sound just like you, Madison and Layla!"

"Yeah, the wicked witches of the East," Damon grunts and we ignore him.

"I totally didn't think of it like that, you're right, they were just like us!" I knew there was a reason I felt so close to them. We reach the front desk, where Leo hands his papers over to the nurse, and then says, "Guess I'll see you sometime." I realise I don't want him to go, certainly not before I can apologise for the other night.

"Damon, if I give you my keys can you go ahead without me? I don't want you to miss your workout. Leo and I can grab a coffee or something." I'm half expecting him to kick off like the old Damon would have done, but he flashes me a tight smile instead.

"Sure," he says, snatching the keys out my hand and not even giving me a kiss goodbye. Not the best look, considering I really want to show Leo that Damon has changed, that I'm not the idiot he thinks I am.

"There's a pub down the road," Leo says. "Pub trumps coffee, any day."

The pub is a proper old-man boozer, with peeling wallpaper, Scampi Fries sold behind the bar, and a bunch of regulars nursing their pints on high-up bar stools. One of them, we spot, is even having a small snooze. I've missed places like this, everywhere since *North Stars* has been so fancy, all sharp glass bars and LEDs. All places where you really feel you have to look your very best, in high-heels and full glam, and not just because there's a swarm of paparazzi outside dying for a picture of you looking horrendous. I order myself a pint of cider and black, reasoning silently with myself that I can have all that sugar because I've not eaten anything all day. This can be my breakfast, then I can have another for my lunch and, maybe one more, for my dinner. I realise I want to stay here, with Leo, for as long as I possibly can.

As soon as we sit down I begin to apologise. "I'm sorry, I didn't mean to be so dismissive of you the other night, it's just—"

"I understand, you're with Damon now. I shouldn't keep interfering in your life. It's not what friends do."

"We've always been something a little more complicated than friends," I say, gulping down my pint. Damn that tastes good.

"But friends first and hopefully, last." This comment cuts deeper than I expected, but I make sure not to show it on my face. "I've been letting my feelings get in the way of who we actually are: proper mates. I won't do that anymore."

I want to point out that he could have been with me, that it's him that was the blocker to us being something more but I don't because perhaps he doesn't see it that way, and besides, he's right, I am with Damon now. Friends it is.

We clink our glasses together and I try to move the conversation on. "So, who were you visiting today?"

"My granddad's best friend, Pauly. He's just moved into Oakdene." He has a white foam moustache on his lip and I have to sit on my hands to stop me from wiping it away, that would feel too intimate. Instead, I tell him and he wipes it himself, muttering "How embarrassing." But it wasn't embarrassing, it was cute. I realise I know so little about Leo's life, his childhood. He tells me how he was basically raised by his grandparents, as his mam and dad weren't around a lot when he was younger. He keeps it vague, and shares that part in a dismissive way that signals that I am not to press any further.

"They're the sort of love story I aspire to have one day," he says, pulling out his wallet, where he shows me a black and white picture of a couple. She's in her wedding dress, a crown of daisies in her hair and Leo's granddad is looking at her, too absorbed by her beauty to notice the camera. "They were together for sixty years. They even died together, just days apart."

"You must miss them so much," I dislodge my hands from underneath my bum to pat his knee. Friends pat each others knees when they're sad, OK? I'm allowed.

"I do, I mean I was fully grown when they both went, it wasn't like I had to go back to Mum and Dad and their chaos. But still, I longed for them. I still do, really. It's also why I have stayed close to Pauly, it's what granddad would have wanted, they were like the boozers in this pub, sinking pints and putting the world to rights each week. Pauly helps keep me close to the pair of them, sharing stories of what they were like when they were younger."

I tell Leo all about my grandma, how I'd go round to her house after school and sit and watch all the gameshows with her, as the pair of us sat peeling potatoes or rolling cookie dough into biscuits. "Nan was head of so many different social committees, she always had so much food prep to do for all these different occasions."

"She obviously meant a great deal to lots of people, just like her granddaughter," Leo says, before downing the dregs of his pint and plonking the glass on the table, his attention caught by something past my shoulder. "Now, come on, the dartboard's free. I bet I can woop your ass."

And just like that the rest of the afternoon vanishes. We play silly games, laughing and sharing stories as the pub empties out and the sky gets dark outside. I'm sad when the last orders bell rings and I realise Damon will have been back from the gym for hours. I wave at Leo as we walk in opposite directions from the pub, an aching in my heart as I realise I might not see him again for ages, but I head home to Damon with the advice from the old ladies in my head. The heart wants what it wants.

But it's Leo's words that I hold close to me later that night, about how I'm like my grandma. I'm falling asleep, tucked neatly into Damon's nook, and smiling, replaying them over and over. Leo doesn't see me as a party girl, or a ditzy airhead, but as a woman who likes to be there for people, to make them laugh, and feel less alone in their own absurd mistake-ridden lives. He sees me not just for who I am, but who I want to be, too.

* * *

Chapter Twenty-Six

Back BF (before fame), I thought spending an hour getting ready to go on a night out was excessive. I'd only ever want to do it if it was spent with my friends, and we pumped the tunes on and pre-drank. Now, before a big event, it's days and days' worth of preparation. Weeks, in Fliss' case. She's been reaching out to loads of flashy designers asking them to send in suggestions for what I should wear to the telly awards, and we made a selection of five that I tried on a week ago. My chosen dress, a midnight blue mini dress with a longer, sheer over-layer encrusted in diamante, has been measured and altered so it fits me like a glove. Which has also meant, for the past week, I've had to be stricter than ever about what I eat, and when. I've had colonics, wraps, massages, the works. Then ever since the fitting, I've been dashing about going to various beauty appointments, getting facials, tans, pedicures, manicures, waxes. Every inch of me has to be perfect. I am not ending up in any Ring Of Regrets or on any 'worst dressed' lists this year. Even if I don't win the award, this has to be my time to shine. It's now only a few hours to go and I've been booked into a salon near the venue where I'm getting my hair freshly toned, blow-dried and styled, before Verity's going to finesse my make-up, implementing her magic touch. Damon is coming to collect me in a limo and we'll walk the red carpet together. This isn't just my moment, it's going to be *our* moment!

The salon has been over-run by reality TV stars, there's Hattie from *Born In Buckinghamshire* over there, her hair already tightly encased in foils and Kim from *CoC* is taking a small nap on one of the sofas, her hair wrapped up in an elaborate turban. The chair next to me is empty and I'm just grateful that Hattie isn't in it, keeping my fingers crossed for either Layla or Madison to occupy it, or one of the other girls from the set that I get on well with.

"Hiya hun! Fancy seeing you here!" Great. It's Samantha. Just my luck. I plaster on a smile, say "hi" back and we marvel over the odds of being sat beside one another in the salon when actually, if you think about it, considering how this is *the* place for us reality lot to get ready in, it's not surprising.

I indicate to my phone in my hand, as if to say, 'would love to chat but have to get on with some very busy and important work' when really, I just wanted to scroll in peace, maybe have a bit of a gossip with Jared, my hair stylist. But now Samantha is beside us and I can't trust her not to spread, or over exaggerate, what we say, so we can no longer chat freely.

"Ah right, yeah unfortunate timing for you, isn't it?" she says and I have no idea what she's talking about so keep the smile glued to my face and pretend I'm not baffled. Remember, it's vital: do not show any weakness around Samantha. "It is," I say. "But we roll. Can't change the press cycle."

Fliss and I had hoped the photos of Damon and me at the old person's home, sorry, retirement village, would drop the day of the awards. So far, it's all been going to plan. Damon can't stop Instagramming and tweeting about his love for me, and while a few #doitforAngelica girls are disappointed I've gone back to him, there are others who have been invested in our love story from the beginning that are absolutely delighted. They see it as a sign that true love sometimes takes its time.

But, when I open up my phone and click onto my fave bookmarked site, the paper that has been so regularly fillings its pages with loved-up me and Damon isn't leading with our charity work. Instead the top slot is…a huge picture of my vagina. It's pixellated out, of course, and another image has a big banner across my actual lady garden, but it only serves to draw more attention to it somehow. Plus for all their 'censored for explicit content' warnings, the story makes it pretty clear where readers can go if they want to see the full, unblurred version. Apparently it's all over Twitter and has even been picked up by some actual porn sites. I bite down on my own tongue, to stop my face showing any emotion, as Samantha is hovering over me, shaking her head. "Just awful, isn't it? I have no idea where they could have got that footage from."

But I know where and when it's from.

"It's from, it's from..." I stutter.

I just don't know *who* it's from.

"That day in the house with the power cut – the one when we were told all the systems were down, that no filming could happen."

It had been a great day. While we didn't mind the cameras following us wherever we went normally and mostly we didn't let their presence limit our behaviour much, as that was the premise of the show: we went wild and let the world see it, there were some things that we didn't do, while aware we were being filmed. All of us always had sex under the covers, so when people say they've "seen me having sex on telly" what they've really seen is some movement under a duvet, on a blurry black-and-white night camera. I also didn't mind it if people saw my tits, and sun-bathed topless in the garden once or twice, but I felt uncomfortable doing anything that made me out to be a sex object. It's not that I judged anyone who did, I mean look at Madison. She wasn't even on camera and she's made the switch from runner to star and made a fortune too by doing the lads mags since. It just didn't suit me. I've done one lads mag shoot since leaving the house and I was so awkward and stilted the entire time. They didn't invite me back, not that I would have said yes, even if they had.

So, while my reputation is that I am a wild child, the reality is: I tried very hard to not do anything too explicit in the house. And now, in a series of crystal-clear shots, there's the full striptease lapdance that I did for Damon that day, trusting the cameramen when they said all the equipment was down. There I am frame by frame, losing my clothes until that last image of me. I feel so exposed and betrayed. "Who would do this?" I ask, unable to hide the quiver from my voice.

"Oh hun, you're shaking," Samantha grabs my hand and holds it, telling me to take deep breaths. I've let myself down, I just can't act in front of her anymore. I feel like someone has stripped my skin off, that everyone in this salon can see the flesh that lies underneath, that they can see even further, my bones, my blood. Millions and millions of people will have seen this by now, watched me strip in what I thought was a private act, something for the man I was falling in love with. *Actually* for his eyes only. That was a crazy day, it was so much fun, and now I feel sick, thinking of what men might be doing to themselves, watching me. I was already viewed as a disposable girl about town by some media outlets, this false impression that the outside world had of me, that I was 'anyone's' and now, they're going to think it even more. I scroll down to the comments and the scathing words swim in front of my eyes. I look away. Am I going to be sick? I can't do that, not here, not in front of everyone.

"Has this happened to anyone else? We all went wild that day."

Samantha shakes her head. "I know. Now we're all scared shitless, I mean I was off the hook too," she lowers her voice to a whisper. "Remember. I was properly crazy...There's so much footage that could be leaked that wasn't meant to get out."

"So why am I the first? Or the only?"

Jared comes over before Samantha can answer, talks me through what he has planned for the day. He clearly has no idea what's in the papers yet and I don't want to tell him. I just want to get my hair done, as normal, as planned. He goes off to mix the colours and Samantha continues.

"We obviously don't know anything, but a lot of the gang think it can only be one person: Leo."

At the mention of his name, my face is drained even more of its colour. I look at myself in the salon mirror, and a ghost stares back.

"Really? Why?" I'd dropped my phone into my bag after reading the comments, to stop myself from looking any further, but I'm conscious I have messages from Damon, Madison, Layla *and* Leo that remain unread.

"For one, he was one of the cameramen so one of the few who has access to all the footage, all the unedited stuff. If it turns out the cameras had turned back on that day, who else would know? Now you know I don't want to ever cast judgement on people without knowing the full story but..."

This is one of the irritating things about Samantha, she always has to preface anything bitchy she says with about a million caveats that she absolutely wouldn't do this but...then proceeds to do the exact thing she claims to be against.

"I heard he's really struggling financially, some kind of falling out with his family and..."

It tracks with what Leo told me about his parents, but he can't be broke? He sorted the money I needed for my parents' house and stepped in and saved me last minute. I paid him back as soon as I got the NuYu cash through and it was a hefty amount, can he really be so skint he'd betray me, for a quick pay-out?

"It just doesn't seem very him,"

Jared's hurried back over, painting stripes of blonde into my hair. "Who?" he asks, sensing that there's gossip, the thing he thrives on most.

"Leo," Samantha says. "One of the cameramen. I have it on good authority that he's been selling stories on all of us, including a pretty nasty one of Angelica, published just this morning."

"What? Let me see!"

"Believe me," I say. "You, of all people, do not want to see my..."

"Vagina?" he asks.

"Full bush," Samantha confirms.

"Hey, it was not full bush!" I say, though I am not sure how this information makes the situation any better. "I'd had a wax. Remember, the strips were hard to come by in the house so we used—"

"Oh yeah, baking paper, instead."

"Not to be advised," I nod "Still, I did a good job. I think. I didn't expect the whole nation would see just how good though!"

I feel sick again. I try to think of other things: puppies, dolphins, chicks in mini hats dancing, anything but the sight of my vagina, splashed all across the front pages. My mam seeing it. My dad seeing it! Sami seeing it and hiding all the copies, in an attempt to protect my dignity.

"How do you know it's him?"

When I'd been doing my amateur sleuthing, Leo's name had come up, but then so had Samantha's a couple of times too.

"Let me look at the story again," she's asking for my phone. "I can't get into mine, it's waterlogged. I dropped it in a flume at a waterpark yesterday."

I guess that rules her out for this particular story. But Leo? Really? I reach for my phone and hand it to her, though I'm worried about her looking at my messages, as if she did she wouldn't be so nice to me. Hang on, why *is* she being so nice to me? It does seem suspicious. She hands my phone back and I open the messages.

```
Looking great in the papers my love, so happy that
the whole world can see what a banging body my woman
has. And it's even better now you've lost the rolls.
Have you seen, everyone online is calling me a right
ledge for getting that lapdance off you? Ben says
it's a great move for me. See ya on the carpet soon,
ya stunna. Dx
```

There's a string from Madison and Layla growing more and more frantic at the fact I haven't read my messages. I reply to let them know I have, and we're trying to figure out who's responsible, asking if they've had any stories leaked about them, or if they think it could be Leo. Then I brave opening the message from Leo himself.

```
I can't believe this has happened, Angelica, I'm so
sorry. You must feel so exposed and betrayed, that
was a private moment that was never meant to be
filmed. I know it's no comfort now but I'm speaking
with all the guys to find out how on earth this foot-
age was captured, let alone leaked. I thought the
cameras weren't even working that day! Sending you
love and strength and I am here if you need to talk.
```

I read the message out loud. "Sounds like an admission of guilt, he literally says 'I'm so sorry,'" Samantha says.

Jared nods, "I'm sorry sweetie, I know he's your friend and it's hard to imagine a man who looks that good being so evil, but I just don't think it sounds like it could be anyone else."

It takes around three hours to get my hair done and the entire time I'm just twisting the idea around and around in my head, flipping between absolutely and no way. Leo has the means (access to information about me, and the camera footage) but I genuinely believed that he cared a lot for me. I don't think you can fake that stuff but, time and again, I'm proven that my instincts can't be trusted. I like to think that most people have a good heart but when you throw money, fame and power into it, the desire for all of those things makes people crazy. When Verity arrives to do my make-up I'm in such a tizz I can barely get the words out to explain to her what's happened. Like many people have already told me today, she instructs me to breathe and slow down. The shaking from earlier hasn't stopped and now everything is blurry, I can't see straight.

Lucky Break

"It must be the stress," I say and Verity looks me up and down and says, "Or maybe you need to eat something? Seriously Angelica, when was the last time you had a proper meal?"

I can't answer her because I can't remember and honestly all this commentary on how skinny I've become is pissing me off, I don't mean to snap but I do, saying, "Oh fuck off Verity, I'm fine with the food, my make-up is for my face not my body, so just do your job, will you?"

As soon as I utter the words I regret them. Who do I think I am speaking to her like that? Verity's been a loyal friend to me since we met on that shoot, and she's been by my side ever since. But my head is swimming with the pressure of the awards, and I still absolutely need to fit into this dress. I can eat something afterwards. I down a glass of fizz that's being handed out to the customers and tell Verity I'm sorry, and that I didn't mean it. "I just feel under so much pressure," I say. "Already I was feeling it, with the award ceremony, constantly hearing that my fame won't last for long, that I need to make the most of it, and I'm so grateful, I really am, but it's *a lot*. I feel like there's a clock ticking over my head screaming: *fifteen minutes of fame, time's nearly up* and I want to make everyone proud and show that I'm more than what people think of me, but at every turn, something's leaked about me and now, and now..." My voice begins to get louder, and people in the salon are turning around and whispering. "MY VAGINA IS ON SHOW FOR EVERYONE TO SEE."

At that I hear someone ask, "*where?*" and spin round on their chair, only for me to see the registered disappointment on their face when they find I'm fully clothed.

Verity pulls a little bottle out of her bag, "Here, you need this," and she shoves it under my nose.

"Is this poppers?" I ask, taking a deep sniff. At this stage I'll try anything to calm down, and at least poppers don't have calories in them.

"No, it's an essential oil, it's this magical blend that always helps me. I reserve it for crises only and..."

She winces.

"I have heard rumours that someone's been selling stories about you. I could do some digging..."

"Journalists protect their sources though" I say, feeling despair.

"I think we can work it out without making someone reveal a source. I've read enough crime novels to know it's all about following the evidence. You said someone had been giving away little stories, they're easy to come by - people talk, pass on gossip. But this footage from the house that you didn't even know existed - this lapdance - who had access to that?" Verity asks. "It can't be many people."

She's right. She looks at me and my empty stomach sinks all the way to the floor.

"Only one person I know could have the personal stuff and the video clips," I say. "Leo."

* * *

Chapter Twenty-Seven

When I was a little girl, I would become so engrossed with my mam's fashion magazines, begging for her old ones so that I could rip the pictures out of them and Pritt Stick them in my diary, creating a collage of all I wanted to be and experience when I grew up. I'd tear out pictures of red carpets and glue them in, then carefully cut out all my favourite celebrities and line them up on 'my' VIP carpet, before getting a biro and drawing me: Angelica Clarke, superstar! Picturing the day when all my dreams had come true and I was swanning down the carpet, with all the attention and photographers on me.

That night has finally come. This year is so different from last year's awards, when we were all new to the scene and were very much the added 'extras' of the ceremony. Whereas, right now, everyone knows who Damon and I are, and they all want photos of us, the fans want autographs and selfies and even the other celebs on the carpet are coming up to us and saying they love the show and they so hope "all that business" with the house can get sorted so there's a second season. People keep coming up and telling me how gorgeous I look, and for once I actually let myself believe them. Jared's made my hair Hollywood perfect, and my skin is glowing from within, thanks to Verity's trickery. But, no matter how many people tell me how good I look, I can know it but I can't feel it. It just doesn't register, or sink in. I'm still shaking from the adrenaline of the evening and the shock of earlier. There wasn't time to cry, or rage, as we had to stick to our glam schedule, so I simply sent a message to Leo saying:

```
I can't believe you would do this, don't contact
me again.
```

Then, because I couldn't bear to see his reply, or excuses, I left my phone in my hotel room. Damon arrived in the limo and barely glanced up from his phone when Ravi opened the door to let me in. I told him he looked dashing in his suit but he didn't say anything back to me, just kept reading out all the comments calling him a 'legend' since the leak happened.

As we stand on the red carpet together, and he finally begins to show me some attention, the flashbulbs going crazy, I realise that little girls might look at this image, of me, of us, and dream of their future lives. I wonder if the women that I idolised felt like this inside: empty. It's not just that I'm hungry, and my body is crying out for a meal, but I am also crying out for a forgotten feeling, a place where I didn't feel so lost. All I've ever wanted is to be here, on this red carpet, with Damon looking on adoringly at me. But my smile feels so fake, like I've just learned how to assemble my face this way, and my brain knows it's not real, so the happiness never envelops me. And, if I've learned how to fake it this way, how can I trust the way Damon is looking at me now? How do I know he's not acting too? I shake my head. I have to get that thought out of my woozy mind, with Leo betraying me and Sebastian out of the picture, Damon has to be my one true love. After all, he's who I've wanted from the very beginning.

I wobble inside the venue and go take our seats. We're on an even better table than last time and there are actual celebrities who we're sharing with, but even though I know all of their faces from TV and movies, my brain scrambles to remember their names. And, of course, because I'm meant to know who they all are, no one introduces themselves. I turn to whisper to Damon to help me out, but he's long gone, having disappeared to the bathroom for a suspiciously long time. I can't tell if my annoyance at him is real, or just fuelled by this immense hunger. And it turns out the extreme dieting wasn't even

Lucky Break

needed, the dress is actually loose on me. I begin to eye up the wine on the table, and crane my neck to see if there's any waiters around who will pour it for me. I've already had about three champagnes, and am beginning to feel that lovely buzz, which is chilling me out. I begin to sway slightly in my seat, so what if the whole world has seen my vagina? As Madison said, "it's a great little purse" and I had at least done that dodgy wax. One of the actors across from me is eyeing me, I can't read his expression. I decide he must think I'm hot. That's the way through this: POSITIVE! MENTAL! ATTITUDE! I decide not to bother waiting for a waiter and pour myself a glass, choosing my water glass instead of my wine glass and filling it to the brim. I gulp down some, it's nice wine, and when the actor opposite tries to speak to me, I am too tired for making small talk so I yell across the table, "I'm very sorry, I can't hear you."

Suddenly, I'm tired of always performing. Why bother being nice to people and making new friends when all that happens is they either think they can fuck you, or they want to sell stories on you? No, I'll just wait here, stuck in my own head, until Damon comes back. I can trust him. He wouldn't sell stories on me as he's a part of them all. I'm having a small dance in my seat, thinking of my lovely old lady friends and their chair Zumba, when Geraldine comes charging over. She pulls the seat up beside me, and begins rattling on about how well I look, though tonight I'm too numb to care. I smile and say thank you, like I've done all evening, while feeling slightly monstrous within. I can't believe the way I snapped at Verity earlier, and she still continued to help me and be my friend. I pour myself more wine. "Careful with that, I have it on very good authority you might be on that stage later on. Weren't you smart, leaking those strip photos of you. The perfect 'before'! I bet the NuYu sales shot up this morning when people were reminded of your transformation."

"I didn't leak them," I say, but it lands on deaf ears. She's still going on and I zone her out slightly until I hear, "though I must admit I don't get why Damon would agree to The Thunder Down Under deal when your whole strategy recently has been to show how in love you are."

"It's not a strategy," I say. "We are really in love." Then I catch up with what's she said. The Thunder Down Under is an Aussie brand of gents' waxing kits that's gone viral – DIY scrotal waxing is now mainstream thanks to their videos, all filmed in stunning Australian settings and using all kind of celebs. I've heard they pay good money, but surely Damon would have told me. Plus their whole brand is about getting smooth for the best sex of your life. Every ad they post looks like an orgy.

"He's what?" I ask, louder than I would have liked, just as Damon returns and two of the neighbouring tables swivel around, hoping to catch some live reality TV action for their own amusement.

"And that's my cue to leave," Geraldine rushes over to the next table, all open arms and air kisses.

"Damon?" I demand as he weaves his way back through the crowd towards our table. "Are you fucking off to Australia?"

"I just didn't want to tell you tonight, on your big night, I thought I'd wait. But yeah, it's been confirmed. Ben's decided to take my image in a different direction, people weren't responding as well to the whole future family man thing as we'd have liked. And the leak, well..." He grins, wolfishly. "The leak showed us how much they like the bad boy thing, so we've decided to run with that. I'm going to be the face of Thunder for a whole year, and it kicks off with six months of me touring Oz as a brand ambassador."

I let it sink in. I'd been planning holidays, trips away together, even thinking about asking Damon to move in...and now he's going to literally the other side of the world? It's like Robbie ditching me all over again. To lose one boyfriend to Australia might be bad luck...but two? What is it about me that makes people want to be on the opposite side of the globe?

"But what about us?" I say, hating how whiny my voice sounds, how it takes me back to old Angelica, who let Damon have all of the power.

"Oh sweetheart, nothing has to change with us, this is all a brand deal. I'll still stay at yours when back home visiting and we can be together. Ben says the good thing about having a bird in the industry is they get it, all the things you have to do to keep relevant and I just knew you'd understand."

He's putting words in my mouth before I've even said them. I shake my head.

"But it won't be fake, you'll be getting your back, sack and crack out for hot Aussie girls. And don't tell me you'll be able to resist all those women..."

"I'll try my very best not to, how's that?" he asks. "Look, I might even put in a word for you with the company – now they've seen you've shown the goods in the national press, maybe they'll hire you for their women's wax and all that."

Why do I still love this man? I just do, I must do, as the thought of him being away for months has left me reeling. But how far am I willing to stretch and bend and alter myself to make him not just say he loves me back, but *show* it. Act it. But then Leo, the man who really did show me he loved me, in so many different ways, has turned out to be a liar. Damon may be an utter prick but at least his prickness lies close to the surface, I know where I stand with him, I just have to cling onto the moments when it's us, alone, nestled in a palace of pillows, laughing about something absurd.

I'm about to say, "If you really love me, I want you to start discussing things with me – actually thinking like a couple," when the lights dim and we're all told to be quiet, as the presenter is coming on stage. I look over at Samantha's table, she's sitting there, all serene and smiling, a woman whose life is going exactly her way. Meanwhile, I'm shaking, on my second (or is it third) water glass of wine, and wondering what I can do to stop the love of my life flying halfway around the world so he can bed a bunch of beauties while showing off his newly smooth scrotum.

They rattle through the categories and I can't concentrate on anything. My head feels like it's full of flies, and at every ad break I want to carry on talking with Damon but he has to dash to the toilet or work the room.

Our category, because it's the newest, is the second to last. The last one is an honorary award, going to a soap star who tragically died, far too young, last year. When I hear that I think how silly it all feels, vying for an award when life can take a turn so quickly. Shouldn't we all be focusing on what really matters? Love, friendship, fun, rather than social media followings and how our lives look on the outside. As right now, my life has never looked better on the outside, but on the inside, I've never felt worse.

"And now for the moment you've all been waiting for," booms the presenter, some comedian who hit his peak in the 1980s. "The Reality TV Star of The Year. Who have you, the viewers, loved the most? Who has outraged you the most?" he chortles. "That's what we asked you and you responded in your tens of thousands. They're sexy, they're scandalous, and they've had a skinful..."

There's then a montage of our shows – for *North Stars* it's mostly our time in the house. I'm up on this big screen running around, so naive and innocent, just having a laugh and then, there I am, sobbing because Damon has gone off with someone else *again*, and, god, I really feel for myself. How is that possible? I feel sorry for the girl on screen and I feel sorry for the girl sitting in this seat right now. Everyone keeps telling me how good I look, how I've 'won' and how different I am to the girl on the show, but they're wrong. I'm absolutely still her inside, only I've lost the essence of what makes me, *me*. I've been so focused on looking good I've forgotten what feels good. I want some of that innocence back, that silliness, to be the girl I was before all the haters commented on my looks, and made me feel I had to become someone I'm not. Yes, there are parts of this new me that I really like. I am more mature, I know how to exercise and eat healthily but recently, I've not been exercising and I've not been eating. I need to find my way back, somehow, to who I truly I am.

I decide I need to crisis call Anika when I get back to the room. She got me through Robbie buggering off, she'll keep me sane whatever Damon big-bollocks decides. I don't even watch the rest of the montage of him and Samantha, Sebastian and Hattie. I just want to get back to my room and sleep.

I'm lost in my thoughts when I feel a jab in my ribs. It's Damon. "Angelica, they're calling your name, congratulations baby, you've done it, you've won!" He gives me a big kiss, our faces filling up on the big screen and I feel so dizzy I don't know where to turn. He guides me by my waist, as I stumble a little, up to where the steps are. I can hear people commenting, "God she's wasted, classic Angelica," and "What a legend, only Angelica would collect an accolade as big as this one off her tits."

We reach the steps and the presenter, whose name I have also completely forgotten, tells Damon he can "take it from here" and he whispers in my ear, "Alright darlin', that's it, one step, two steps" until I'm on the podium and the lights are so blinding and there's a silence, and then some awkward giggles as I realise I'm meant to say something. I need to give a speech! Thankfully, I'm granted a little bit of time as, from the audience, I hear, "this is BULLSHIT!" The camera men quickly scramble to get their lens on what is happening and we see on the big screen that Samantha has stood up, knocked her chair to the ground and is storming towards the exit. It gives me a little time to try and straighten my thoughts out, remember who I need to thank, so when the spotlight is back on me, I manage to say: "I really do care, I'm just so overwhelmed, I've lost what I want to say," and someone from the audience jeers, "you're slurring!"

I ignore them and carry on. "I, first of all, want to thank the love of my life Damon—"

The same person heckles, shouting. "You're an idiot, he's been shagging anything that moves."

This time I find myself addressing them. "You're not the one dating him, so shut up." That gets a small cheer but I spot a few faces, including the actor on our table, just looking at me with pure pity. "And, the *North*

Stars house, everyone, the production team, the cameramen…" I trail off, thinking about how, just hours ago, I'd thought I would namecheck Leo in my speech. "And, of course, my girls Madison and Layla, I want to cause chaos with you until we're eighty and, Reed and Marc and most importantly, the two people who I wouldn't be here without, who I know are watching from home, my mam and dad."

It's at this point the spotlight gets brighter and I suddenly feel like I've gone blind. I stumble backwards, just one step, but the light keeps getting brighter and brighter until a wave of pain hits me.

Everything turns to black.

* * *

Chapter Twenty-Eight

All I can see is a bright, bright light. Even stronger than that glaring spotlight, the last thing I saw. It's overwhelmingly bright, I want to tell someone to turn it off but discover I have no voice. I can't speak, or even croak. Is this it? Am I meeting my maker?

There's a flashing blue light now, some voices calling my name. Again, I find I can't answer them, although I so want to. I want to ask what's happened, where am I, why am I witnessing all of these different moments in flashes and fragments?

I'm in pain. I'm in so much pain. My whole body feels shattered, and every time I try to move lightning bolts of agony flash all the way through me. Won't someone help me? I need help. There are these shadows around me, I can't speak to them, they bend and warp and suddenly, I'm floating. The pain has gone. I feel myself letting go – of all the anxiety and the stress, the lust and the jealousy – I just let go of everything and shut my eyes.

I wake up to the scent of roses, of lilies, a rush of blooms fills my nose and, for a split second, I wonder if I am in a garden somewhere. Or is this what heaven smells like? But then I open my eyes further and I see the white ceiling, the harsh strip lighting, the blue hospital curtain yanked around my bed. Is this groundhog day? Have the past few weeks been a hallucination, and I'm still recovering from my nose job? I try to lift an arm to my face but nothing is moving. Am I really awake? Can I make a sound?

"Hi," I try to croak and I hear my mam's voice in response.

"Angelica, you're awake! Oh thank god, love, we've been so worried." I feel wet tears on my cheek and know I am crying. I feel so disconnected from everything and I can't remember how I wound up here. I try to swivel my head left and right but I am in too much pain to manage. I look ahead, see one leg in a cast, floating above the other. "What happened?" I manage to struggle out.

"Oh honey, can't you remember? You went up to collect your award, we were so proud, I was watching the live stream at home with your dad, he's just gone to get me a can of Diet Coke, actually hold on, I'll just tell him..." She disappears from my eyeline for a moment and I desperately want her back. I can hear her shouting, "Jim, Jim she's awake!"

Then I can feel her presence back by my side. "Then, they still don't know how, one of the spotlights came loose from the lighting rig and you were just there in its path, like a startled rabbit in the headlights. You fell backwards off the podium. At first we thought maybe it was a joke, a stunt you'd practised and you'd appear, laughing, on another side of the stage or something. I think the whole audience did. But then you didn't appear and oh god, I was sick to my stomach with worry. They stretchered you out of there – thought you might have broken a vertebrae or worse. I've been out of mind, furious with the awards for almost killing you. If you hadn't fallen, if it had actually hit you, I dread to think what would have happened..."

I hate to think of that too, how panicked she and Dad must have been. Panic caused by me. As it's all beginning to slowly come back to me, I remember not eating that day, drinking all the wine possible. If I hadn't drunk on an empty stomach, and starved myself for weeks, would I have fallen? Maybe I could have just sidestepped that stupid light. Would I have worried Mam and Dad so much? Probably not. Guilt floods through me, amplifying the pain.

"I'm sorry," I croak.

"Don't be silly, my love. You have nothing to be sorry for, those stage managers on the other hand, are a different story! Mind you, the team did get you medical help so quickly. You were knocked out cold, they said. We were just watching on in horror at home, as it cut to an emergency ad break. Your dad was going wild—"

"I was." He's appeared, somehow. How long has he been here? "I was yelling 'I don't want to see an advert for Persil I want to know my daughter is OK' and then, the phone rang—"

"I've never got up so quick in my life," Mam says. "I rushed over and they said you were being taken to hospital and we better come quick, so we piled in the car."

"Worst journey of my life."

"Sssh, Jim, we don't want to make her feel bad. But yes, it was horrible. I cursed every red light, every traffic jam. I just wanted to be here, with my baby."

"Then we got here and the doctor confirmed that you'd been knocked out but had come round soon enough, and they'd just put you back under as a precaution – to check for swelling on the brain and all that, nothing too serious. They are going to run more tests but we're not to worry. You've got bruising to your spine, your coccyx and ribs, oh I can't remember, there was so much medical jargon floating about, I tried to write it down as your mam was just too in bits to listen and, yeah, you can see, your broken leg."

Mam's stroking my hair, and I can feel my eyes drift shut again. "You need to get as much rest as possible, the doctor said you're very, very lucky that your injuries aren't worse. Honestly, you could have died. But someone, somewhere is looking out for you. Anyway, I'll stop blabbering on and get some fresh water for all these flowers, have you properly seen them? The room is covered in them, so sweet of him..."

Then, I'm asleep again. I dream of rose petals floating through the air, Damon lying on a bed of them, I see him blowing petals at me, holding out single red roses. But then his finger is cut by a thorn, the dream is taken over by a wash of red, blood fills the television that is my shut eyes, and I'm swimming in it, screaming. I can't get out, I'm drowning.

"Ssssh, shhhh, you're OK my love, you're safe, it's just a bad dream." I wake to Mam's voice. "Oh you were tossing so much, well as much as you can toss with that cast. I think it's all the painkillers, they'll be sending you a bit loopy."

This time I can look around the room a bit more and Mam's right, it really is adorned with flowers. These absolutely massive bunches of all my favourites: lilies, roses, but also daisies and sunflowers. There's also a blanket on my bed patterned with smiley faces that's brand new, and someone who knows me well must have brought it here. It makes me smile so much.

"Damon?" I ask.

"Tsssk," Mam says, barely hiding the disapproval from her voice. It's confusing as I thought she'd let go of her animosity towards him, that she understood I loved him and that was enough. "Let's not talk about him just yet, you need to rest. There's a boy ban on the ward! Enforced by me, and your bouncer of a dad."

"That's not fair!" I wail and Mam smiles. "I want to speak to Damon, can I at least have my phone?"

"You need to eat something first, sweetheart," Mam says gently, passing a tray of food from the side.

I know she's right. These last few weeks, I've not been controlling my eating, it's been controlling me. If I hadn't have ended up here I might have ended up needing help. But suddenly I can feel my appetite coming back. I eat the little pre-packaged croissant without thinking about calories. Instead, I'm thinking about Damon. I ask for my phone again.

"I need to let Damon know I'm awake," I say. "Have you found my mobile?"

"You must be on the mend, there's my boy-crazy girl back." She glances at Dad. "We went and got it from your hotel when we packed you a bag. We wanted you to have something comfier than your awards dress. What do you think Jim, can she have her phone?"

"I'm a grown woman!" I say, but it comes out as a squeak.

"I'm not sure," Dad says while beckoning Mam over to where the pair can whisper but luckily not out of earshot.

"I don't think she can find out just yet," I hear Mam say and Dad replies, "but she'll be unbearable if we don't give it to her."

He's right, they may as well just succumb now or I'm going to whinge until they give in.

"Fine," Mam roots in her handbag. "Here you go."

The first message I open is from Anika. She's furious at me in the way that only your oldest mates are allowed to be.

I could kill you, Angel-face, if you hadn't nearly done it yourself. You need some serious self-care, girl. Get well soon – and when I say that I don't just mean your bust leg, I mean take care of yourself properly. I need you well enough to get mortal with me when we dock back in the UK soon XXX

The next ones are from Madison and Layla. There's a load of silly memes wishing me better and saying that as soon as I'm able to have visitors they're going to come, and is it appropriate to bring prosecco onto a hospital ward? The fact they're being so normal is exactly what I need. I don't like lying here, feeling like an invalid and prisoner in my own body, robbed of my autonomy. I just want to be treated like standard up-for-a-laugh Angelica, and that's exactly what Madison and Layla are doing. They also say a few cryptic things like…

Dunno when you'll read this but please do give him a chance, he's been proper done over.

I don't know who the 'he' is but as I scroll down, through the hundreds of messages I've received, I'm looking for one name and one name only: Damon. But he doesn't appear. Surely this must be a mistake? Even Sebastian has sent me a lovely message telling me he thinks I'm fantastic and he knows my strength will carry me through! So has Mam deleted the messages from Damon? What's happened to them?

"Mam, where's Damon?"

She sighs and pulls up a plastic orange chair, so she's at my level and looking right into my eyes. "Oh honey, I'm so sorry to tell you this, but he's already on a plane to Australia."

"The Thunder Down Under?" I click on the brand's social media page and see the last post – a big photo of Damon's beaming face in a first-class plane cabin with the caption: Guess Who's Going to be Balls Deep? I think I want to vomit. I don't know if it's my injuries, the drugs or Damon's dumbass grin. His girlfriend almost died and yet he didn't think he could delay an intimate waxing sponsorship deal?

"Did he call?" I ask.

"Sorry love, we just got a message via that slimy creep…"

"Ben?"

"Yes, yes, that's it. Ben. We called Damon multiple times on the drive down and it was just going to voicemail. Eventually, frantic with worry, I got in touch with Layla who put me in touch with that Ben. How rude is he? Anyway, he brusquely told me that Damon won't be contactable for the next few hours as he'll be on a plane. I was so confused, he was with you when you fell but according to this Ben fella, the plan was always going to be a late night flight after the awards and, well, baby, he caught it." Mam grimaces, seeming genuinely sorry to be the bearer of bad news.

I still can't believe it. "Does he know how hurt I am?"

Mam bends over and retrieves a bunch of newspapers from her bag. I'm on the front page of them all:

TELLY TUMBLE – Fans pray for Angelica as she's rushed to hospital after falling off podium on live television

PRAYERS FOR OUR ANGEL – award-winning star in critical condition after lighting near-miss disaster

Each story is accompanied by an unflattering screenshot of me falling backwards, my mouth wide open in horror, pics of me and Damon on the red carpet earlier and then shots of all the fans outside the hospital lighting candles and laying down flowers, as if I've legitimately died.

"People have travelled far and wide, everyone's been so sweet," Mam says, before adding, "it's all a bit melodramatic, but we know you'll love this drama."

I manage a smile. "I do, it's like I'm at my own funeral but still alive to hear all the nice stuff! But if Damon knows how hurt I am and he still chose the brand deal, I just don't get how he could do that."

If strangers can come to the hospital to pray for me, then surely Damon, the man who has told me he loves me and would do anything for me on multiple occasions, can give up an advert opportunity. But he hasn't. His actions don't match his words and, in that instant, it's like everything becomes clear. His actions have *never* matched his words. There's only one person that Damon has loved, or ever will love, and that's himself. Why have I wasted so much time on him? Don't I deserve someone who loves me back? The cards surrounding me from friends and family, alongside the hordes of fans waiting for me outside, prove that I do. It's funny as I should feel sad, but I've been heartbroken by Damon so many times before, and in this instance, having survived something so much worse than him, I can see he doesn't deserve my tears either. I feel sad...but for him. His life is going to be so miserable, if he keeps chasing all these false markers of success and never succumbs to loving and being loved by someone. He'll wind up one of those sad regretful types in Verity's makeup chair. All I've ever wanted is to love and be loved, and lying in this hospital room I see I've achieved that. Sure, I don't have the 'one,' but I have lots of ones, in my mam, my dad, Madison, Layla, my fans. How lucky am I? It doesn't have to be all about romantic love; friendships and family are just as important, I feel that now.

"But all the flowers? These are my favourites. I thought they were from Damon."

If Damon didn't do this, then who did? Mam and Dad just look at each other, as if they don't know what to say.

As I look around at the beautiful flowers in their rainbow of colours, I hear a noise. The door opens and there, framed in the doorway, is Leo.

I've never seen him look this way before - there's concern in his eyes, whether it's out of worry about me or fear of what I'm going to say, I don't know. What I do know is that my last message to him was like slamming a door. But alongside his look of concern, there's a fierceness, as if he's here to put himself between me and anything that could ever hurt me again. His sleeves are rolled up and I concentrate on the muscles of his forearms as I can't quite bring myself to meet his eyes again. I can feel my heart pounding, a fierce if foolish hope growing that maybe he's come to say what I know now I've been waiting to hear.

I have to stop myself remembering how his arms felt around me, how it felt to kiss him and remind myself instead how damning the evidence against him is.

Mam looks nervous and says her and Dad will be waiting outside.

"Do hear him out, love," she says, as she retreats.

I'm trapped in this bed so I've got to listen to him. But I can't promise I'll forgive him.

Chapter Twenty-Nine

Within seconds, he's standing beside me.

I take a breath to try to stay calm. "What exactly is it that you have to tell me?"

"I'm so glad you're OK. I've been waiting in the hospital, I told your mum I'd wait here until you were awake and ready to see me. I can't play it cool anymore, Angelica. When I thought you could be gone it tore my heart out. I told myself I'd just come here to see that you were going to be alright and maybe convince you that it wasn't me who sold those stories on you. I would never, ever do that to you. But I couldn't leave it at just that. I knew I needed to see your beautiful face again. And I know you probably still hate me - and you'd be within your rights when you hear the full story, but please let me try to explain myself."

It's like the world has turned to glass - these next words from him could either shatter everything or make it shine.

"My love, Angelica, as you are just that, my love. You don't know how hard I've tried to move on from you, to forget you but the times we've spent as friends, and yes, as more than friends, have been the best days of my life. I can't move on from that. I can't forget that. I once told you I'd wait for the day when I hoped you'd realise you feel the same way as I feel about you. I've been waiting all this time and I need you to know that nothing's changed the way I feel. I think I fell in love with you in the house, watching you each day, being your true, funny, messy, absolutely beautiful self. Then the world fell in love with what I saw and suddenly

I knew I'd be at the back of a long queue. But I'm here, Angelica. And I will always be here for you."

It's such a beautiful speech, I can't help but begin to cry. Even though it hurts. I remember what the ladies in the home told me, what Verity told me, about love and finding the right person. Someone who will love you no matter what, in all stages of your life, however you look, through the ups and the downs. And, when I think about it, that's always been Leo. He has worshipped me since the very beginning and all I've done is try and change myself, to fit in with what Damon wanted me to be, what I thought the public wanted me to be. I've been chasing a false dream too, and it's time to stop. I don't need to dream any more - Leo is here in front of me. Then something catches at my throat. What did he say about me having the right to hate him? If he's here to prove he didn't sell the stories, what else has he done that could make me hate him?

"The thing is, I'm not just Leo Right, the cameraman. I *am* a cameraman and I love it, but I'm also the son of Theodore Wright…"

"Teddy Wright? As in the owner of the production company?"

"That's the one. The 'most powerful man in television.'" He does quote marks with his hands as he says it. "And quite a shit dad, if I'm honest. He didn't raise me, my grandparents did, like I said. He was never around, just parading a string of different women in front of the press, after Mum died."

"So, if you're the son of one of the richest men in the UK, then why did you need the cash for stories about me?"

"Like I said, I didn't sell the stories."

"Leo, you've just proved that you've not been straight with me, and no one else would know both the personal stuff *and* have access to the show's cameras."

"I know I should have told you who I was from the start, but I wanted a chance to just be a normal part of the crew. I wanted to understand this business from the ground up, not just because of who my dad is. I wanted to earn respect. But over the summer, I've been trying to build bridges with my dad, I've been visiting more, staying at his place and well, it hasn't always just been me there."

I know the painkillers are slowing my thoughts down but I'm still not following.

"It's Samantha. She's known from day one who I really am and was trying to get with me for months. I knew she didn't really like me – she just thought I was useful. But I've rejected her so many times and it's made her mad…and then she stopped, so I thought that maybe it was all in the past. Until I realised she'd set her sights on someone else: my dad. She's been staying over at his, I even caught her looking at my phone once, though she pretended she'd it picked it up by mistake. I've been such an idiot. And it gets worse, Angelica, I'm so sorry."

What could be worse than Samantha screwing Leo's dad? Ugh. Could she become my mother in law?

"It was me that told my dad I'd discovered loads of footage on a hard drive – from the power cut day. Some of the cameras had reserve batteries and kept capturing freeze frames that we didn't know existed. I knew we had to delete what was on them – I told him I was going to. He must have told Sam. She'd have been able to send them to the press. I feel so guilty."

I'm the one who feels guilty for ever believing Leo would sell me out. It's like a tornado of emotion has hit me - I'm furious at Sam, but overjoyed that Leo isn't yet another in my long line of disastrous men. "It makes total sense it was Samantha, I'm sorry Leo, I should have trusted you."

"You don't need to say sorry," he says, wrapping the blanket around my shoulders. "Just tell me when you're better, and not high on painkillers, that you'll think about what I said just now. I meant it – every word. And I know I'm not famous. Or tanned. And I've never even considered waxing where the sun doesn't shine but…I love you, and sometimes, I think that you love me. Or could, if you let yourself. Do you feel it too?"

I want to pause, to tease him a little but find I absolutely can't. It all comes out in a rush. "I do, Leo, I really do, you make me feel so safe and loved. And yes," I lower my voice for the next part. "I think about that day under the angel so often. You make me so hot. Or as horny as I can feel with one leg in traction and covered in bruises that make me look like the undead."

We laugh but stop as the same thought is clearly stuck in both our minds. But I want to be the one to say it first. "And this time, there's no more waiting. Damon is definitely out of the picture for good. It's you, Leo, it should always have been you."

He leans over me, and runs his hand gently across my cheek. "Does this hurt?"

I move my head and murmur, "No," and he moves closer. As his lips meet mine, I feel like a firework is exploding in my chest…and everywhere else. I push up, meeting his mouth hungrily and wishing I could hold him. I'm already imagining what I'm going to do to him as soon as I get out of here. Then, as he takes me in his arms and I feel the warmth of his skin against mine, something whirs and the bed rises and I not-that-gently headbutt him. Laughing, he untangles the remote control from beneath me and just watches me. I figure if he can make me feel this sexy when I'm in hospital-issue pyjamas, we've got it made. True, I'd have preferred my Hollywood Happy Ending moment to be located somewhere a bit more glamorous than the fracture ward, but I am surrounded by roses and kissing a secret millionaire so it's still more romantic than by the bins round the back of a dodgy nightclub (where I've definitely been known to kiss a few frogs before). My heart is racing and for once, my head isn't trying to convince me not to listen.

Mam and Dad come in at that moment, and stand there grinning, and I'm too happy to even find it embarrassing. "Did he tell you the news?"

"That it was Samantha all along? Yes he did, that scheming cow, honestly, how sad of her to spend so much time trying to bring someone else down."

"Not that, we mean the show! It's back!"

"What?" I can't believe it.

Leo, it turns out, has also been using his repaired relationship with his dad to rebuild the burned down *North Stars* house and commission a spin-off series, with me as the central star.

"The channel have agreed the slot and the budget. I'm just wrangling with my dad on the exact format, but I think it's going to be incredible. We'll have to keep our relationship hidden a bit longer as it's all about you as a single guru, giving advice to a whole new cast of housemates on how to be happy on your own and get over toxic exes, basically," he explains. "But it's only eight weeks of filming and I'll be one of the crew, so we'll still see each other every day."

"My next gig!" I say, and the panic that's been filling my body for weeks begins to simmer down. I feel like I can breathe properly again. "I thought I might have screwed everything up falling over at the awards, with no show to return to, I thought everything I'd worked for from the day of my *North Stars* audition, scoring my lucky break, that I'd lost it all. It would all be over."

"That was never going to happen, people love you too much," Leo says. "But once this is filming, it does guarantee more telly time, which means people will get to know you even more. And all the audience favourites from the first series are going to come back as advisors and mentors."

"It's amazing, thank you, Leo."

He smiles tenderly. "Thank yourself, it's all your doing. The whole #doitforAngelica thing really made it an easy win and sign off. Now, what I've also got signed off is permission to take you for a celebration dinner, a porter is on his way with a wheelchair now. So, what would you like?"

I know exactly what I need, and what I crave. A desire I've been squashing, that I can't deny any longer. A girl wants what her heart wants, and I'll let go of any of the worries about what it could do to me. It's healthy to indulge in your desires, after all… "A large kebab. Extra garlic sauce."

* * *

Epilogue

Hot gossip!

The reboot of *North Stars* is returning to your screens and it's going to be more explosive than ever before! Rumours had been flying round the TV biz that the new series would be focus on a new set of hot, young talent who were single and *not* ready to mingle, all being coached by the heartbreak survivor herself, Angelica Clarke.

But according to a document sent anonymously to our showbiz desk, the new series looks set to have a different premise. *North Stars: Take Two* won't focus on Angelica's newly empowered single life, but will instead see her ex, Damon Green, return from Oz to rekindle their fire.

Our insiders have it on good authority that Samantha, the voice of season one, has been having an off-screen affair with the most powerful man in television, Theodore Wright. While we can't help but ask, *what is it that made you fall for 86-year-old millionaire Teddy, Samantha?* He's said to be head-over-heels for the bombshell who is also now set to present a late-night spin off show, *Zoom In*, that will feature all the footage too scandalous for primetime. The new series is shaping up to be more outrageous than ever, and this time, there's nowhere to hide from the cameras…

Acknowledgements

I've been dreaming up the stories of these characters for so long so it feels really special to finally bring them to life. I hope you love them as much as I do.

Thanks to everyone at Bold and HarperNorth, and to the booksellers up and down the country for getting this into readers' hands.

Thanks to Katie Innes for helping organise my thoughts and crazy stories and for telling me if they got too outrageous!

Special thanks to my family and friends for always believing in me – I knew if I made them smile with this story, I'd be halfway there.

And finally thank you to everyone who's been on this journey with me, for always supporting my books and telling you how much they mean to you. I love hearing from everyone who's reading them.

Harper North

would like to thank the following staff and contributors for their involvement in making this book a reality:

Fionnuala Barrett
Imogen Gordon Clark
Sarah Burke
Alan Cracknell
Jonathan de Peyer
Anna Derkacz
Tom Dunstan
Kate Elton
Sarah Emsley
Simon Gerratt
Monica Green
Natassa Hadjinicolaou
Emma Hatlen
Jess Haycox
Jean-Marie Kelly
Taslima Khatun
Megan Jones
Rachel McCarron
Monica Green
Alice Murphy-Pyle
Genevieve Pegg
Dean Russell
Claire Ward
Florence Shepherd
Bobbie Slade
Eleanor Slater
Hilary Stein
Jack Storey
Emma Sullivan
Katrina Troy

For more unmissable reads,
sign up to the HarperNorth newsletter at
www.harpernorth.co.uk

or find us online at
@HarperNorthUK

Harper North